the luckiest

MILA McWARREN

interlude ⭐ **press**. • new york

interlude **press** • new york

Love does not begin and end the way we seem to think it does. Love is a battle, love is a war; love is growing up.

—James A. Baldwin

Prologue

A *voicemail message left by Jasmine on Aaron's phone around noon on January 1, 2015:*

"Oh, honey, you better sit down for this. Alex just sent me a text message with a picture of an engagement ring on her finger. I can't believe they're actually gonna do it—they're way too young! And I'm not seeing either one of them until we go back early for rehearsals and spring auditions, so I'll get to David before I see her—he better watch out." Jasmine sighs and jostles the phone. "I can't believe you're already back up there and I can't just come over and bitch about this. Why the hell didn't you stay in Houston until after New Year's?"

An email dated February 10, 2015:

To: David, Jasmine, Nik, Aaron, Stephanie, Tu, Mia, Camille, Natalia, Nicole, Shelby, Jennifer, Bianca

Dear everybody,

So hopefully by now you've all had a chance to get used to the *absolute awesome* that is me and David getting married. I am so ridiculously excited, so if you still think it's weird or antifeminist or we're too young or whatever just keep it to yourself, because I need your help planning a wedding.

We're fighting years of family tradition to keep my mother's hands off of it because we're trying to keep it small, really, honestly small, not Tejano-small, because it's nicer and cheaper. Also, nobody needs the drama and I actually learned something from my mother's utter craziness during my quince, and she didn't even seem that disappointed when I told her. Jasmine gets to be maid of honor and take care of my fractious ass because if it weren't for her (dot dot dot) and Nik will be David's best man because he *is*. Both of our attendants, I'm pretty sure, will rue the day.

What I would really like to do is have the most amazing, romantic, laid-back summer wedding. I want it to be in a pretty place, and I want to have flowers and lemonade and champagne and lots of tinkly music and dancing in bare feet, and that's really about it. And I want my friends to be involved. I want everybody who's getting this email to know that they're special to us. So what I want to ask of you guys is that you help us—help us plan our wedding, help us get it ready, be a part of it. You guys are the most talented people I know, and we love all of you.

So if you're game, let me know. The weekend we've picked for the wedding is the 27th and 28th of June (yes, this June, you losers—no long engagements for us) and I know it's pretty soon after the end of school for a lot of us, but I really like the idea of finishing college and starting my grown-up life with David for real.

More details later, once I've come down off of this cloud. And finished my lab work.

Love and in love,
Alex

⌒⌒

Another email dated February 10, 2015:

A—

Just a private follow-up to ask you to be my HBIC. Your mom is the only one I know who actually taught her kid to do anything remotely useful, and I need to ruthlessly exploit that. And besides that, you know you are my own personal style guru. Bring your A-game, baby, and thank you for getting over everything that could have made this hard, because I need you.

Love you—the other A

An email dated March 3, 2015:

To: David, Jasmine, Nik, Aaron, Stephanie, Tu, Mia, Nicole

If I've heard back from you in the affirmative you're on this email list, which I've entitled CAMP WEDDING 2015 for lack of a more epic title—all my epic thoughts are filled up with finishing my thesis and deciding what we're doing about last names. (And thank you, but it's more complicated than just doodling them in the margins of my notebooks. *You* try being a feminist with a name like mine and marrying a proud man!)

But I wanted to let you know that we have a location! Stephanie has already come through and offered us her family's place down in Galveston, and oh my God, y'all, it's so perfect! When we were in high school we spent a week there for a school paper thing (Steph was our editor, of course), and so let me tell you: That house is pretty amazing. (It is *seriously* swanky—I have no idea why Steph went to that shitty high school with the rest of us broke-ass losers if her parents can swing that place.) There is a lawn right next to it and one of those stone jetties into the Gulf. I'm pretty excited and it's beginning to come together in my head, so let's all say a big thank you to Stephanie and her parents. THANK YOU, MR. AND MRS. AND MS. BAXTER! (This is such a huge deal. My mom called her mom. It's embarrassing that that is still happening but there you go.)

What this means is that, since we have the whole house we can spend some time there before the wedding whipping things into shape, and apparently we have the go-ahead to move into the house as of Saturday the 20th. There are six bedrooms and some of them will sleep like three or four people (dibs on not sleeping in a bunk bed), and if you're going to be helping us get things together you should totally come spend the week with us so we can make things. It'll be like the biggest house-party-slash-crafting-session ever. Jasmine will get high off of magic markers and Aaron will spill glitter everywhere and then pronounce it festive. I can't wait.

The address is at the bottom of this email. Google Maps works, and you can park anywhere on the street. Let me know when we can expect to see you, and good luck finishing up the semester! (And, I think for everybody on this list: Have fun at graduation! Can you believe it?)

Alejandra Valeria Martinez Garcia-Williams (is a terrible name)

A response to the previous email, sent reply all four minutes later:

Aaron—

My parents will not appreciate another glitter explosion; my dad is still vacuuming it out of furniture and every time he does my mother has to leave the room to spend some time talking to Jesus. Find a new decorative angle, please.

*** Ms. Stephanie Baxter

Medill School of Journalism at Northwestern University, Class of 2015

A digital portfolio is available upon request

"The minute you settle for less than you deserve, you get even less than you settled for." —Maureen Dowd

An email dated March 4, 2015:

Dear all:

Glitter is so 2010 and also completely inappropriate for a summer wedding. I knew that even during the incident of which we no longer speak (so nice job, Alex). Who *do* you think you're dealing with?

I'll probably be there last—I need to be here as much as I can for work and I want to go home for a day or two because I haven't been home since Christmas. You can probably expect me on Sunday night. I'm booking my flight next week, assuming my last grant check comes in on time.

Looking forward to taking my place as Emperor of All Things, etc.,
Aaron

ALEJANDRA VALERIA MARTINEZ GARCIA
&
DAVID MARCUS WILLIAMS
invite you to share in their joy at their wedding
Saturday, June 27, 2015
at six o'clock in the evening
at the home of Rashawn and Vanessa Baxter
Galveston, Texas

A post from the blog A Lone Star in Manhattan, *Thursday, June 15, 2015:*

After six months helping my friend A plan this wedding, I'm headed home for it tomorrow night. The itinerary goes like this: Mom for a couple of days, the fancy wedding house for a week, then Mom for a few more days, then home.

A's wedding is going to be gorgeous because we're going to make it that way. And it's going to be joyous because she is the most alive person I know, and she's crazy about her husband-to-be. And it's going to be sweaty because she's getting married outside, in Texas, in June. We cannot have everything, I guess.

I am going to be gracious, because I motherfucking *am*. My mother would be appalled if I behaved in any other way; we may be poor, but my mother was never desperate. I will tell myself that, over and over, and those of you who are there will all remind me as necessary. Right?

⌇

A post from the Year One *blog on the "About Our Students" page from the website of an MFA program based in New York City, Friday, June 16, 2015:*

I really wanted to be able to make these posts; I read last year's Year One posts every week—I almost said "religiously," and that would be accurate; it was a part of my Sunday morning—and when I came to the admissions open house back in January I stood on the other side of the room and looked hard at Gillian. While it's not quite right to say I wished her *dead,* I did imagine, for only the briefest moment, that the cheese she was eating might go off if I wished for it hard enough, and then this program would be down a student, and who better to fill the shoes of a female Jamaican poet than a gay white boy from Texas? (This story reflects even more poorly on me if you know how kind Gillian has been to me since the day I hoped the Boursin would do her in. Let us not dwell upon those details.)

Of course, now that the opportunity is upon me, I'm freezing up and have no idea what to say. I wanted to be asked to write this blog; I wanted *so badly* to be here and I was beyond honored when they asked me to do some of the writing for the department as part of my funding package. "It's an honor," the department secretary said. "It's a chance to work on developing your voice," Gillian said. "They're giving you money for it," the rest of my incoming cohort said ("you lucky bastard," was the part they did not say). "For fuck's sake, you actually think you are a memoirist and you even managed to convince other people you could pull it off, so get over yourself already," the imposter who lives inside my head said.

Maybe that's the best answer to "why the MFA," then: to make me get over myself already.

So hi. I'm Aaron. I'm twenty-three and I just graduated from NYU with double majors in English and history. That's me over to the side; Beth (that kind and incredibly patient woman you get on the phone every time you call here panicking about your application) took the photo, and I think she captured something of the real me in the crazy expression in my eyes, although I don't think they've ever looked that blue and I suspect she used a filter. I live in Brooklyn with some roommates; I don't have a boyfriend; I was a vegetarian for four months before I realized I love my own sense of pleasure much more than I love animals; I like wearing colors, but I'm usually wearing black because sometimes I still feel like a poor relation. I grew up in Texas and I'm a first-generation college graduate, and staying in New York to do my MFA is about so much more than my reluctance to ever leave New York and move back in with my mother, I promise.

I'll be your voyeuristic window into the first year of the MFA program until spring 2016, when the department chooses somebody else, or until I fail miserably and spectacularly. If I do wash out, it will be from too much work and too much coffee, not enough sleep and not enough social contact, and what a dull student blog that would be to read. I'll try to do better.

I'll be back home for a wedding starting tomorrow, and while I'm there I will be convincing everybody who has known me since I was thirteen that I am now a serious New York writer. When I get back here, I'll start convincing you, too. Just wait and see if I don't.

Sunday

Aaron's eyes are gritty by the time he pulls to a stop outside the house, and he winces as his headlights bounce off cars he's known since high school, now decorated with a few more college bumper stickers. He sighs and closes his eyes against the glare from the bumpers and tailgates and leans back against the headrest with a rueful grin; only a few years ago, two hours wouldn't have seemed like such a long drive, but he's been in New York long enough to become unaccustomed to that much time behind the wheel.

He'd meant to get away from the house he grew up in by noon, but his aunt Karen had called the house to dangle one more lunch at his favorite café in front of him; his mother had urged him to spend some more time with her and the thought of one of those burgers before he had to face the music was too good to pass up. And then while they were at lunch, his cousin Josh had called his mom from work, wanting to see Aaron one more time before the wedding, and his aunt Karen had mentioned that she had a half-gallon of the newest Blue Bell flavor at her house—chocolate with a marshmallow swirl and a whole bunch of chocolate-covered nuts, she said—and Aaron had sat there, surrounded by the kitsch, in the favorite restaurant of his thirteen-year-old self and stared at the bowl of pickled jalapenos next to his plate and *felt* it, felt the pull of home in the sweet cream of a half-gallon carton. He can't ever admit it to anybody, can't bear to say out loud, that it still works on him like that, but the fact is it's damn good ice cream, and he can't get it in New York, and Häagen-Dazs and Ben & Jerry's aren't the same at *all*, no matter what his friends and roommates may argue, and there are some things a native Texan is never going to pass up, especially in the middle of summer.

Once he'd been back to aunt Karen's so Josh could come by and then made it back to his mom's house one last time and he'd eaten more than one man should ever be allowed, it was almost eight when he got on the road. This was unfortunate—he hated driving after dark, always had—but leaving his mom's house was harder since the breast cancer scare two years ago. His mom blew off his concerns when he finally mentioned them, but to Aaron's eyes she looked drawn, tired. When he had a minute to talk alone with Karen, she insisted that his mom was fine, that the doctors' reports were all normal and Aaron was seeing the aging process, which seemed accelerated because of his long absences.

Maybe she's right—some days it seems as if everything is changing so fast—but his mom is still a year shy of fifty, and Aaron worries about her. It's his job, worrying about her; it has been for years, because who else is going to do it?

This whole trip home is a mess.

He doesn't want to feel this way; he wants to be happy for his friends and happy to spend some time with them, so he sits there in his car—his beloved old Chevy Tahoe that his mom pays the neighbor kid in Easter banana pudding, Thanksgiving pies and Christmas tamales to keep in excellent condition so it's always ready for him—and he waits and listens to music on his phone for just a minute more.

He's had six months of lead time and over an hour on the road— almost seventy-five minutes of estuaries and salt marshes, oil refineries and smokestacks, the crush of cars on the bridge to the island, and beach-town Sunday night traffic—to get used to the idea of what's waiting for him inside this house and he's still stalling. He hasn't seen most of his friends since Christmas, and he's excited to be with the people who make up the rest of his family and with whom there's been far too little time over the last few years; but he also knows that Nik is inside.

When he thinks about Nik, he sighs, and even then he feels his face stretch into a smile. Sometimes he hates that this is still his reaction— sometimes, when he's drunk, he decides that he's done all the thinking and had all the heartbreak over Nik that one lifetime could stand. Sometimes he writes about it, long rambling essays that are half sepia-toned reminiscence and half personal screed, and he's pretty sure that nobody who has ever read them recognizes them for exactly what they are: little love letters of rage. But leaving New York for his mom's house and then leaving his mom's house for here has been like tripping out of one set of worries only to rush straight into another. He's not sure he's ready for this one; he's not sure he's ready to take on Nik, not yet.

They've seen each other plenty over the last few years, and for the most part those visits have been fine. But they were just parties, dinner, quick evenings out being young and stupid. He's looking now at spending a *week* in a beautiful beach house with his ex, the one who broke his heart and then disappeared—only he never had the courtesy to disappear *properly*, the bastard—while they help their best friends plan their wedding. And Alex and David deserve, *deserve* a week of laughter followed by the best day of their lives, and Aaron can't wait to see them. He can do this. But dear God, it's going to be hard.

Aaron is rubbing his eyes again, when he feels a tap at the window right beside his head. He jumps and looks out the window; thank God, there's Jasmine's toothy smile in the yellow glow of a sulfur streetlight. He grins at her, turns down the music and rolls down the window. "Hey there, pretty girl. Want a ride?"

"Mister, get your ass out of that car and give me a hug. Five *months*, Aaron! Reading your blog is not the *same*!" She pulls at the door and he's laughing, turning off his ignition and whipping off his seat belt so he can slide out of the car to squeeze her tight.

Sticky summer air settles heavily against his skin, and he sucks in a breath full of cigarette smoke, the patchouli in her hair and the salt of sweat and seawater; the combination feels like home. He's known her since they shared a table in the fourth grade, and they've had their ups and downs; but from the time Jasmine Sawyer declared herself Doris to his Montgomery after they watched the original *Fame* when the new movie came out—because they'd *desperately* needed a palate cleanser, and possibly new eyes altogether—they had been there for each other. She'd held his hand and listened to him cry over his mom and his dad and his grandparents, over the injustice of high school, over Nik, over difficult living situations and arguments with roommates and disagreements with professors and issues at work and so many boys. She'd hated her brother and hated her parents, and for a while there seemed to hate everybody; and then she learned to love a few people and gave up her Torrid wardrobe, to his eternal gratitude.

She's his very first *girl*, the original model, and he'll never be anything but glad to see her—even now, when she's a little too thin in cutoff shorts and a loose embroidered top. Her dishwater blonde hair is in messy braids, and the ring in her nose glints silver above her bright smile.

"How are you, princess?"

"I am taking it one day at a time, Aaron," she says, her sigh heavy.

"Oh no. Alex? Or Mitchell? Or—oh God—not Alex *and* Mitchell? *Scandalous!*" Aaron has known since middle school that if he can get her to laugh, everything will eventually be okay in the world.

"Oh good lord, do not give me those mental images," she says, smiling and shoving some loose hair out of her face. Well, it's a start. "Both, actually—we're 'on a break' again, although he'll be here on Saturday. And Alex—she's fine, she's just kind of *crazy* excited about this bride thing, and we need Ritalin or something, because that girl—"

Jasmine is interrupted by an ear-splitting, "AARROOOOOOOOOON OH MY GOD AARON!" Alex rockets down the front porch steps, barefoot in a pair of cutoff jeans and a tank top, trailed by an only slightly less enthusiastic Stephanie and then by David, who beams from ear to ear and strolls sedately behind them.

Alex hits Aaron like a truck, and he staggers back into the side of the Tahoe under the weight; both of them are giggling. He hasn't seen her since Christmas break, when he'd been over at her house helping her pack for New Year's at David's just days before the proposal they'd all known was coming but nobody dreamed would come so *soon*.

She pulls back, still laughing as her dark hair falls across her face, and God, she's so *happy*. College has been so good for Alex; *David* has been so good for her. The little gothy girl he'd known is still under there—earrings still dot all the way up one of her ears, a sparkling little trail buried under all that hair—but her sarcasm is blunted. Aaron's been on the opposite trajectory, but he's pretty sure that's what happens to some people when they fall so completely in love that they can't wait for what happens tomorrow.

Stephanie hugs him and squeals at him. They'd been together just weeks before, when she was in town to talk with an editor her advisor knew at the *Voice* and a reporter her parents knew at the *Amsterdam News*. Her parents financed her trip. Aaron had swung by for lunch between the two meetings and noted how she glowed with the certainty of her own success, the thrill of the chase and the chill of a spring breeze against her cheeks. She'd tucked her hand into his arm and marched them up the street; her white coat was stunning against her dark skin. She was perfectly sure that the world would make room for her, but Aaron thought about how he still didn't feel confident enough to take up his own share of the sidewalk.

David finally strolls up with his hands in his pockets, his usual easy, friendly smile spread across his handsome face. He looks almost exactly the same as he did the first time Aaron met him years ago on a boardwalk, standing under a Ferris wheel; the only difference is that this time, Aaron isn't distracted by David's cute best friend standing next to him.

"Aaron, it's good to see you, man. I'm glad you're here," David says, and holds out his hand for Aaron to shake.

It has never *not* been a little awkward, these last few years. Aaron first met David years ago, back when David and Nik were next-door neighbors and went everywhere as a package deal—long before Nik and Aaron became a very different kind of package. Then Jasmine and David met again during their first semester of college, when Jasmine won a spot in a student a cappella group—the first extracurricular activity she pursued there, to Aaron's great surprise. What started with a simple text message—"You will never guess who was at my audition today! That cute friend of Nik's, the black guy with the ears and the gorgeous smile?"—spiraled so far that sometimes Aaron can't believe it actually happened, is *still* happening. Jasmine and Alex were roommates, so once Jasmine brought Alex and David together there were endless opportunities for them to be thrown together, and there was no stopping them. And that had forever changed Aaron's relationship with all of them.

It's gotten easier, sure—he and David have a different kind of friendship now than they did when David was just Nik's best friend. Aaron comes with Alex—that deal was sealed a long time ago—and David and Nik are the same way. They've figured out how to make it work, and David has never said a word to Aaron about how awkward it must be for him, but Aaron has always wondered what Nik and David say to each other about him. He's seen them with their dark heads bent together at parties and dinners, and sometimes one or both of them will look up at him while they're talking and give him a little embarrassed smile before looking back down and he knows they're talking about him.

But now, as David shakes his hand and welcomes him to his wedding, Aaron appreciates him for what he is—a good man, a kind person, the person one of his dearest girls is going to marry. David is good for her, stronger than Andy ever was: a rock who doesn't need Alex to do or be anything except his partner. Aaron pulls David a little closer, into the kind of manly hug they've been exchanging for years now. They may not be close—they can't be, there's way too much in the way—but this they can do.

David goes to the back of the Tahoe and pulls Aaron's bags out while Alex and Stephanie continue to buzz around Aaron, chattering nonstop. He meets Jasmine's eyes over their heads and raises a brow, and she rolls her eyes and mouths "later" at him before she lights a cigarette. It takes him a second to remember that—right—she was telling him her story. He blows her a kiss, then grabs her arm and drags her to the back of the Tahoe so he can help David.

The house still looks the same, and Aaron remembers moments of weekends past. He swears he can still see a hint of shimmer in the den carpet, and recalls making promotional posters for the newspaper with Stephanie the summer before their senior year, trying to find new writers to inherit their baby, and the fight over the big glitter canister that he'd definitely ended by dumping it over Stephanie's head. "There, fine, you're the biggest star of all. Are you happy *now*?" he'd sniped, and she'd stood there, her big brown eyes blazing with fury. It's a good memory, and not only because of the way Nik laughed at them after he'd pulled Aaron from the room and kissed him until he calmed down.

Now, Stephanie and David hustle Aaron up the stairs to one of the bedrooms lining the main hall. He's back in the room he shared with his cousin Josh the last time they were here, and Stephanie tells him he's here on his own this time. They've moved in an extra table for Aaron to use as a workstation—right by the window, so the light will be good—and he moves to it to set up his sewing machine and start unpacking. David waves and leaves, and then it's back to Stephanie talking a mile a minute about everything that's happened since the last time they were together: the editors who have called and then not called; her plan to go back to look for an apartment; her thoughts on what kind of job she should take while she's waiting for the real thing to happen; the scourge of the unpaid internship and her parents' feelings on the topic; how her mother thinks she should come home to Houston and work there, or maybe Dallas, or maybe Atlanta—any one of the Southern cities with newly thriving black communities, with a heavy emphasis on *South*. It's the usual chatter, the stuff they're all talking about now that graduation has come and gone and they are supposed to be adults.

While he sets up and Stephanie continues to monologue at him, he thinks about the last time he was in this room. Josh wasn't part of anything they were doing for the newspaper—that had never been his thing—but was there that weekend ostensibly because he was Aaron's ride, which was ridiculous, because Aaron had his car and had been driving it for over a year; it was the easiest thing they could think of to tell themselves and all the parents. It was much easier than admitting that Josh and Stephanie couldn't stay away from each other, but also had *no idea* what to do with each other. Nik had come down during the day, and so had Andres and Joe, and Aaron remembers that week-long visit as the last burst of childhood. Stephanie's mother had been there, supervising everything they did with that tight smile on her face, and Aaron never woke up and noticed Josh missing; midnight visitations could not have happened with Mrs. Baxter around. One night, though, Aaron woke up in the small hours to see Josh sitting in a chair by the window with his feet propped up on the wall, slapping the cord of the blinds against the glass over and over. Aaron remembers asking him, "What are you doing awake?"

Josh hadn't looked at him, hadn't paused in beating out his rhythm when he said, "Trying to figure out if I ever want to be good enough."

Idiot that he was then, Aaron didn't want to ask what he meant. He never did find out, although now he has some ideas of his own. That same chair is still by the window.

It's oddly soothing, being chattered at by Stephanie, and by the time he finishes attaching his foot pedal and settling his odds and ends on the table, he feels at home. He works hard using skills both picked up from his mother and self-taught, a variety of things that will help him keep his head above water. He can sew, bake, cook, decorate; he has earned style, grace and sophistication through his own explorations rather than been given them by virtue of his birth. Aaron has always thought of Stephanie as something like his photonegative, and he doesn't only mean the colors of their skin. She'll never be the hostess her mother wants her to be, but she has always been very determined to be very good at one thing: Journalism. And she is.

He is gazing out the window into the deepening darkness, still absentmindedly listening to Stephanie, when Nik's car pulls into the last empty spot in front of the house.

Nik steps out of the car and into the circle of a streetlight, and Aaron freezes. He's definitely shifted into summer Nik—khaki shorts, faded gray T-shirt with the ubiquitous orange longhorn on the front, aviator sunglasses propped on his head even this long after dark, hair a little wild. He looks a bit like the frat boys he knows Nik can't help hanging out with, happy and careless and filled with life, and so different from the kid he was back when they met that, despite everything, Aaron can't help but feel the strangest surge of pride. Nik is tanned and smiling, and Aaron's whole body longs for him. Just for a moment, he wishes he could still be angry; surely that would hurt less. For now—as he has for years—he just feels abandoned.

"He looks good, doesn't he?" Stephanie's voice is soft beside him, and he tears his eyes from Nik so he can turn to face her.

"He always does."

He always *has*; it's part of the problem. From the first time they laid eyes on each other, back when they were awkward high school freshmen, Aaron has thought Nik is cute.

That day, Aaron was sitting on the band bus next to Alex, his stupid shaker hat resting on top of the saxophone case clenched between his knees while he leaned against the window. They'd just pulled into the parking lot at the stadium for a marching band competition, and there *he* was, short and scrawny and standing five feet from everybody else, but grinning at his feet with his trumpet dangling from his left hand as if he'd forgotten it was there because the joke he was telling himself was so funny. He looked up as the bus trundled by, just some Indian kid in a marching band uniform, and for some reason Aaron smiled at him and Nik smiled back. Six months later, Aaron was sitting in a classroom with nerves swimming in his belly, preparing for a regional social studies writing contest, when a boy named Nikhil Warren found his assigned seat next to him and Aaron recognized him. And even then, even before they were friends, even before they finished growing, even back then, Nik had looked good to him.

Aaron knew Nik intimately for just a few years, but they were important ones, and there was a time when Aaron was sure he knew everything about Nik. They grew up together in all the ways that mattered, and Aaron understood everything about Nik and somehow never got bored—he's still not sure how that worked, and has never found anything else quite like it.

There are only two mysteries left about Nik, really: Aaron will never understand what made Nik stop loving him, or what he did to make Nik shy away just when Aaron needed him the most. And he'll never know why he smiled at Nik that first time—it was out of character even then, when he thought nobody would be able to tell he was gay if he stayed quiet and hid in plain sight. That easy smile is even more anomalous now, but still he leans against the window, looking down at Nik, and knows he's smiling; he can feel it stretching his cheeks.

When Stephanie talks again, he startles even though her voice is soft and conspiratorial. "He broke up with Ollie, did you know?"

"I heard—we talked at Christmas, a little bit." It had been a good conversation, actually—they've been getting better. At Christmas they'd stood in Alex's kitchen and laughed, talked about Nik's application package for grad school and his student teaching. Today will be the first time Aaron has seen him since then, and he's not sure what to expect.

"Do you think—" she starts, but he cuts her off.

"I don't see how. Nothing's changed."

"That's exactly my point." Her jaw is fixed; her chin is stubborn. She's so resolute, so eager to convince people that she knows exactly what needs to be done. She's always been like that: When they were in preschool she had firm opinions about snack time. Even if it's what makes her such a powerful journalist, it's still irritating as hell; even though he's known her for way too long and clearly sees the way her frustration makes her vibrate and her tight curls shake, he doesn't like having to butt heads with her every five minutes. Stephanie is the only person he's ever known who elicits this combination of furiousness and fondness just by the way she loves him. He kisses her forehead.

"No. No, I mean everything's changed. I'm there, he's... wherever he is." Her eyes want to argue when he pulls away, but that's nothing new. "I mean it, Steph—don't. Leave it alone."

"Okay." And her voice is so gentle, so sweet. This is why, despite everything, he loves her. "Are you going to be okay?"

He feels anxious and brittle. His face wears a pathetic rictus of a smile, but it's the best he can do on what suddenly seems like far too little notice. "Stephanie Baxter, I'm going to be fabulous." He turns back to the window, and Nik is looking up at him. He's too far away for Aaron to make out his expression; the light from the street and the porch is too dim to be much help. But Aaron can see him raise his hand in a little wave and smile brightly. Aaron feels his own expression warm and he nods back, slowly, just one time, before he steps back from the window.

Stephanie squeezes his hand. "Get it together, A.W. They went to get food—let's face the audience and eat dinner."

Aaron looks in the mirror. His fair hair is a little poofier than he might ordinarily wear it, thanks to the humidity, but that's nothing unusual on the Gulf Coast. No tan, not unusual either. But out of all his button-down shirts, this one makes his eyes look the most blue instead of pale gray, and the washed-out jeans he usually wears during summers home fit him well; his skin is clear and the circles that appear and disappear under his eyes seem to have taken the summer off. If he wishes his jaw were a little more square and a little less elfin, well, that's hardly anything new. He gives himself a smile and a little shake, and then they go.

Downstairs, the room is full of people. Tu Dao, always the shortest member of David and Nik's mini-United Nations gang of friends from their high school days, went with Nik to pick up the pizza; now, Aaron almost runs smack into him as he steps off the stairs. Tu ended up at Purdue and hasn't been back often, so it's been years since they've seen each other, but when Tu shakes Aaron's hand with a friendly but solemn smile, Aaron is unsurprised to learn that Tu is as earnest as always. It seems easier to deal with now, though. Tu always seemed so adult, even when they were in high school, and maybe Aaron has caught up to him. They chatter about internships and school and, after they collect slices from the boxes already strewn across the table and are still leaning against the sideboard closest to the stairs, carefully balancing their paper plates amid and atop a collection of picture frames and figurines, Nik comes over with drinks. He passes Tu a Sam Adams and presses a Diet Coke into Aaron's hand.

Beaming, Nik asks, "Hey, Aaron. How's your mom?"

"Hey. I think she's fine—it's possible I overreacted. That's what she and Karen are telling me, anyway." And just like that, it's done; he's made first contact.

Nik keeps smiling; his expression is warm. His tan shows off the gray-green of his eyes—Aaron doesn't know why he is still so surprised by them. "I'm really glad to hear it. Hey, we should talk later, catch up a little!"

Aaron nods, says, "That sounds good," and then Nik is gone again, off to pass out more drinks.

When Aaron turns back, Tu is looking at him a little sadly; the smile has faded from his eyes. Aaron feels his face go hard, cold, and he's ready to throw up his usual defenses when Tu asks about what comes next for him.

His grad school patter comes easily by now; he's already performed it twice for neighbors and friends of his mom's in the few days since he's been home. It's such a relief to talk about nothing of consequence with somebody he barely knows anymore.

PAPER PLATES AND PIZZA BOXES have been shoved into too few trash bags. Mia has just discovered the dual blenders Stephanie's dad keeps behind the bar. Aaron leans against Jasmine and loses himself in the blur of voices and the whir of crushing ice. Jasmine strokes his hair and he lets his eyes close, but then Alex staggers to her feet and addresses them all.

"Okay, people, this is a full house, so cool it for a minute. I have very important news to share."

"Actually, can you—give me a second," Mia says from the bar, while she uses one wrist to shove dark wavy hair from her eyes. They all watch her as she shakes a blender pitcher, whacks it against the bar—Aaron's eyes cut to Stephanie just in time to see her cover her wince—and then sets it on its base and blends its contents one more time. The last chunk of ice gives, and then the noise is a steady, slushy roar. "Got it. Okay, go!"

"Thank you. Okay, Mia is making drinks, but I wanted to let you know that our last member has arrived! Our Wedding Boot Camp can finally begin!" Aaron grins down at his lap at the capital letters in Alex's voice and joins in a round of cheers, then gives her jazz hands that make Jasmine laugh into his shoulder. "I have a list here somewhere..." David hands her a piece of paper. "Right, so here's the job list."

"Stephanie is our hostess, so she's in charge of rentals and basically making sure we don't burn the place down. Jasmine will *do my bidding* for the week, which is awesome, and actually, so will Aaron."

Stephanie snorts. "Good luck with that." Nik elbows her in the side. Aaron raises a brow at him, and Nik is *still* smiling at him. He doesn't miss the way Jasmine draws in her breath.

"Nik belongs to David, and of course he's doing the music, and Tu is acting as photographer." Aaron shoots a glance at Tu; he'd had no idea. "Mia and Nicole, my all-time favorite sorority sisters, are doing the food like the bosses they are, and Mia will also be bartender the night of the wedding, which is why she's my favorite." There's a general uproar, but then Mia rounds the bar and starts passing around margaritas and they quickly agree that no, that's totally fair.

Aaron takes a sip and licks at the salt along the rim of the plastic cup—classy, as always with this crew—and Jasmine murmurs, "Keep that up. He's still watching."

"Oh, shut up and drink faster," Aaron hisses under his breath, staring into his cup until his eyes cross as he takes another drink.

"And I think that's about it," Alex finishes. "I wasn't kidding when I said I wanted this to be a simple thing, just a big house party, really. But I trust you guys, and I know you'll make it beautiful."

Aaron looks up again and gives her a wink.

"In the meantime, though, we have this house for a week, because Stephanie's parents are *awesome*. Stephanie, what should we do?"

The suggestions start off silly and quickly devolve; Aaron stays quietly tucked into Jasmine's side and accepts a second margarita, resolving not to think about how all the salt and alcohol is going to make him feel tomorrow.

Twenty minutes later they've reverted to high school form, having fired up the karaoke machine that the Baxters always keep up to date, and are deep into a round of musical silliness that's rapidly becoming sillier as Mia dances behind the bar and keeps both blenders humming and the margaritas coming. Alex never could sing three notes on pitch, but somehow she and David have *killed* "Ain't No Mountain High Enough," leaving Aaron and Jasmine nudging each other and pulling faces at how adorable a pair they make. David and Jasmine have mugged their way through the love theme from the last Disney movie—leaving the rest of the room groaning—and then, somehow, Aaron has a full cup in his hand and is scrolling through the most recent additions to the machine. He smiles to himself and, against his own best intentions, chooses the poppy, sarcastic, strangely biting "Blank Space."

Aaron can feel Nik watch him while he slides one hand down his own torso, mugging for his friends and pretending to be drunker than he is, and, high on tequila and the best song to come off a record he still hears everywhere almost a year later, he takes a risk and makes and holds eye contact while he dives into singing about a doomed relationship and wonders along with Taylor Swift if the high was worth the pain. Nik leans back, lets his eyes drift up and down Aaron's body and gives him a smirk just this side of filthy; maybe Nik has already made up his mind.

They've done this before, flirted and teased around everything they don't say. They did it every time they saw each other for almost a year once long ago, and then the last night of the summer after their freshman year in college ended in Alex's bedroom, both of them gasping and pressing their frustration into each other's skin. Aaron lightly dragged his teeth down Nik's dick without breaking eye contact, and Nik tugged Aaron's hair a little harder than necessary to bite a bruise into his throat, and the next morning Aaron woke up sore and sticky and got the hell out of there as quickly as possible. They'd never talked about it, had escaped back into their lives at school; then, by Christmas, Nik was clutching the hand of a boy named Oliver as if it was a lifeline and refusing to make eye contact with Aaron. Aaron didn't forget, but he threw himself into life in New York and kept his head down, putting one foot in front of the other.

Aaron finishes the song and Stephanie snatches the mic out of his hand, crooks her finger at Nik and launches them into a reprise of their performance of "Dancing on My Own" from the homecoming weekend they all spent here at the house back in senior year. Stephanie still has questionable rhythm and tragic pitch—she loves to sing, which is why they have a karaoke machine in this house, but it's one thing she will admit she doesn't have much of a gift for—but there's a reason Nik majored in music at The University of Texas, and his voice has come a long way.

Somehow, this deliberate throwback to a memory that was never anything but happy seems different than what Aaron has just done. He sits on the sofa, flanked by Alex and Jasmine, hating them both a little for participating in it even while he smiles. Nik dances—how can you *not*, with this song—but he still watches Aaron, gives him a little head-tilt during the chorus, and it's charming and devastating and infuriating.

Jasmine leans to murmur, "Oh, I see how it is."

"Oh, shut up."

"*You* might not be desperate, but I'm not sure about him. He's coming hard, baby."

Aaron catches the reference to his blog post from last week and elbows her in response, but he doesn't stop watching Nik. Aaron watches him bounce and grin and flirt—those eyes continue to be utterly ridiculous—and though he knows he is being drawn in, he leans toward Jasmine and mutters, "And he'll be coming alone, because I'm not doing this with him again."

"That would be easier to believe if you weren't still staring at him. And if I didn't know how long it's been since you had a boyfriend."

Aaron pinches her leg. The song ends; Nik sits. Aaron spends the rest of the night in a dance that should be heartbreakingly familiar—long glances, eyes skimming over each other—but Nik is doing it all wrong. The last time they did this, and every time Aaron has done it since with somebody strange and mysterious, the dance has been about confidence, about tests and teases, about reeling him in with stops and starts and hot-and cold-running interest. Nik's eyes are anything but cold—Jasmine was right, he's coming right at Aaron, muted but constant.

Aaron drifts off against Jasmine's shoulder, a sweaty cup of melting margarita in his hand and the look in Nik's eyes burned into his brain.

When he startles awake to a shout of laughter from Jasmine just a few minutes later, Nik is gone.

In Their Own Words

A post from the blog A Lone Star in Manhattan, *Sunday, September 18, 2011:*

(I had to write this for a class and thought it might be worth putting up here. Those of you who know me: Keep your comments kind, please. It's not like I can ask the same of my TA.)

I grew up in Texas, one more displaced son of the Great State. I've been in New York for three months now, and I'm starting to notice distinct families of response to that piece of information, and all the ways it disappoints people.

The politically-minded extend their condolences. It's a fair response, and one that I guess I appreciate; I've been out since I was sixteen and there's not much to hide, and I was born just before George Bush's stupidest son decided politics might be fun. I haven't lived a day of my life without knowing who he is, and that deserves some sympathy, I think. What those people can't ever know, though, is how much every one of those condolences comes across as pity for the unknowing rube, and I don't think I deserve to be pitied, at least not for that. There are certainly things about me that might be pathetic (I'm learning more of them every day, but here's one: express trains still confuse me), but however tragic my general circumstances might be, being a bumpkin doesn't seem like one of them. I got out of Texas as soon as I could, but those people can't know how much my family loved me, how much my friends took care of me and how many very happy memories I have from there. I disappoint them with my smile, with the way I brush off their concerns, but who can care about a stupid governor with a mother like mine?

The science and tech people ask about computers in Austin, or oil exploration in Dallas, or space or medicine in Houston. I am hopeless: All I know about Austin is what I learned when I went there to compete for the state championship in feature writing, I've never even been to Dallas, and all I know about NASA is that my first boyfriend's father worked for them as a contractor and was often stressed out. I grew up just a few miles from the Johnson Space Center and we visited every year because it was a cheap and easy field trip for a broke school district. I have memories of watching the news in a fifth grade classroom after a space shuttle fell apart as it crossed our state, and I remember some of the girls crying because we'd been on one of those field trips just a few months earlier. I was good at math as a kid, and people were already telling me that I could be an engineer if I wanted, but that day all I could think about was those poor people who had died, probably just because somebody messed up a fraction. It was the beginning of the end for me, and I disappoint those new friends with my now terminal lack of interest.

The more geographically ignorant, particularly those who grew up in the city and have never traveled outside of it, ask me about horses. Every time, they ask about the horses, half convinced I rode one to school. I never have an answer except to tell them that, no, there were buses and cars, thanks. There are lots of cars, especially in a city like Houston, which seems to collectively think that a longer commute time is a good solution to overscheduling and overcrowding—if everybody has their own car, the logic seems to go, there's plenty of downtime during the day, all by yourself. I got my first car the day I turned sixteen, and I'll admit that I still miss it, here in the city—turns out that quiet time is pretty valuable.

Here's a secret, though: I've never been on a horse, but I've spent plenty of time on the water. As you get closer to the coastline, horse trails and pastures give way to bayous and salt marshes, little bays of brackish water that reach their fingers into land and wind through towns and neighborhoods. They bring snakes and frogs and truly terrifying mosquitoes, but they also bring an ease of transport that we took full advantage of—you can get a boating license when you're only thirteen and a used aluminum flatboat for two hundred bucks. There's a boat slip at the end of even our poor little neighborhood, and when I was a kid I played there, throwing pieces of gravel into the gray water and poking sticks at swarms of tadpoles.

When I was an older kid, the boat slip made space for other adventures; one impossibly steamy summer day my boyfriend sent me a text that asked me to meet him there in fifteen minutes, and remembering him riding up in a dilapidated boat with a grin splitting his face still makes me smile. We lost a lot of hours on that boat, and a few other things besides. I think I'm always disappointing new acquaintances when I tell them that I don't know anything about horses, but that I do know several different types of knots and how to replace a pull starter cord on an outboard motor.

Texas did its share of disappointing me, too; for a place so big, it seemed there was never the right kind of room for a person like me, and maybe I can blame its politics for that. It's a greedy state, so needy for glory that it doesn't share well, which makes it hard for its more promising young people to leave it behind. I never did develop much of a mind for science, but I do remember that gravitational pull increases with mass, and I blame that phenomenon; I also harbor a grudge toward the state for everybody I had to leave behind to escape its orbit. But I learned a lot from that time on the water: How to push into a solid mass of humanity like this city and make space for myself; how to jump right over small waves to get where I'm going; how to tether myself to one solid thing to stay safe in a storm; and how to drift, aimless and happy and content, when the company and the circumstances are just right.

Monday

Monday starts with a walk with Alex, Jasmine and Stephanie. Aaron is already sweaty by nine a.m. New York can get warm in the summer, but it's nothing like the swampy heat here, although at least at the beach the breeze keeps things a little more comfortable. The girls chatter about the wedding and the house—what needs to be cleaned up, what they need to add or move, if the rental order for chairs is enough. Alex and Jasmine brought Alex's mother here in the spring to meet with Stephanie's mom Vanessa and show her the house in the last push to calm her down, and much of the big planning was done then. But now that they actually have to *do* it rather than talk about it, the wedding prep seems more overwhelming. Aaron's glad he grabbed one of the clipboards the Baxters keep in the kitchen when he walked out the back door, and the girls grin at him and then each other every time he takes down a note. He has no idea why, and he's not sure he wants to ask.

The house is beautiful, and, since none of the guests will make it past the bathroom in the front foyer on the ground floor, they don't have to worry about keeping the whole place ready for the wedding itself.

The lawn is broad rather than deep, sweeping down to the beach in the St. Augustine grass that means home to him; he hadn't even known there *were* different kinds of grass until he sat on a blanket in Central Park and noticed how fine the grass there was.

The grass ends in a low picket fence with the pickets spaced wide to let in the breeze, and then the Gulf spreads out; the water is gray but gleaming in the morning sunlight. The homeowners' association raked the beach this morning, as they do twice a week, and so far there are no footprints; runners prefer to be closer to the water, where the sand is packed better, and the tide has come up enough to wash away their tracks. On Saturday the wedding party will set up a bower just over the dunes, and that's where Alex and David will get married. Then they'll have the reception on the lawn. The noise permits have been filed, the parking and use of the beach have been cleared with the homeowners' association, all of the furniture and tents have been rented, and Alex's mother is spending what she would have spent on the hall and church rental to re-sod the Baxters' lawn after it's all over.

The day passes with lists and consultations and endless discussions; Aaron is convinced that Alex, Stephanie and Jasmine have forgotten something he'll be called upon to fix, and he doesn't want to scramble at the last minute. Alex's initial conversations with the florist have left things pretty much in order, and her vision is not complicated: She wants a stolen moment of summer, full of wildflowers and greenery, and Aaron will wrap her bouquet of daisies and brown-eyed Susans and delphinium—because bluebonnets are out of season and unavailable; she asked, because of course she did—in a swath of handspun ribbon he's brought from New York, a remnant of silver-shot raw silk captured from the end of a one-of-a-kind bolt that a new friend had put aside for him. Her eyes widen when he pulls it from the canvas bag he's tucked into his sewing box, and he has to quickly whisk it away and rewrap it before the tears in her eyes fall onto it and ruin the silk.

Over lunch he fiddles on his laptop with designs for the wedding program, runs fonts by Alex and Jasmine and measures the borders and margins of the paper Alex has chosen in order to make sure, make *double* sure that it's right before he emails the file to Kinko's with a request for completion by Friday.

And then, when lunch is over, David comes in from outside, sweaty and a little bit sandy. He wraps his arms around Alex and drops a kiss on the top of her head, and instead of fussing about the sand she turns in his arms and leans into him with her whole body and whispers, "Holy shit, we're getting married!" Within minutes they've taken off upstairs to get David cleaned up; apparently Alex needs to help. Aaron shakes his head as he shuts his laptop, but he can't blame them for wanting to enjoy what they have.

Back at college, when they first met in their a cappella group, David intimidated the hell out of Jasmine with his easy confidence, which left her feeling defensive and unsure when he was around. She denied it; in long phone calls Aaron stood up for him and told Jasmine what a nice guy he was, and she told Aaron he was crazy and then dragged Alex along to their end-of-semester party for backup. Alex argued with a group of the guys for fifteen minutes about the treatment of women in popular music, and continued the debate with David long after the rest of them wandered away; by the end of the night they ended up making out on the back porch while Jasmine's friends gave her endless rounds of holy hell for bringing the cute girl who snagged a perfectly acceptable guy out from under them while they were still planning their moves.

Jasmine called Aaron the next morning, pissed at Alex, pissed at her girlfriends and *really* pissed at David, whom, she had decided, was the real problem. Dragged out of bed by her phone call while trying to sleep off his own disastrous Last Night before he had to pack for home, Aaron assured her that it was just one of those things that happened in college. He reminded her that Alex and David really didn't run in the same circles, they shared *no* mutual friends and years from now Alex would still be with her high school boyfriend Andy; everything would be out in the open and they would all share a laugh about that one crazy night in college. He believed it, too, and kept telling her the same thing over the long, awkward Christmas break when Jasmine and Alex hadn't been talking, and Alex and Andy had done everything *but* talk, and Aaron did his best to stay out of it.

Only that never happened, that happily-ever-after for Alex and Andy, because Alex and David ran into each other during their first week back at school in January. They sat together at a talk that both of their psych professors had offered as an extra credit opportunity, and then they went to lunch at the Student Center food court, and then they ditched their afternoon classes and went to David's dorm room. A week later, Jasmine came back to the dorm room she shared with Alex to find her sobbing on her bed, clutching her phone to her chest—she'd just called Andy and broken off with him, because she was *gone* over David. Jasmine had looked at her, gone downstairs to the dorm store to get ice cream and then come back upstairs to clean Alex up and call Aaron on Skype. That night, after the call ended, he'd felt shaken—if not Nik and him, he'd been *sure* Andres and Alex were the real thing. But maybe none of it had been real; maybe they'd all simply been using each other until they could get out of the crappy little suburb that had always felt a little like prison. This thought never seemed true, not even then, but sometimes he wondered.

The real horror of the situation didn't hit him until that summer, when he'd made it back to Texas, walked into a cookout in Alex's backyard, and seen Nik standing near the grill. David saw him freeze and came over to greet him as if Alex's home was his own; that was the first real sign that this awkwardness was Aaron's brand new normal. Going to separate high schools had always been hard, at least right up until the moment he and Nik broke up; then he'd been grateful that he had a separate group of friends to carry him through the last few weeks of school. A year later, with David in the picture, all of that had changed.

And now they're getting married, and it will be this way for as long as he and Alex are friends—and he's never planned on an expiration date for that. And now Alex and David are upstairs sharing a shower, and, as Aaron packs up his laptop, he tries hard not to think about where Nik is in the house.

In the late afternoon, Aaron chops vegetables for a salad while Mia and Nicole bump hips and prepare pasta and a simple sauce. He listens to their ever-larger plans for food before he stops them and reminds them that he's taking the kitchen on Wednesday night and on Thursday and Friday mornings for work on the cake. They share a look, and he's not convinced they believe him, but they continue their planning and he makes a mental note to press the point later.

Jasmine strikes up a conversation with Mia and Nicole about people they all knew at college and what they're up to on Facebook, and so Aaron ends up between Stephanie and Nik at the dinner table. He and Nik pause as they recognize the seating configuration, and then sit down, and Aaron tries to laugh off the awkwardness as he shakes his head and pours wine for all three of them. Before December he hadn't really *talked* much to Nik for years, and God knows Stephanie can talk enough for all three of them. Most of what he knows about Nik's life now comes second- or third-hand, and if Aaron only keeps his Facebook open in the hope that one day Nik will change his mind and reactivate his own account, well, long and lingering pain is just a part of having a serious ex. After last night, though, he's a little thrown, and Nik doesn't seem to be in a hurry to decode any of his own behavior for Aaron.

Aaron smiles at Nik and is opening his mouth to ask him something, *anything*, when Stephanie turns to him with a chirpy, "How's Josh?" Aaron frowns down at his dinner before he looks up at Stephanie. "He's fine. He met a girl and it looks like it's getting serious—he was talking about rings at lunch yesterday."

Stephanie's head snaps back. "Rings. Oh, holy... wow. That's... I mean, is she new?"

He looks back at his plate; he had *really* hoped this wouldn't come up. "Not too new—I met her at Christmas. She's all right—she's pretty—but at least when I met her, she seemed to think that he was some great catch, so that should tell you something about her judgment and taste level." He knows this is an asshole move, and that Josh deserves better, but whatever happened between Stephanie and Josh was too weird, and he doesn't want to encourage anybody to pick it up again. He doesn't know the whole story; all he knows is that he stopped answering Josh's questions about Stephanie a long time ago, and Stephanie seems to ration out her own questions. Both of them know how to use the Internet.

Stephanie laughs a little too loudly and bumps his shoulder. "Don't be like that about your cousin! He's a good guy! Are they coming to the wedding?"

"I think Josh is; he's on weekdays at the refinery. I'm not sure about Meg—the girl." He knows Josh is coming; he saved the address to Josh's phone before he left the house yesterday. But he doesn't want Stephanie to feel crushed at the thought of seeing her sort-of-ex, who's all but engaged to somebody else, and he might as well give her time to get used to the idea.

But it isn't a problem, apparently, as Stephanie grins and claps her hands together, "Oh my God, I can tell her the best stories! Soooo, what about you? Are you dating anybody?" She gives him a look and oh, God, she's trying to be sly. God save them all.

"Stephanie, I saw you *three weeks ago*. You're the most frequent commenter on my blog and you are a compulsive Facebook stalker. Have you heard me mention anybody?"

"Noooo, but I *do* see tagged pictures of you; you just always delete the tags so they're harder to find later. But you do look like you're having a good time!" Now it's Stephanie who refuses to make eye contact; she smirks down at her salad, even when he gives her his best "shut-it-now" expression, the one he *knows* she can still read. He has no idea if Nik realizes that Stephanie has just called him a slut; he can see Nik out of the corner of his eye, but he's focused on dinner. His body is turned toward Aaron and obviously following their conversation, but he doesn't react to any of it.

"I see people, I go out, but there's nobody serious, nobody... yeah. What about you?"

She lifts her eyes from her plate, finally, and fixes him with a look of triumph that makes it clear that was *absolutely* payback for not telling her about Josh and Meg earlier. "Oh, you know—work is an obsession, especially now that I'm headed to New York. And you, Nik? Anybody new after Oliver?"

Aaron can't believe it—*Stephanie Baxter just breezed through an opportunity to talk about herself.* Suddenly, this whole bizarre conversation makes sense; he would bet his entire collection of journals that she has her eye on getting them back together. Aaron shivers.

"Oh." Nik drops his fork and rubs his hands up and down his thighs— how interesting is that tell? Aaron thrills a little, that he can still read Nik's body language: Nik is nervous. "Ah, no, that wasn't a great breakup—I'm on my own for a little bit."

That part of the story is new, so Aaron offers silent thanks for Stephanie in interrogation mode and takes another bite of pasta while he waits for her to do her job and drag the rest of the story out of Nik. Is it just him, or is Nik really bad at breaking up? Because that would explain so much.

"Oh, I'm so sorry! You always looked very happy together. What happened?" He barely keeps from scoffing into his glass of wine; if by "very happy" you mean "attached to each other at the face," then sure, they had seemed delighted to be together. For most of their sophomore and junior years of college, so many of Alex's parties and dinners had included the dubious thrill of seeing his ex hanging all over somebody else. It had sucked. It *still* sucked when he thought about it, even though the worst was last summer, when Nik had been in Dallas with Ollie most of the time. It was hard to see Nik, sure, but that didn't mean Aaron didn't miss him when he wasn't around.

Aaron turns to Nik; he wants to watch him while he answers this question. Nik is looking into his wine, swirling the liquid so that it almost reaches the lip of the glass. His face is passive, expressionless, even as he sighs. When he finally answers it is slow, deliberate. "I don't—it was never quite right. I think we both really tried—we were good for each other. Ollie is the kindest person I know. But when one of you is hung up on somebody else it's never going to work, and eventually you get tired of trying to force it."

Stephanie coos behind him, "Oh, Nik, I'm so sorry! That's terrible."

Nik turns, gives her a wry smile and says, "Thanks, but we really are both better off." His eyes flick over to Aaron's and the smile fades and they're left just staring at each other.

"There was somebody else?" he hears his own voice say quietly.

Nik looks at him for a long beat before he angles his body toward him and responds in a hush. "Well, yeah. It sucked, for both of us, but I think we're both right where we need to be." Nik's smile is tentative, strained, and Aaron can't stop looking at him.

Stephanie, of course, has apparently missed this altogether and has been working her way through another bite of olive oil and rosemary pasta. "And graduate school is next for you too, I heard? Where are you going to be?"

Nik glances at Aaron. His smile falters before he says, "Well, actually, I'm going to—"

Alex yells, "OKAY! STATUS REPORTS!" Chat time is over, and this is going to be a working dinner.

There's not much to tell this early in the game—he and Stephanie give their report from the beach this morning and Stephanie goes on and on about the neighborhood and how difficult the homeowners' association was to wrangle until Aaron pokes her in the side. Tu announces that they've reached the end of acting like idiots and pretending there isn't a photographer in the house, and that he will start casual snaps tomorrow in preparation for Alex's formal portraits on Thursday morning; everybody bitches about having to stay "on" while they're trying to get things ready until Alex guilts them into submission. Nik says something quick about the music planning getting underway, and he and Jasmine share a nod, and then Mia and Nicole talk about the menu again and he has to pay attention to that, to press his point about the cake before the kitchen schedule turns into an absolute nightmare.

The conversation devolves again, with everyone newly focused on the week's tasks. During his argument with Mia and Nicole about plating, Aaron glances over and sees Alex and David, leaning back in their chairs and presiding over their happy minions, and shares a smile with Alex. People get up and move around to be closer to somebody they have to talk to. Jasmine and Stephanie clear plates.

Stephanie comes back as the rest of them are draining the last of a bottle of wine, a maniacally gleeful expression on her face and a remote control in her hand. "You guys are not going to believe the video Daddy helped me put together. High school highlights in five minutes!" she chirps as she waves the remote. Despite groans and mutterings, everybody pushes their chairs away, eager to get on with the mockery.

Aaron is laughing at Jasmine's muttered, "That girl—we're going to need to slip Valium into her drinks in a day or two, too," when Nik slides back into his space and stops Aaron with a hand on his arm and a low whisper. "Stay behind—I need to talk to you."

Aaron's belly flips. He winks at Jasmine and tells her he'll be along in a minute, shaking his head at her cocked eyebrow. Once everyone has filed out of the room, Nik goes to the corner where his bag sits against his guitar case.

"Listen, this has to be quick, but—David had me put together an arrangement of something he wants a bunch of us to do at the wedding as a surprise for Alex." Nik pulls out a folder filled with sheet music, flips through it and finally hands a sheet to Aaron. "There's a solo part in it for you, if you're interested. Do you still sing? I mean, for real?"

Across the top of the page in Nik's scrawl is his name, which brings back memories—so many notes, old love letters—and Aaron skims the rest. Nik's right—there are a lot of parts here that he's well suited for, but the song... "Oh my God, I'm going to have to make sure both her mascara *and* her eyeliner are Oscar-grade waterproof."

Nik just grins. "Yeah, should be a showstopper."

Aaron glances up with a smile to see the look on Nik's face—a bit awkward, thanks—and finishes skimming his copy of the full arrangement. "It's a big arrangement. Who all's doing this?"

"A mix of people—a bunch of my high school friends, although Tu is sitting it out because he never did any of the music stuff, and he really wants to get good pictures—he's going out tomorrow to get another tripod because he wants to get several angles of film on it. But, yeah, everybody David invited from that group has already been looped in, plus a few people from their a cappella thing in College Station that he thinks can really do it justice—he says some of their guys will join you on the tenor, but some of the parts can be only you, if you want."

Aaron frowns at him. "I don't sing, Nik. Not really. I haven't been in a chorus since middle school—I'm not you guys. You *know* that."

"No, I know, but you know you have a good voice. And Alex would *love* to see you up there with us—that's why David thought you should have some solo parts."

"I thought *you* did the arrangement."

Nik smiles at his feet. "Well, you know I've always liked your voice." Aaron remembers: silly, giddy nights singing along with George Jones and his mom while they washed the dishes, Nik grinning and kissing him when Aaron sang about how lucky he always got with Nik. "You always will—so, so lucky," Nik had whispered, hot against his ear, while his mother had pretended not to notice. It's a good memory, and it leaves Aaron unable to fight the little bubble of joy that pops up; he knows that joy is written across his face.

"Come on, man, say you'll do it. It'll be awesome."

It will be *spectacular*, as long as… "You think we can have it all ready in time?"

Nik's grin doubles in size, and Aaron's grows to match. "I do—everybody's freaking out to make it happen, and we've already had Skype practices to get started. They're all coming in for the party on Thursday, and then on Friday we'll sneak away to do a last-minute rehearsal on the mainland. Just tell Alex you have to help us with clothes or something. Jasmine knows—she's been helping a *ton* with some of the chorus guys so David doesn't have to worry about it too much. It should be fine." Nik looks confident, and it's a good look on him.

Aaron's palms sweat; between Nik's smile and the pressure of performance, there's a lot to take in. It's been a long time since he felt singled out in this way, and singing was never something he was confident about. "You heard me the other night—you really think I'll be okay?"

Nik takes a breath. He looks as though he wants to say something, and then catches himself. More than anything, Aaron wants to know what he wanted to say. Instead, Nik puts his hand on his shoulder and says, "Aaron. You're never anything less than good at anything you do. I don't see any reason this should be any different."

Aaron shakes his head. "I can't believe we're singing in each other's weddings. Well… I mean, not, you know—*each other's* weddings," he says, waving the sheet music.

"No, that would be horrible," Nik says, with a sad smile. "But yeah, I know what you mean. It's really… yeah."

"Very *adult*," Aaron ventures, because wow, didn't *they* somehow get from friendly to strained in a hurry.

Nik looks at him, his eyes suddenly serious. "Yeah. It's time, I guess—time to move on, to finally give up the playing around and go ahead and grow into the people we really are."

"I guess," Aaron says. The moment is serious, solemn, and there's been too much tension tonight. He has to break it. "But before we do that, wanna go see the people we used to be?"

Nik grins at him and waves him forward. "Lead the way! But here, give me that first." He tucks the music away. "I'll give it to you tomorrow, when you're less likely to leave it on the end table for Alex to find." Aaron rolls his eyes.

In the living room, Stephanie is running a video of newspaper headlines from high school, narrating as she goes. *Of course she is.* Stephanie has always been the most irritating person Aaron knows; she's infuriating, but so familiar that she's become very special to him, in her own way. It isn't always easy, though; last week in the city, over sushi, she'd described the last of her meetings as "not quite an interview, but definitely a little more than just a courtesy meeting," whatever that meant. And even though he has known for a few years that Stephanie is a marketer by nature and at least half full of shit at all times, especially when it comes to competing with him and her own judgment of her success, it is still hard not to be jealous. Years after they fought over headlines and editorial duties on their high school newspaper and slugged it out all the way to the Texas State Championships in feature writing, she is doing it; of *course* Stephanie Baxter will be the one to make a successful career in journalism happen, while he dicks around in grad school. She has that *thing*, that natural bulldog nature that makes her a great journalist.

But then, after so much laughter and sweetness and joy in her company, and after the sushi and drinks and dancing—which she paid for, naturally; it's always been good to be friends with the princess, and years of etiquette classes organized by the Jack and Jill mothers had some advantage—it was also good to sit down to his laptop in his crappy little apartment and write about the experience, to pour everything he had into words about his friend and rival and turn bitter memory into pithy memoir, to remember where his own voice lived now. That night he sprawled, drunk and so full he could burst, on his bed in Brooklyn and, laptop at hand, spared a moment to be grateful to her: In addition to all the other gifts she so graciously bestowed, she had made him feel like a real writer. He felt a solidarity with all the others, in their various garrets. He'll never be Hemingway—that homophobic asshole—but for a minute, then, he knew the cruelty of the city, the grasping sting of competition and how it rubs right up against the sheer, craven gratitude for the wealthy friend. Their relationship has always been full of love, but it has always been complicated, too.

Now he watches her, smiles and shakes his head at her, even while he settles down in the house she's provided for Alex's wedding.

Aaron and Nik squeeze into the narrow spot left at the end of one of the sofas farthest from the TV. Aaron leans hard against the arm; the full length of his leg tingles with awareness of the inch or two of space separating him from Nik. Alex wrestles the remote from Stephanie, reminds her that "this is a *group* activity," and holds up a DVD case Aaron recognizes: Alex's senior year digital media class project, an edited collection of a bunch of the video she'd shot over the course of their high school years.

Aaron smiles in surprise; he remembers this project, remembers her doing it and bitching about it, but he hasn't seen it since she put it together. He'd almost forgotten about Nik's silly high school hair, slicked down the way his mother always liked it, but mostly he just can't believe how young they all look. There's a lot of Alex and Andres on this video, because God, Alex loved him, but there's Stephanie and Josh, and Jasmine and her high school boyfriend Joe; it's the three girls, Aaron and the people who came with them. And there are a few shots of David in the background, because he was with Nik so much of the time, and for years if Aaron went somewhere, Nik was there too.

They look young, but they also look... so happy. They were so transparent when they fell in love with each other, and he can't help smiling, bittersweet as it is, because they were only babies. But he's still never felt anything else like it, and, as puppyish as his crush was when it began, it grew into something that still has the power to move him.

"Hung up on somebody else," and, "the people we really are," Nik had said. On the screen is Aaron's babyish face next to Nik's, their cheeks pressed together in the middle of a group of their friends. Aaron was so self-conscious and anxious then, felt so much safer in a group than on his own. He's not ashamed of how he felt about Nik, not embarrassed as he can still sometimes be about his fumbling attempts at aborted relationships. Being with Nik was his first time out, and while it lasted it was profoundly real. Aaron had been so lucky, and he can finally simply be grateful.

There's a section Alex edited to look like photographs piling up on each other, so she could work still photos into the video. He remembers her swearing a blue streak trying to figure out how to get that to work; now he's glad she managed it. There's a whole series of stills of them on the Boardwalk the weekend before school started their junior year. He and Nik had been friends for about a year by then, keeping their friendship going with phone calls and weekends and the odd intramural competition—being so involved in school activities had helped them get to know each other. But that weekend was special: Aaron had come out to Nik a few days before, just after they ran into a guy Nik knew from his Gay-Straight Alliance at school, and that night, on the Ferris wheel that stood at one end of the Boardwalk, Aaron gathered up the courage to take Nik's hand for the very first time. It was the culmination of over a year of longing, and the beginning of almost two years of what is still the most important relationship of his life. And there it is, a photo of everybody who was there that night, one of those mass-selfies that make up about half of his photos from high school. Their cheeks are all pressed together to fit into the frame and he can see the flush high on his own, and remembers that Nik kissed him for the first time the very next night, in Nik's car in front of his house.

As the last of the photos of that night fades into video from junior year football season antics, Nik's hand comes to rest where Aaron's arms are folded. Nik's fingers are warm and calloused and gentle. The tips of his fingers slide over the back of Aaron's hand and glide down to follow the length of his fingers one by one. Then they trace back up. Aaron doesn't know what this is, but he follows the advice of the warm liquid of his belly and moves his hand closer to Nik, letting it rest in the small space between them so that the backs of his fingers curl against the side of Nik's thigh. He can't bring himself to look at Nik, but it's okay because Nik turns Aaron's hand to stroke lazy, drifting circles into his palm, starting at its arches and running down to trace over the bones of his wrist before spiraling back up. *God, his hands.* The moment is a sweet reminder, not just of that night on the Ferris wheel, but also of the few times they'd been able to share a bed, of Nik drawing those same circles down his back so long ago, lazy in the afterglow. Aaron's whole hand feels extra sensitive, as if every pore is trying to absorb Nik, every hair is reaching out to understand, every square centimeter of his skin is aware of Nik and the mystery of his thoughts. Every movement feels significant, laden and slow, so that when Nik slides his fingers between Aaron's own and rubs heavily, deliberately against the juncture of his fingers, loops their fingers together and slides down until they are fingertip to fingertip, Aaron feels it in his dick and can't help it—he has to turn his head to look.

Nik is staring at him, one cheek resting on the back of the sofa and the other lit by the TV. Nik's eyes are dark, his mouth is soft, and their hands slot together palm to palm, fingers interlaced, as Nik's thumb rubs the side of Aaron's hand softly and steadily. For a time after their breakup they'd been so careful not to touch each other; that time has been over for a while, but Aaron is still very aware of where the lines are, of what is a friendly touch and what is something else, and this, this isn't like a hug or a pat on the shoulder or even perching on somebody's lap when there aren't enough chairs. This is deliberate, a statement of intent, and the look on Nik's face makes Aaron want to brace for impact.

Aaron can't take the intensity of Nik's gaze, so he turns back to the television to watch without seeing and concentrate on the feeling of their hands. He's almost twenty-three years old, and the first boy who ever held his hand has taken it again, so sweetly, and it doesn't seem to matter how much sex he's had in the interim, how many ways he's opened his body or seen others do the same for him, because he's suddenly right back at sixteen, when hand-holding seemed the most intimate thing two people could do. He's simultaneously terrified and desperate to feel and remember every moment of contact. It had seemed like such a chaste thing to him in recent years, holding hands, and he hasn't done all that much of it in the last couple years. But this is Nik, and everything about the way he's touching Aaron feels intimate, sexual and exploratory, as if when Nik touches his hands, he's thinking about touching him *everywhere.*

Aaron looks back to see Nik facing forward again. It's funny—they've known each other for so long, they still know so much about each other, and right now all that means is that Aaron can see the trouble etched across Nik's brow, and at the corners of his eyes and mouth, but can only guess at the cause. He squeezes Nik's hand and rubs his thumb across Nik's knuckles just once, and Nik turns back to face him.

The music changes just as their eyes meet in the low light in a moment pregnant with possibility. Aaron feels heavy with it; his body is boneless and pressed into the cushions with the relief of inevitability and the promise of this man's body on his. Nik holds his stare, and his lips purse lazily in a soundless whisper of Aaron's name; his mouth is still so beautiful. Aaron is thinking about leaning over to taste it, just to see, when everybody bursts out laughing and David says, "Oh, man, I can't believe Nik is missing this."

The moment is shattered; a second too late, Aaron realizes what the music change indicated. A moment was captured on this video that he only just now remembers: He and Alex were in the backseat of Nik's car on the way to the grocery store to get supplies to make queso, Nik driving and David in the passenger's seat, when Chamillionaire came on the radio and David and Nik launched into performance mode. Alex was carrying her camera everywhere still, and she had captured the absurdity of the moment by focusing tightly on Nik—this clean-cut Desi with his short hair and spread-collared shirt, driving his mother's Volvo and screaming out lyrics about the police—and then turning the camera on her own grimacing face.

He turns back to the TV and sees Alex roll her eyes one last time before the video cuts to Andres and Alex at a homecoming dance.

Nik squeezes his hand one more time before he extricates his own. He gives Aaron a weak smile and turns to face the room. "Yeah, laugh it up, Williams—you're still sporting the same haircut from high school."

Aaron feels off-balance, as though he's reeling, until Nik pushes back toward him, sliding his whole body a little closer and pressing into Aaron. Aaron keeps breathing and laughs at Jasmine mugging for the camera in a Santa hat with red and green streaks in her bleached blonde hair.

As the film wraps up, while everyone laughs at Alex pulling faces at the camera during senior spring break—just before prom, right before it all fell apart—Aaron slides his arm back and around Nik, drapes it over his shoulder and holds his breath for the instant it takes Nik to nestle into Aaron's side and relax there with a sigh.

A few moments later, Nik stifles a yawn, and his hand comes to rest right above Aaron's knee. Nik's fingers brush the inseam of Aaron's shorts, while his thumb idly traces the shape of Aaron's kneecap. It shouldn't be so sexy, but Aaron can't help leaning down, only for a second, to bury his nose in Nik's dark hair and breathe deeply. *He's changed his shampoo.* Maybe—maybe he's remembering it wrong. It's been a long time.

Aaron thinks about everything they're not saying, and about how much he doesn't *want* to say any of it, not yet, how he wants to stay in this moment of potential for as long as they can. It doesn't look as if he can dodge defining what this moment means for long; he's not ready to answer questions about what's happening between them, and though they've somehow flown under the radar so far, their friends are starting to get restless and soon will be looking around for the next interesting thing to do.

Aaron brings Nik's hand to his lips, and Nik's fingers squeeze around his own when Aaron presses a soft, slow kiss into his knuckles. "Later," he whispers into Nik's hair, and Nik nods against his shoulder before Aaron urges him to shift his weight so he can stand.

He stretches. "Mmmm, I think last night is still catching up with me, and we have a long day tomorrow, ladies. I'm for bed." Nik looks at him and then face-plants into the cushioned arm of the sofa with a muffled groan; Aaron can't help reaching down to ruffle his hair. "'Night, all!"

Jasmine gives him a look, and Alex and David look at him and Nik and each other speculatively, but Stephanie is captivated by her own performance on the screen and everybody else is eating popcorn and seems to be amused by her, so they wave him on.

His bed feels bigger, emptier tonight. But there's a lot to think about, and he lets himself smile just a little while he stares up at the ceiling and finally falls asleep.

In Their Own Words

An email exchange between Aaron and Nik, August 14, 2010:

Hey Nik.

Last night at the Boardwalk we were talking about that game-leveling guide. Here is the link.

It was good to see you and to finally meet the rest of your friends. Alex and Jasmine liked y'all.

Really, that's what you're saying this morning? You sound like an alien. What is wrong with you?

Hey Aaron,

Thanks for the link. Obviously that conversation about a video game was the most important thing that happened last night.

Sincerely,

Nikhil Warren

Thanks for making this easy, Nik. Your compassion is overwhelming. But fine.

You disappeared pretty fast after we got off the Ferris wheel. Were you mad at me? Or upset?

My mom was on her way and you know how she gets if she has to wait. And the whole thing was kind of weird because everybody was there? If I had a chance to do that over again, it would be when it was just us.

I'm sorry. I couldn't wait anymore. I thought it was kind of perfect but I guess not.

It's okay if you just want to be friends, but I really wanted to try. I never did that before, so thanks for at least not freaking out. It will be an okay memory, I think. :-)

That is not at ALL what I want, Aaron. It was perfect in every way except for that one. I just didn't know what to do—you already know I'm a dork. I feel like I'm making you feel bad and I'm sorry—that is not what I want.

Are you going to make me say it?

I think you better.

I was really glad when you held my hand—you have really nice hands. And you're right—it was pretty romantic.

Before, when I imagined a boyfriend, I never thought he could be as cute as you. Now when I imagine a boyfriend, he IS you.

Wow. Okay. Now I'm blushing. And smiling.

I am smiling a lot.

Because I like you so much, Nik. You are a big part of my life and you are a big part of my coming out and I just LIKE you. I like how you get excited about things and I like how smart you are and I like your eyes, which just keep getting more gorgeous. I like how you like your little sister and how you aren't shy or weird about it. I like that you're a good trumpet player and I like that you don't care who knows all these things about you. I like that you let ME know all these things about you, and also that last night you let me hold your hand.

So will you be my boyfriend? Because you also have a really nice mouth and the next time I see you I want to tell you more things I like about you and then go from there.

I haven't been able to stop smiling since last night. I know what you mean.

Band practice lets out in 20 minutes (Mr. D is going to kill me if he sees me emailing but it's worth it) and I am coming straight to your house if you say it's okay.

It's okay.

Tuesday

Aaron Wakes to Alex letting herself into his room; she's still dressed in boxer shorts and a tank top, and her hair is tied in two low pigtails.

"Good morning," she whispers.

"Morning. What time is it?"

"It's a little after eight. I think everybody else is still sleeping, but I couldn't stay in bed any longer. It's dress day!" Her voice is hushed as she makes her way over to the bed and flips back the covers to slide in next to him. She doesn't look likely to go back to sleep, though; her eyes are bright and her expression is filled with barely suppressed excitement. Aaron smiles.

"It *is* dress day." He yawns into his hand and rolls toward her. "When's the last time you tried it on?"

"Not since the final fitting. I didn't want to ruin it."

"Mmmm, admirable restraint; I'm impressed."

"I'm not a moron, Aaron."

"No, I know. Sorry." He scrubs at his eyes, willing himself to wake up a little more. "I just… it's your wedding dress. It's a big deal."

"I know." She grins at him. "Can we do it now?"

He pulled a face. "Now?"

"Please? Please, please, please?"

Alex is so cute like this, pigtails and all; she's always been able to get him to do anything, and she knows it. "Fine, okay! Where is it, anyway? You haven't been keeping it in your room, have you? For David to see?"

"Are you kidding? He doesn't have a romantic bone in his body—he'd be peeking at it without even waiting for me to leave the room."

Aaron thinks about the serenade and suppresses a smile. "It's wrapped and hanging in Jasmine and Stephanie's room."

"Hmm. Is she up yet?"

"Not sure."

"Go get the dress and bring her back with you. We'll do the fitting in here—you can change in the bathroom."

He's up and out of the bathroom when she struggles to clear the doorway with the dress still wrapped in its bag. Her face is lit up, excited, and he can't even resent the early morning wake-up when she looks like this.

Jasmine drags in and face-plants on his bed while Alex gets dressed. "Doesn't she need your help getting into that?" Aaron asks.

"At this hour, she can bring her undressed self out here if she needs help."

"Remind me never to ask you to be *my* maid of honor," he quips, even as his hand strokes her hair while she snuggles more deeply into his discarded pillow. He hates that it's probably going to smell like the smoke she dragged in; their friends must have been up late last night.

Alex shuffles out of the bathroom with her arms twisted behind her, and Aaron zips her up, while Jasmine cracks an eye and squints up at them.

Aaron spins Alex around and holds her hands out to the side, looking her up and down. "Cups sewn in?"

"Yep. The seamstress did that, and added detachable straps, and took it in at the waist and the hem."

"How does it feel? Can you sit?"

Alex perches on the edge of the bed, holding herself tense and upright, and there's not so much as a pucker at the waist.

"No, I mean *really* sit. Are you going to sit like that while you're half-drunk and exhausted from dancing?"

Alex slides back onto the bed, sprawling against Jasmine. Jasmine laughs and shoves her, and Alex leans back harder, throwing her arms out to the side and stretching.

"How does it look when I'm *really sitting?*"

"The dress looks like a dream. You, however, look like you've just puked from too much champagne. You're the bridal cautionary tale."

Alex turns her head to face Jasmine. "Remember how sarcastic and bitchy he was in high school?"

Jasmine slings an arm over Alex's shoulder. "We're so lucky he grew out of that."

While they're giving him shit, he grins and digs his phone out of his pocket, and the moment they look back his way he snaps a photo. Jasmine's hair is everywhere, Alex slouches in her wedding dress and pigtails, and there's not a swipe of makeup to be seen. They look gorgeous.

Alex comes after his phone with vengeance in her voice until he grabs her by the shoulders and bends to look into her eyes. "Your dress, girl. *Your dress,*" he says, and she crushes him in her arms.

When she pulls back, Alex says, "Yes?"

He nods. "Absolutely. Now. Shoes, hair, makeup, jewelry?"

She grins at him and claps her hands. "Shopping."

Two hours later, they've made their excuses to the rest of the house and made it to the Galleria in Houston, chatting a mile a minute in the Tahoe while the radio drones beneath their voices. It feels familiar, a comfortable kind of exciting. Alex and Aaron have finally heard the entire, inglorious last chapter of Jasmine-and-Mitchell, and Alex has given Aaron the "ask me later" look, so he knows there's something missing.

Just as they pull into the underground garage, Jasmine says, "You know, the hell of it is that Mitchell isn't even... I mean, he's good in bed, don't get me wrong." Aaron pulls a face at her in the mirror. "And we have a good time when we're together. But I don't think..."

He pulls into a parking space, and Jasmine's last words hang in the air when he turns off the ignition. "He's not your love story, princess."

She looks at Aaron, then at Alex, and her jaw hardens. "Maybe not everybody gets a love story."

"That's probably true," he concedes. "That doesn't mean I'm accepting anything less than that for any of us."

Jasmine raises a brow. "That's very interesting. Tell me about your love story, Aaron. You been holding out on us?"

Alex chimes in. "That's a very good point. Are we actually in the *middle* of your love story?" Her grin is positively terrifying.

"I have no idea what you're talking about," he says, tucking his sunglasses into their case.

"You had your arm around Nik last night." Jasmine says this as if she's presenting facts in a courtroom.

"Shut up! When I saw them, they were just holding hands!"

"Ohhh, girl, you missed it, then. Aaron had his arm around Nik's shoulders, and Nik's hand was clutching his knee, and they both looked like were ready to pass out in each other's arms. That was some grade-A sexual tension."

"Ladies," he interrupts before Alex can respond. "We need to stay focused. You—" he jabs a finger in Alex's direction, "are getting married in *five days,* and you'll be walking down the beach in bare feet. Which is a choice, but I'm not sure it's the one you want to make. And you," he says, sweeping his gaze to Jasmine, "are the maid of honor, and you still don't have a dress, for goodness' sake. Now. Priorities. Everybody out of the car."

Alex sweeps around the car to take his arm as he locks the door and sweetly says, "That's okay, honey. We have a long drive back."

NINE GRUELING, EXHILARATING HOURS LATER they're back in the car. Jasmine has shucked off her shoes and is rubbing the balls of her feet, and Alex has collapsed in the back seat to loll her head against the window. They're all exhausted, but it's been a good day. They've found perfect little ivory slingbacks with a low heel for Alex to slip on after they're back on the grass, as well as a thin jeweled headband—"It's like a crown. Stephanie will try to steal that from you; guard it with your *life.*"—that Aaron can attach veiling to. For Jasmine they've bought lavender chiffon—the flowing skirt shows off her killer legs and the halter-style neckline leaves her glowing shoulders bare—with nude shoes that make her legs go on *forever.* There's new waterproof mascara and eyeliner, and probably too many accessories, bags and hair combs, and everything they'll need to sparkle. They're going to be *perfect.*

They've cleared the Loop and are headed toward the coast when Jasmine abruptly turns and says, "Okay, spill it."

Aaron is quiet, until Alex's sleepy voice says, "Really, Aaron. We sort of need to know. It's time."

Aaron silently focuses on traffic, then sighs and says, "I don't know what to tell you. Yeah, that happened. No, I don't know what's going on. That was all Nik." He glances at Jasmine, who doesn't seem impressed. "What do you want me to say? If I'm looking for a fuck, it's not like I'm going to be looking in his direction? Because that's true."

"You mean you won't do that *again*." The only thing Jasmine had ever said to him on the subject was, "You both deserve better from each other." She had always liked Nik and had thought he was good for Aaron. He always thought she might have a bit of a crush on him—nothing that could be a problem, and it's not as though he could blame her, but still. Jasmine spent most of high school boy-crazy, at least until she settled down with Joe, and Aaron is not sure that many guys escaped her eye.

"I do. There was nothing about that that I want to do again." Even as he says it, he knows it's a lie. He *wants* Nik's hands on him, wants to taste his red mouth and his tan skin, wants to bury his own hands and face and dick in him and stay there for as long as he can. But that's always been true—he has wanted Nik since he was just starting to understand what that meant—and this simple desire is not the point, anyway, because Nik is not somebody it will *ever* be that easy with.

Alex slides forward to lean between the seats. "What if it's not about sex, Aaron? What if he wants to be with you?"

"First of all: it's *always* about sex, at least a little. And if it's more than that, how is that supposed to work? I don't have any idea where he's going to grad school, but you said he was happy in Austin; I can only guess he'll stay somewhere in Texas. It's not like there aren't any schools here, and you know what his dad is like. My work is the opposite of mobile and, besides that, fuck, I *love* New York."

Alex doesn't meet his eyes in the rearview mirror, and just like that his heart splinters. He hadn't realized how much he'd been hoping, in some small, immature way, that the new connection with Nik *could* be something. Alex looks uncomfortable, maybe even sad, and he knows: It isn't happening. Last night had been wonderful and very exciting, but it can't happen.

"More than you love Nik?" Jasmine throws back.

He bristles. "What are you even *talking* about? I haven't been in love with him for years."

Jasmine gives him a look. "Do you think you're funny?"

He gives her a look of his own, but she goes on. "Look. Aaron. I know you're not that boy from high school anymore, that you're not still an uptight little overachiever who only wants to get the hell out of here. You have moved up and on and I don't even want to know how many men you've slept with, because there's having a good time and then there's full-on-slutty, and it makes me sad to think about you that way."

He rolls his eyes.

"Fine, you make that face, but I remember the boy you used to be, that sweet boy who just wanted somebody wonderful to love you, and baby, *you found him.* You found him five years ago and the two of you managed to fuck it up, and he's still here, and he still makes you crazy. Do you know what I would give to feel that way about somebody again? You're a fool if you're too chickenshit to at least *try.*"

Aaron drives.

When Alex speaks up; her body is still, so he knows she's serious. "She's right. And Aaron, you still make *him* crazy. I can't... you *really* need to talk to him."

He sighs. "You don't understand. I'm not that boy anymore, and besides that—" He breaks off and is quiet before he says, "You don't know how fucked up that whole thing was by the time it ended. Just be glad it's better now. At least we can be in the same room. It's better if nobody pushes it."

Alex locks eyes with him in the rearview mirror. "That's bullshit. That boy is still a part of you. And I know more about that breakup than you realize, Aaron. Not that *you* ever told me anything."

He narrows his eyes and his gaze darts back and forth between the road and the mirror. "What do you know?"

"Nothing you couldn't find out, if you had the balls to do it," Alex says with a look of defiance, as she throws herself back into the seat.

They're quiet for the rest of the drive.

When they pull up to the house, it's after nine. The windows are ablaze with light, and they can hear people laughing from the back decks that face the water. Nik is sitting on the steps facing the street, fooling around on his guitar with his laptop open next to him.

Aaron shakes Alex awake and they all go to the back of the Tahoe to collect their packages. The girls leave Aaron to struggle with everything that isn't Jasmine's dress. Nik laughs and closes his laptop, trying to stop Alex from grabbing a sneak peek at his playlist. "It's not ready yet, Alex! Thursday, we said Thursday!"

"It's my wedding! It has to be perfect, Nik! Just a hint?"

Jasmine, bless her, rolls her eyes and says, "Come on, Bridezilla. Let's get you inside before your sense of entitlement swells any more—Aaron's not going to be able to bake the cake *and* alter your dress again before Saturday." She pokes Alex with her dress hanger.

"Oh, fine. I see how it is. You invite your friends to help you with your *very special occasion* and then they tell you nothing." Alex makes a face at them and walks into the house, chattering about how eager she is to "hang this thing up."

Aaron sets the bags on the porch and drops next to Nik. "Working on the arrangement?"

"Mm hmm, yeah, tinkering a little bit—no real changes, just thinking about the balance of voices." He picks out the opening notes of the song on his guitar. "How was your day?"

Aaron sighs. "Insane. But, on the plus side, Alex is finally fully dressed for Saturday and we found a dress for Jasmine that I need to take up a little tomorrow. I think their clothes are mostly done, although they still need to think about hair and makeup. I haven't done makeup in years, since theater in high school."

Aaron's voice drifts softer and lower as the notes come up behind him, his own accompaniment, and the guitar sounds beautiful as it echoes against the houses. He watches Nik's fingers move over the frets and strings, strong and square, and thinks about the way they touched him last night.

Nik picked up the guitar during their senior year of high school, and Aaron remembers watching him learn to curl around the instrument, remembers the night they'd been so into each other that neither of them noticed when Nik's fingertips began to bleed until he left trails across Aaron's torso. The calluses are still there, and Nik is still beautiful in motion, so *easy* and at home in himself when he plays.

Nik's playing stops, and when Aaron looks up Nik is watching him. "Aaron, can we take a walk, talk or something?"

Aaron looks at him, thinks about all the different kinds of trouble they could get each other into, and sighs. "Yeah. That's probably a good idea." He pauses and stares down at the way Nik's hands have curled around his guitar. "I know a place—come on."

Nik tucks his guitar behind one of the giant porch pillars, and Aaron pulls him up, then drops his hand as they walk the few minutes to a wooden walkway to the beach. The moon is out, the mosquitoes haven't started swarming and it's quiet but for the sound of the water against the shore and the long grasses that cover the dune blowing in the breeze.

"This is where Alex wanted to have the ceremony—it's a beautiful spot, and I can't blame her. But it's far enough from the house that we thought it might be a problem, so it's been axed. I think it has, anyway. I think Tu wants some pictures here."

"How is this walkway still here after hurricane Ike?"

Aaron shrugs. "The HOA rebuilt, just like everybody rebuilt their houses. Stephanie says that it's so low-lying, they have to rebuild all the time anyway. Some people have enough money to keep throwing it at the same losing proposition, I guess."

"They should. It's pretty," Nik says and drops to sit on the bottom step, kicks off his shoes and lets his toes dig into the sand. Aaron shrugs again, kicks off his loafers and joins him. Nik takes his hand.

They sit there for a long time. Now that there's no audience, Nik has brought both of his hands into play, using one to cup Aaron's hand while he traces patterns across Aaron's open palm with the other, following the lines. He starts out looking almost blissed out, but the longer they sit, the more troubled his face becomes.

"Nik," Aaron starts. When there's no response, he says, "Nik, what are we doing?"

Nik keeps looking at their hands, although he stops the stroking and clasps Aaron's hands between both of his own. "Aaron, I... God. I've thought about this so much, I think about *you* so much. I want to be with you. I still... don't you? I thought maybe—Alex said she thought you—I just..."

Aaron has *never* seen Nik this flustered. When Aaron found out Nik was gay, it was from a chance meeting with a kid from Nik's GSA; it seemed to cost Nik *nothing* to say it out loud. To hear him tell the story, he came out to his parents—traditional and pushy and loud as they both are, each in their own, very different ways—without seeming to spend a moment worrying over it. This was the boy who'd once told him, so tenderly and easily, that he *loved* him. *He must be really thrown for a loop to be this inarticulate.*

Aaron knows the feeling—he's reeling, but after everything they've been through, all the ways they've hurt each other, it's so much easier to say, "A lot has happened. We can't go back now and change it all—all of that *happened* and I can't do this for just a few days, even for a very romantic long weekend. That summer at Alex's house—we shouldn't have done that. I don't think we should do it again, not here."

Aaron pauses and watches the water wash gently against the stone jetty a few yards ahead of them. "I was watching us last night, in those videos. I don't know if you were watching, but I was. What we had was *real*, it was intense and as solid as anything can be at that age, and then it was over." He waves a hand, encompassing the water and the two of them there. "This is just... a crazy summer daydream, it can't—"

"It was you. And—Columbia," Nik interrupts. Aaron blinks at him, confused. "Stephanie asked where I was going to grad school. Do you remember, last night at dinner? It's Columbia—I got into Columbia. I'm going next month to find a place to live, and from August on, I'm living in New York."

The line of Nik's jaw is determined, set. And all of a sudden, Aaron gets it: Nik is coming to New York. He might be years too late, but he's finally doing it, he's taking that first step and he's going to be *right there.* Aaron still has no idea what it means, and he's *angry* that Nik can still do this to him, and he has so many questions and, somehow, absolutely nothing to say.

"Congratulations," Aaron finally offers. "I—it's a good school, I think."

"Columbia, NYU and Brooklyn. Those were my top three choices, although I applied to Cornell and Rutgers too, just in case. I just—*Aaron.*" Nik's voice is strained; he looks so animated, and a little bit broken—he looks as if he's about to cry. "I don't want only this weekend. I don't want to fall into bed and fuck around and I don't want to hurt you. Can we try, just, let's see—"

Somewhere in the middle of this monologue, Aaron gives in. He's desperate to shut Nik up, frantic to get out of this, so Aaron does what he knows and he kisses him.

It's gentle, messy at first because Nik's still talking, but his voice rolls over into a low moan as his hands push into Aaron's hair to hold his head in place. Aaron may have initiated the kiss, but Nik makes it his quickly, turning Aaron's head and sliding his hands down to cradle Aaron's face. The last time Aaron tried having a boyfriend, he had done that a lot, too; it had always felt presumptuous, fake, feigned. He'd forgotten how much he loved it when Nik cupped his jaw, splaying his strong, gentle fingers over Aaron's temples as if his face were something precious, something beloved.

Aaron opens his mouth, needing the kiss to be stronger, deeper, because all he can think is they're here, they're here again and this is *everything.* He *wants,* God, he wants it *all,* and when Nik licks into his mouth, fierce and wet and hot, Aaron groans from the bottom of his belly and pushes, urging Nik onto his back right there on the walkway. Nik slides his hands back into Aaron's hair, gripping and pulling him along with him, whining into the kiss and God, he goes, he's going, nothing could keep him away.

Aaron rolls into a straddling position so that he's on his knees over Nik and can get his hands into Nik's hair and lean down over him and plant kisses all over his face, across his eyelids and his jawline and down to his ear. Nik is moaning and breathing harshly—"Oh, God, oh my God, Aaron, please, please"—and he tightens his grip in Aaron's hair and pulls him back in for another kiss. Aaron can't help it, he knows it's too soon, but he carefully slides his knees down so that he can grind against Nik, just one time, because he fucking *needs* it. Nik rips his mouth away and groans so harshly that he sounds gutted, so Aaron rolls his hips again and Nik's moan echoes through the night; one more time and Nik is pushing, rolling them and Aaron is lying there on his side.

He blinks at Nik, who is lying there beside him propped up on an elbow. His mouth is dark in the moonlight and wet, so wet, and his eyes are huge. His words and his breath come out in stutters.

"Jesus fuck, Aaron, you—fuck." Nik's hands push into Aaron's shirt, pulling it out of his shorts to reach underneath, and the roughness of Nik's hands sliding across his belly makes Aaron gasp. Fuck, he's so hard. His hips buck up once. Nik is watching him with wide eyes and his hand stops.

Aaron whines and reaches for him, and Nik comes to him but settles into the crook of Aaron's shoulder and whispers, "Shhh, shhh, listen."

Aaron groans and Nik shushes him by pressing soft kisses against the skin of his neck. God, he still wants to fuck, to lay his hands all over Nik and relearn every inch of him, and he wants Nik all over him, wants that hand that still rests on his belly to slide and tease and pinch and press. But it's good, lying here—he can see the stars, and hear the way he and Nik are breathing, ragged but easing up. Nik starts talking.

"God, I want you. You—you're so fucking hot for it, and I can't wait to watch you fall apart and see how it compares to what I remember, see what you're like now, what you've learned. I still jerk off thinking about how you looked when you went down on me for the first time—remember that day?" Nik rubs slow circles on Aaron's belly.

Of course Aaron remembers—they were in a hurry before Nik's mom got home from work, and he felt nervous and a little scared and was sure he was doing it wrong, and his jaw had ached, but the taste and the *feel* of

Nik were incredible. And he gets it—Nik is slowing them down because he has things he wants to say—but still. He grabs Nik's hair and drags him up into a kiss that starts out hot; that memory is an important one for him, too. His first taste of cock, and it had been a heady vindication that yes, this, *this*. The memory can still make his mouth water.

Nik pulls away, panting. "Fuck. But, also, I… I'm—*I'm in love with you*." Nik looks at him, his face drawn and pleading. "This… if we're really, really lucky, and we still work as well as I think we will, and this all works out… as ridiculous as it may sound, I want this to be my last first time, Aaron. I don't ever want sex with you to be about relief and gratitude. Well, at least not yet. I don't know, I just… just slow down," he says, brushing some hair out of Aaron's eyes before flopping down on his back and finding Aaron's hand.

Aaron blinks at him, waylaid once again by Nik's bright and effortless admission. It's so *tempting*, is the thing. Aaron's not that sweet, romantic boy anymore; he told Alex and Jasmine as much just an hour ago. But they must have been right—that boy must still be in him somewhere, because he's so fucking eager to just *take* what Nik is giving him, to snatch it up with both hands and run with it.

But it's terrifying, too. Three years ago he'd ended a relationship with Michael, beautiful, sweet Michael, who had carried him through the end of his freshman year in college and then been dumped for his trouble because he told Aaron that he loved him. Aaron couldn't say it back, didn't even want to and had been annoyed by the presumption.

He should feel that way now. It's too soon for Nik to say these things, way too soon, but Aaron can't be angry. He can't, because everything in him just wants to hear Nik say it again. Aaron wants it for his younger self, so he can be right, so Nik can be *wrong* to have left him; but he wants it for himself now, too, so he can be loved, so this man who had never left his mind, never left his *heart,* can be his again.

Nik has turned his head to the side and is watching him; his anguish at Aaron's silence seems to deepen by the second, and Aaron says, "Nik, it's been so *long*. How can you say that? Do you even… what does that even *mean*?"

Aaron turns to look at the sky. From the corner of his hooded eyes he can see Nik still staring at him, his eyes bright.

Then Nik takes a deep breath and says, with his voice quiet and earnest, "It means that I still think about you, all the time. It means that I sit beside Alex and wait for her to say your name." He pauses and chances a quick glance up at the sky and then back down, and the rest comes out in a rush. "It means that I dress to see you and I plan what I'm going to say and then I watch you and wonder what you're thinking, and wonder if you're happy. I wonder who you're sleeping with and hate him, hate *them* on principle, because if I had you in my bed again, just one more time, I'd never let you leave in the morning. It means that I fell in love with you five years ago, when we were still mostly kids, and nothing about that has changed—except for how it *has,* because I feel like I know you better now, understand you more even as I see you less often, because I've watched you grow and I've grown a lot myself. It means that I talked to my parents about you before I came here this week—both of them."

Aaron turns his head to look at him, and Nik holds the eye contact with a fierce grimace. "It means that, when I gave Ollie that lap dance at that party, I was hoping you were watching me. And it means that, until I learned how to shut up when I was drunk, I said your name one time when I was having sex with Ollie, because even though we were young, *so* fucking young, oh my God, sex with you was... what it's supposed to feel like. For me."

Aaron steals glances at Nik's open, honest face while he listens, and he wants write this down because goddamn, you don't get declarations like this often and he wants to keep this one *forever,* but he's also... he's *melting,* is what it is. He's falling, all over again, because after everything, after everything that happened, he somehow let himself forget about this, about Nik's absolute willingness to risk himself, to lay it all on the line. And then Nik starts talking about sex, about that night they jumped in David's pool and swam in their underwear, and Nik had ground his wet ass against Oliver. Aaron had wanted to *die* for wanting Nik and hating him. And then Nik reminds Aaron, all over again, of the heat of his body, of the way he felt against him, and that's it.

Aaron pushes up and rolls them, pinning Nik under his body and God, their clothes are going to be ruined at this rate, but at least it's just one more of Nik's faded UT T-shirts and a pair of khaki shorts rubbing up against the rough planking as Aaron leans down and kisses him, hot and dirty, pushing up to his elbows so he can get his hands into Nik's thick hair.

Aaron pulls away, kisses down to Nik's jaw again and whispers, "No more being quiet—let me hear it," before sucking a kiss into that spot low on Nik's throat, the one he'd first found on another summer day so many years ago.

It still works—it lights up Nik's body and brings him surging up against Aaron, calling out for him. "Aaron, fuck, shit—oh, God, Aaron, Aaron." Aaron's going for it now, taking the ride that Nik is giving him, and it's so juvenile, just rubbing against him as if they are teenagers again; but there's time for more, and this is where they started out, and it's so *hot,* stripped back to that place where they can't get enough of each other. Nik clutches at Aaron's back; his words give way to panting and deep groans while his hips work and his leg comes up to wrap around Aaron's ass and pull him closer, tighter. Aaron rolls his hips and licks, his tongue hot and wet, up Nik's neck to suck and nip at his earlobe. He can feel Nik's nails through his shirt when he finally goes tense all over and moans long and loudly—and if the sound doesn't carry clear across the beach, Aaron will be shocked. And he just... doesn't care.

He rolls off Nik and pulls him close so he'll be able to breathe as he comes down—Aaron *needs* Nik right here with him, but can't bear to crush him. Nik's breathing is still far from steady and his eyes are screwed shut, and Aaron can't keep from rubbing gently against him; Nik post-orgasm has always been arousing as hell, so loose and flushed and happy.

Aaron is already thinking about the next time, because this summer he's not stopping at once—he can't wait to get Nik naked, to bite the curve of his bicep and trace his belly with his tongue and dig firm fingers into the muscles of his thighs, to see more of his skin, stretched out under the lights, and the thought makes him groan and snake his hand down to press against the front of his own shorts. Nik's eyes drift open at the movement and he's suddenly alert, grabs Aaron's wrist and drags his hand away and replaces it with his own. Nik's eyes stay locked on Aaron's as he begins to stroke, and Aaron can't look away from Nik's messy hair, his dark eyes and wet mouth; the look in his eyes is intense, possessive. Aaron falls onto his back, gasping for breath, but with his head turned to Nik, staring.

"Aaron, you—fuck, I need to—" and Nik is reaching for the button on Aaron's shorts, pulling it open and using his wrist to push down the zipper so he can wrap his hand around Aaron's dick. His hand is warm, his callouses create just the right kind of friction, and he starts pulling right away. "Fuck, you're so—"

Aaron looks from the ripple of Nik's forearm to his face, his mouth, his eyes locked on Aaron and says, "Oh, God, *Nik*." And that's it, he's gone, spilling over Nik's hand and all over his clothes, and he's warm and his *toes* tingle and his shoulders ache from arching over and over into Nik's hand until he can't take it anymore; he needs to lie down and he lets his arms fall to his side.

Nik flops down next to him and wipes his hand on his wrecked T-shirt, and together they gaze at the sky, lost in their own worlds and waiting for their breathing to slow down.

Aaron finally breaks the silence. "You swear more than I remember. You never did that."

"Mmmm, better to say 'fuck' than 'Aaron'—I think it's become a habit." Aaron smiles. "You've grown into your dick."

Aaron laughs, hopeless and a little broken; he has, Nik's right. "And you're broader, too. And hairier." He rolls onto his side to look at Nik and props himself on an elbow. "I like it. I like all of it, although you should feel free to shout my name when you come." He drops a kiss on Nik's neck and takes a deep breath, then noses at Nik's skin. "God, you're still so damn *sexy*."

Nik pulls him into a kiss as he breathes out Aaron's name; his voice is full of sweetness and gentle affection, and Aaron can't help it, he *wants* it. Aaron's so tired of regret; maybe he'll regret this later, but for now he can't bear to think of that. Except . . .

He breaks the kiss. "Seriously, you can't ever tell Stephanie about this. Or Alex. Or David."

Nik just laughs. "You have overestimated the level of sharing in that friendship. What, are you thinking about how you'll have to lie to Alex?"

Aaron smirks. "I'll tell her someday. It'd be a nice anniversary gift, don't you think, telling her that, on the spot where her bridal portrait was taken, we consummated our burning passion for each other days earlier?"

Nik smiles at Aaron gently, so earnestly. "Tell her it's where we 'made love.' You'll get the bonus of turning her stomach," Nik says.

Aaron runs his fingers through Nik's hair and looks at him. There are so many things he doesn't trust himself to feel or say right now to. Instead he kisses Nik, dragging "Stay with me tonight?" across his lips, feeling the risk in every word and every sweet meeting of their mouths.

Nik nods. "Not yet, though. Stay here for a minute."

Nik pulls Aaron into his strong arms and pillows Aaron's head against his broader shoulder. Aaron listens to Nik's heart beat slow and steady, the warm sound of his body's contentment mixing with the lapping of the water against stone. When he lets his body go soft, languid, content... that's when he knows he's in trouble.

In Their Own Words

A POST FROM *the blog* A Lone Star in Manhattan, *Monday, October 3, 2011:*

So. Let's talk about sex (baby).

Just to be clear, let me define my terms. If activity occurs that could conceivably lead to orgasm and somebody else is involved and actually knows about it, then it counts. Don't get too excited or too disgusted; I'm not dishing details. But I suddenly realized just this afternoon that this is a thing I can do now. It's not like it happened without my knowledge; I was there the whole time. But if I want to I can have cereal for dinner, I can skip a class, and I can get laid—whenever I want to. How amazing is that?

I'm gay, so a whole host of things about sex came as a bit of a surprise. But the *second* time that sex made me reevaluate the world and my place in it was just after I started fooling around with my first boyfriend. I'm sure we all went through this, but for me it was still a revelation; for weeks I was sure that every person I saw might have been doing something naughty just moments before. Who knew what kind of filthy thoughts the library aide might be having? It was so egalitarian, and I kind of loved it; I loved the mystery just as much as I loved the power.

It's been a while. I learned a lot, I went through some adjustments, and now it looks like I'm looking at tracking down partner number two. It's so different to think about this now. I feel as if I already know myself, and the whole process isn't the mystery it used to be. Now I understand the power of sex; now I understand how I work, and what it's like for me. And that's great, but suddenly, now that I'm thinking about this, it's as if

I'm that kid again. Every man I lay eyes on is a potential partner; I'm not saying I want it to, but it *could* happen. I could have Lucky Charms for dinner, I could skip my eight a.m., and I could take that cute boy in my tech and media lecture back to my room.

The world is a miraculous place.

But that brings me back to the beginning: what is sex to *you*? Do you have a working definition? Because the only thing keeping me from implementing this plan immediately is that I have no idea what's expected of me. The last time I did this it was with somebody I had known for a long time, and we talked and talked and talked before anything ever got really good. I'm not up for that right now. So I guess what I'm asking is: Oh my sweet lord, what am I in for?

Wednesday

Aaron opens his eyes to sun streaming into the window and groans, just a little, at the ache in his back. He and Nik woke up sometime after midnight, stiff and sweaty, and hauled themselves up to wander, bleary-eyed and half asleep, back to the house. All the bags were still sitting on the front porch, as well as Nik's laptop and his guitar, and he heard laughter coming from the living room. They'd only just managed to shove everything inside the front door and stumble up the stairs unseen before they stripped down to their underwear—Aaron had thrown Nik a fresh pair—climbed into Aaron's bed and passed out again.

Aaron is glad to have a few minutes to lie here, quiet and still, before he has to get started on the day, because he has a lot to think about.

Nik says he still loves him.

Some small, dark part of him thrills at this, because for so long he thought that Nik didn't, that he never could have loved him if he'd done what he had. The whole thing had been so confused and so fucking *painful,* and the last few months of high school—from the moment Nik had come to his front porch late one night in April and tearfully dropped the bombshell that he wasn't going to New York because he was staying to go to the University of Texas instead, right up until Nik's prom night, when they fought on that porch all over again and then broke up—was a period Aaron tried not to spend too much time considering. There had been so many arguments, so many miscommunications and so much painful confusion that by June he'd been bitter and resentful and so fucking eager to get out of Texas that he decided to find a summer job in New York and left town as soon as he could.

He jumped into the city the way so many had, happy to be there not just for everything the city itself had to offer, but also as part of his grand escape plan, and he drifted through that first summer almost numb to everything he had left behind. Determined to get some good writing out of the whole thing, he started a blog and spitefully titled it *A Lone Star in Manhattan.*

Everybody had advice on how to deal with the breakup, once the actual event was over and he was left to put his life back together according to an undetermined pattern. His mom told him that life was long and he was young, and to wait and see what happened next. Jasmine told him to do what he had to do to get Nik back. Alex said he should give it some time, go see what New York had to offer, but not take for granted what he'd had with Nik, because it was special—just like her and Andy. The writing had been Stephanie's contribution: "Use the experience, Aaron," she'd said. He might have hated her a little for it, but she wasn't wrong; it was how he first started to think of himself as more a memoirist than a journalist, and look where that has taken him.

Aaron threw himself into the city with everything he had, his body and his brain and his words, and it helped. Michael, too, had been a gift, but once Aaron realized it wasn't ever going to work the way he wanted it to—would never *feel* the way he wanted it to— he'd taken control of that part of his life and stopped letting other people in so easily.

Going back to Houston was never going to be easy, but going straight from a breakup with Michael at the end of his first year in college to almost constant contact with Nik over the summer made everything much more difficult. Once that summer was behind him, once he'd allowed himself one last fling with Nik, he felt so *different*—harder, more brittle, but determined to stop feeling bad about himself. Nik was his first love, but also his first hookup, and he wasn't the last.

Nik stirs next to him, and Aaron turns to face him. This is not a view that Aaron has had enough of in his life—he's seen a fair few men wake up, some of them better-looking than Nik, but none so absolutely fundamental to him and to how attraction works for him. Nik's hair is a mess; his jaw is dark with stubble where it hangs slightly ajar. Aaron has seen Nik like this only a time or two; chances to share a bed were rare in high school, and that had been one of the things they daydreamed about when planning to end up in college together. That time seems so long ago, and it's bittersweet to remember.

Nik's eyes flutter open, and Aaron watches him come back to himself; he can see the second Nik realizes Aaron is watching him, because suddenly he's wearing the most beautiful, sleepy smile. "Hey," Nik whispers. His voice is rough, and when he's sleepy he has a little more Texas in his voice than usual, so the vowel stretches long and lazy.

"Good morning," Aaron says back, and then they lie there, breathing together, inches away from each other and unable to stop staring. Nik reaches out to touch Aaron's face, feathering his fingertips across his hairline, over his ear, down his jaw, and Aaron shivers as those fingers delicately move down his neck, tickle his collarbones, slide over his shoulder and gently tug.

"C'mere," Nik mutters, sleep thick in his voice.

Aaron smiles. "I don't know, I'm pretty comfortable here. Maybe *you* should come *here.*"

Nik squeezes his shoulder and pulls harder, saying, "Columbia, remember? You can move the three inches this morning." Aaron just rolls into it, too stunned to continue resisting.

He settles against Nik's bare shoulder, his face turned toward Nik's, and his hand hesitates before it rests on Nik's chest and splays wide across his heart. Aaron plays with the hair on Nik's chest. There's more than he remembers, and it's thick and dark and—on Nik, at least—so appealing. His legs tangle with Nik's, and the arm that's wrapped around him sweeps over his back, cups his shoulder and pulls him in a little tighter.

Nik groans. "God, you feel good." He drops a kiss on Aaron's hair, then lets his head fall back to the pillow and sighs. "You feel really good. Let's never get out of bed."

Aaron laughs. "They'd just come looking."

"Let them. It's worth it. I'm not looking forward to letting you go again, even if it's only for the day."

They fall quiet, waking up to each other, stroking gently and breathing together. There's so much between them; so much that's already gone by, but so much potential, too. Aaron is ready to let the past go, to carry on and move forward—he wants this so badly he would compromise just about anything—and he can finally admit that to himself. Still, he has to ask: "You have to tell me what happened. Back then."

Nik is quiet for a second, but he doesn't act as if he doesn't know what Aaron's talking about, at least. He drops a kiss to Aaron's hair and sighs. "My dad. My dad, and sort of my mom, and money."

Aaron is quiet while the whole story spills out: about how Nik's dad hadn't wanted him at NYU; about how the end of the shuttle program and the killing of that particular fatted calf scared the shit out of Nik's dad and just about every other engineer in the area who had ever worked with NASA; about the scholarship at the University of Texas, his grandfather's legacy there and his dad's insistence that Nik take what was on offer, because he wasn't interested in raiding his retirement to fund Nik through four years of living with his boyfriend on the East Coast.

It began when Nik started applying to schools, but it didn't come to a head until that one night in April, only an hour before Nik ended up on Aaron's front porch, and it ended with a fight that involved Nik's mom and dad and didn't stop until his little sister Alisha came into the room crying and Nik left. It's as messy a story as any Aaron has ever had to tell about his own family, and Nik's bitterness is evident in the telling, especially when he talks about his little sister, the baby Aaron remembers being so full of laughter. Yet Aaron is stuck on one question: "Why didn't you *tell* me all of this?"

Nik scrubs at his face with his free hand. "Because you never asked," Nik says with more bitterness in his tone.

Aaron starts to pull away, but Nik holds him with the hand clasped on his shoulder and says in a low voice, "No. We need to do this, but no running away this time. Stay here." Aaron is stung; his mouth sets in a hard line, and the hand on Nik's chest pulls into a fist. Nik's hand covers it; his thumb brushes softly and tenderly across Aaron's curled knuckles. "Please. Aaron, you *left* me, come the fuck on," he whispers.

Fuck it, that might be fair. And anyway, maybe Nik's right. The contact keeps Aaron a little looser, makes it impossible for him to build up a good head of steam, and as earned as his indignation might be, being close to Nik feels too good to let go of quite yet.

So Aaron stays there, body taut, staring straight past Nik and into the wall, and says, "I left *you*? What are you *talking* about? You told *me* you weren't coming with me to New York. I must have asked why a hundred times that month, and all you ever said was 'It's not possible' and 'I can't.' 'Believe me, it's not that I don't want to' and 'Aaron, I love you, it doesn't have to be like this.' And what you asked was always 'How could you do this to me? Don't you love me?' It wasn't—I just *couldn't*."

Nik sighs again and lifts his hand from Aaron's to rub his eyes as if he's waking up with a headache; Aaron knows the feeling. "It's stupid, I know—within six months I felt like an asshole about it, because I let the whole thing happen, so that much is totally on me. But I didn't know how to tell you how fucked up it all was. I wasn't used to money being an issue, for one thing, and I was *so* embarrassed about that. And it was harder then, dealing with my dad—so much of what went on between me and him left me feeling like it was all my fault, and my mom was pretty much useless with that, at least at first—she didn't know what to do either. She's apologized for it since then, but man, talk about too late.

"By then Dad was angry about *everything* and had taken to saying snide things about you, about us, and I just… I couldn't *tell* you how bad it was—how could I do that? You always came to *me* with stuff that was upsetting you—it felt so weird to even think about throwing all this stuff on the table. And I thought… I mean, not to be a dick about it, but I know you loved me, Aaron. I *know* you did, I felt it, and I *never* thought it could get that bad. And then once it was done, once you left and left *me,* I was just… God, *so* angry."

"Nik, we told each other *everything.* I told you about my *dad.*"

"I know. I *know.* But this was hard for me like nothing had been before, not really. And I told myself that if you ever came to me and just *asked*, if you seemed like you really wanted to listen, then I would tell you, because I would know you were ready to hear it. But you never did. You assumed, right from the start, that it was something I was doing to you because I wanted to, and it was—God, Aaron, do you know what it felt like to know that you trusted me that little? After everything?"

Aaron lies there for a long time. Nik's thumb continues to rub across his hand, and Nik's other hand comes up to sink into the hair at the back of Aaron's head, to hold him there. Aaron thinks back, lets himself really probe those six weeks of painful in-between.

Most of what he remembers is feeling incredibly injured, because Nik is right—that's *exactly* what it felt like. It seemed Nik had done this *to him,* as if he'd thrown away everything they had, and the thing that's most fucked up is that now he's heard Nik's story, of *course* that's what happened. He can't imagine that he ever thought otherwise, because Nik is right about that, too—Aaron does know him, has known him for years. Right now it seems absolutely insane to have thought, all these years, that Nik turned on a dime and decided to be cruel, to simply change his mind. Aaron has no idea how he could have ever *thought* that—and then, maybe he sort of does.

When Aaron was little, he thought he understood how love worked. He knew that you found your person and you stuck it out, even though sometimes it could be hard, and even though sometimes you might fight and yell, and even though sometimes it could be ugly. Love was a mixed blessing: Sometimes he would watch movies with his mom on the sofa and she would be in her soft chenille robe, and love looked so beautiful, and sometimes there was singing, and always the focus and the kisses and the hands were soft. And then sometimes he could hear his parents fighting, usually late at night while he was supposed to be sleeping, and sometimes there was crashing or glass breaking or words he wasn't supposed to say and nothing seemed soft except his pillow, so he tugged it over his head so he could sleep.

And then, when he was seven, his dad was suddenly gone, and then when he was nine he was back, and there was this long period when he wasn't sure how many parents he had, this long stretch of back and forth when most days it didn't really matter but sometimes it really did. Until one day, Aaron's dad said something smart and mean about how Aaron was maybe *too* much like his mother and his mother didn't like that, *at all.* Her face went hard and terrifying and she told his dad to go, chased him out of the house without ever having to raise a hand. There was nothing soft about her then.

It took a long time for Aaron to make sense of what had happened way back then, and it wasn't until after he came out to his mother and she just smiled and ran her hand over his hair and said, "Of course you are, baby," that he understood some of it. He mostly never thinks about any of that, and he certainly hadn't connected it with what happened with Nik before, but maybe some of that is in there, somehow. They say that you learn how to love from watching your parents, and while his mom had a lot to teach him, his dad remains a mystery. Maybe he learned some things he wasn't supposed to.

Now Aaron tries to imagine what Nik might have been through, how it must have felt to have his own dreams shattered and torn away and then to have his boyfriend refuse to work through it *with* him, and he's suddenly so, so ashamed. God, he'd been such a self-righteous dick at eighteen. He really hopes that's been beaten out of him, because if he's lucky enough to have people who still care about him after all of that, then they definitely deserve better.

He lifts himself onto one elbow, and Nik's hand tightens again but he keeps his gaze steady on the ceiling. Aaron cups Nik's face in his hand and pulls his head around so their eyes can meet. Nik's eyes are a little glassy with unshed tears—his face is so open, so pained.

"Oh. Oh, Nik. I am so sorry," Aaron says, and of all the heartfelt words they've ever exchanged, these might be the ones he means the most.

Nik whispers, "Me too." And who cares about morning mouth, really, because this kiss is sweet and tender, poignant and healing and so *honest.* Nik's other hand comes up to slide into Aaron's hair and hold his head there. Aaron deepens the kiss and, just for a moment, imagines what it would be like to never let this man go.

They kiss for long, sweaty minutes; the bedroom heats up as the sun rises and Aaron has to throw off the covers and then kick them down. The kisses are long, lush, exploratory, and Nik keeps breaking them to say Aaron's name or to just look up at him. Nik's eyes have gone golden-green in the light, and Aaron can't get enough of the feeling of Nik's hair between his fingers; it's growing out into thick, wild waves, and he loves it. Aaron finally shifts so that he's more on top of Nik than not; he can feel Nik hard in his underwear and God, that seems like *such* an amazing idea—he wants to kiss him and kiss him until they can't take it anymore, until they're desperate for it and they can break apart together.

Nik suddenly rolls him, and Aaron is afraid it's going to be a reenactment of last night. He doesn't *want* to slow down to talk again, he's through talking. But Nik gathers both Aaron's hands and brings them over his head, leaning his weight on them and hovering over him. He looks beautiful and happy and wild. And then he murmurs, "Yeah, I have you where I want you now," before diving back in to kiss him again and gently rock above him.

Nik had quipped about what Aaron might have learned while they were apart, but this is a new side of Nik, this kind of raw sexual aggression, and it makes Aaron gasp and wish for his hands to be free so he can cling, clasp, pull Nik closer. Instead he simply takes what Nik wants to give him, which appears to be everything.

Nik lowers his head and works his way down Aaron's body, starting at his ears and his jaw and his throat, sucking softly across his collarbones. He's dropped Aaron's hands to push further down the bed, and Aaron is sliding his hands back into Nik's hair when they hear, from the hall, "WEDDING CAMP 2015! FUCK YEAH, RISE AND SHINE, WEDDING BITCHES." Alex bangs her way down the hall, knocking on doors and throwing them open as she passes. Aaron's room is at the far end of the hall, but she's moving fast—

Nik looks up at him, eyes wide. "Did you—"

Alex hits the door and tries the knob, then jiggles it again. "Aaron?"

Aaron clears his throat, looking up at Nik as he does, mentally thanking his long history with the *weirdest roommates ever* for ingraining some good instincts.

"Put the coffee on, Alex—I'll be down in a minute."

After Alex stomps away, Nik collapses against him, giggling, and says in a low voice, "You're a genius. I'll never doubt you again."

Then Alex is back at the door, knocking again, this time a little more quietly. "Aaron? Have you seen Nik?"

Aaron's mind goes blank, and it's a good fifteen seconds before he can just say, "Coffee, Alex!"

It's quiet for a few seconds—maybe he's gotten away with it.

"Aaron!" Alex is going for faux-scandalized, but her excited giggling is sort of ruining it. "Oh my God, Aaron, do you have a *boy* in there?"

"Alex, darling, I'm getting in the shower now, and if you don't have coffee by the time I make it to the kitchen, you're eating Sara Lee on Saturday. You're not the only bitch in this house," he calls, but it's hard to get the attitude right when Nik is crushing him, trying to muffle laughter in his shoulder.

"I understand," she calls back, a little more subdued.

"Thanks. And hey, babycakes—between us?"

"You got it, mouse." If Jasmine is his Doris, then ever since a long, sweaty Tuesday after their freshman year in college when they'd holed up at his house and watched the entire *Tales of the City* miniseries, Alex has been his Mona. Only with, as she'd said then, "Strictly theoretical lesbian action. And oh my God, why don't I have her *hair*?"

Nik gazes down at Aaron; a grin lingers at the corner of his eyes. "Not gonna happen this morning, is it?"

"Alas, no. Although—you're welcome to join me in the shower?" Aaron hopes he will, even though the shower is small—to get his hands on all that skin he'd put up with a lot.

Nik looks as if he's considering it, too, and his eyes go a little hot. He pushes himself up to his knees, and runs his hands all the way down Aaron's body, shoulders to hips to knees to feet, two slow parallel lines of contact and warmth ending with a double squeeze to his feet while Nik sits back on his heels. "I hate myself for saying this, but I think later? I wanted to get a run in this morning, and maybe not being in the kitchen for the first round of breakfast isn't a terrible idea."

Aaron watches him, stretches a little and runs his hands down his own torso to his hips, where he lets one hand drift over the front of his underwear, shapes it to the length of his cock and shows off a little. He knows they need to go, but that doesn't mean he has to like it or make it easy.

Nik groans and dives back on top of him, muttering, "God, you're evil."

Aaron laughs, pushing at him. "No, no, okay, maybe a little—I just wanted you to *feel the pain*."

Rolling his hips, Nik sucks at Aaron's neck and says, "That's what we're calling it now?"

They both collapse into giggles. Eventually they giggle themselves out, and the mood is still, intimate. Nik looks down at Aaron, his eyes warm, and says, "I am so happy to be back here."

Aaron lets the words hang in the air, basks in his contentment and watches Nik back. Finally he pushes some of his hair out of his eyes and says, "I can't believe it's happening."

Nik kisses Aaron's forehead, his nose and his chin and then leaves a sweet, lingering kiss on his mouth. "We'll work on that. You going back to your mom's on Sunday?"

Aaron nods. "Just for a few days, then I have to get back."

"So we have over a week now, and then at least two years, and Aaron, we're going to make the very most of all of it. Then we'll see what happens next."

That's something he can spend the day mulling over, so Aaron kisses Nik and smiles when he gets up. Instead of pulling Nik back to bed, he wraps a robe around himself and looks both ways for Nik before ushering him out and watching his underwear-wrapped ass dash down the hall. It's a delicious way to start the day, really.

WHEN AARON MAKES IT DOWN to breakfast, Alex not only has coffee ready, she's sliding a pile of scrambled eggs, potato, and sausage onto a tortilla for him. He smirks as she puts it in front of him along with a mug of coffee; it's so good to drive her crazy, and he can't help it—he's *happy.*

"Okay, mister: spill," Alex says as she slumps into a chair, both hands wrapped around a mug of coffee, her eyes locked on him.

"Where's everybody else?" Alex flips open the tortilla and adds more pepper before he wraps up the breakfast taco and takes a bite.

She rolls her eyes. "We have maybe three minutes before they're all in here, so either do it now or we can discuss this with an audience. I'm sure Stephanie would *love* to know—"

He laughs. "I always forget how good you are at blackmail. You've gone soft—five years ago you'd have had my neck under your boot already."

"Flip-flops aren't nearly as intimidating, it's true, but I can still take you out, Mister Wilkinson. So, again: spill it."

He pretends to be absorbed in stirring more skim milk into his coffee so he doesn't have to meet her eyes. "I don't know what to tell you; I don't think it's quite ready for prime time." He takes a sip of his coffee and sits back in his chair. "But... something, anyway."

Aaron shrugs. Alex must be able to tell he's not just being cagey, because she sits up and claps her hands together with a little smile and God, it's so like Stephanie he can't help but laugh and shake his head. Alex's time with her sorority sisters has changed her, and not all for worse, but it's sometimes still unexpected.

"And he told you about Columbia?"

"Why yes, *Alex,* he did. And how long have you known about that, by the way? Yesterday's conversation makes a whole lot more sense now, but a little advance intelligence would have been useful."

She smiles. "No way, *Aaron.* That was his bombshell to drop; he's been waiting for months to do it." She pauses and reaches to squeeze his hand. "It's been hard, watching both of you. David and I have... *so* many conversations, you have no *idea,* and David always wants to stay out of people's business and I don't know what they talk about when it's just the two of them, but... I'm really glad, for both of you."

She's gone *so* soft, so sweet, so daffy, in love. It's lovely, if also a little embarrassing. He doesn't tell her to slow down, to not jump to conclusions.

He just lets himself pretend he understands what he's doing and lets her come along for the ride.

He should have known better; trust Alex to take the wind out of his sails with the very next sentence. "So, is he still good in bed?" she asks, a mischievous leer on her face. Last summer he'd gotten drunk at a party and used the opportunity to tell both Alex and David about his sex life, both with and after Nik. It was another reason to be angry that Nik hadn't been around that summer, as far as he was concerned.

"Funny you should ask—I was about to find out when some shrew started banging on my door," he says with a raised brow.

"Oh shit, sorry," she says, eyes wide. "If I'd known I was interrupting *that* glorious reunion, I'd have… well, no, I would still have done it. Just maybe half an hour later?" she says, biting her lip and raising her brows.

"Half an hour? Hell no—after all this time?" He gives her his best sexy face, which can still make her laugh, and thinks about everything he's not telling her about last night.

She's still laughing when almost everybody else—everybody but Nik—floods into the kitchen in one giant herd. Then she's up from her chair in a shot, giving him a wink as she pulls huge boxes of frozen waffles out of the freezer.

Aaron quickly finishes his breakfast so somebody else can slump into his chair and leans against the sink, listening to the chatter fill the room and lazily swiping a sponge over his plate. It seems as though they missed quite a lot last night, another in a long string of drunken Cards Against Humanity battles that have taken the place of their games of Apples to Apples from high school. Stephanie is cheerfully recounting her all-time favorite cards played in response to "What never fails to liven up the party?" to a defeated and increasingly overwhelmed-looking Nicole when Nik bangs through the kitchen door, sweaty and still breathing deeply.

He walks to the cupboard and stretches to grab a clean glass, and Aaron can't be bothered to turn and see if he's the only one who notices how Nik's running shorts ride up his thighs when he does that, because *fuck* his legs are still tight from the run. He comes to the sink and steals the tap from Aaron to fill his glass. He smells like grass and sweat, and

Aaron concentrates very hard on getting the last bits of egg off his plate and trying to listen in on the conversation behind him. Nik finishes the first glass of water in one go. As he pours himself another, he murmurs under his breath, "Good morning again."

Aaron clears his throat, turns to Nik and says, "Good morning. Good run?"

Before he takes another drink, Nik smiles at Aaron over his glass and says, "It was all right. It's beautiful out, but it was hard to get out of bed this morning."

Aaron wants *so badly* to kiss him, to lick that mouth, cool from the water, and curl his hands into Nik's wet, sweaty hair. It's a feeling he's grown used to, over the last six years. The difference now is that he *can*, again; at least he thinks he can, but it's really, really unlikely to go unnoticed, and they haven't talked about this enough yet. Just for a little while and as much as he can, he wants to keep it theirs.

So Aaron says, "Yeah, I know the feeling," and gives Nik a small smile of his own. He puts the last of his dishes in the drainer and says, "I'm gonna go get those bags out of the hallway," and leaves the kitchen.

He's made it to the entryway and bent to pick up the bags they'd left there when he hears footsteps behind him. Still bent over, he turns his head to see Nik standing beside him.

"Hey, *hey*," Nik says, placing a hand on Aaron's lower back. "What was that?"

Aaron looks at him, at his hurt and earnest face, and *fuck it*. He stands and immediately crowds Nik against the front door, one hand sliding around his neck to twine into his hair, the other sliding down his thigh to pull those shorts up and work his hand under so he can cup Nik's ass, and pulls Nik into a kiss that's wildly possessive. He licks into Nik's mouth lewdly, suggestively, and Nik's hair is damp around his fingers and so are his shorts, limp and clinging from sweat.

It's been so sweet so far, but suddenly he thinks of how Nik smells right now, how it would be to bury his face in his crotch and lick the sweat from his balls, and he feels filthy, wanton. He drags his hand from Nik's hair and slides it under the waistband of Nik's shorts and beneath his underwear to get a good handful of his ass, round and strong and sticky with sweat. He licks his way down Nik's neck, lapping up salt and fastening his mouth to the column of Nik's throat, feeling the vibration in his mouth when Nik lets out a low moan. They're out of control and it's *perfect*.

Nik's head tips back to hit the door. "Oh my God, you're gonna kill me. Come upstairs with me," he gasps.

Aaron can't stop his hands from kneading Nik's ass. "I can't— everybody will know."

"I *really* don't give a shit. Do you?"

It's a terrible idea, it really is. This week is about Alex and David, and they don't need this drama. They're locked in a *house* with these people, and there is bound to be some teasing, mocking hell to pay, but Nik is gently rocking against Aaron, who squeezes him tighter, using his hands and hips to grind back, hard. Nik moans.

Aaron pulls away, scrubs at his face for just a second and bends to scoop up his bags. He's already on the third step when he turns around and sees Nik collapsed against the front door wearing a look of confusion. "Well? Are you coming?" he says.

Nik swears as he picks up his guitar case and laptop and hurries after Aaron.

They're not doing a great job taking care of their things, because as soon as they're inside Aaron's room they drop everything by the door. Aaron locks the door and immediately pushes at Nik's shorts and underwear, and Nik swears, toes off his shoes and throws his shirt on the bed just in time for Aaron to push him down on top of it and kneel to mouth at his dick. He licks around and over and laps at his balls while still trying to get Nik's socks off. Nik moans, "Please, *Aaron*," and then he's completely naked and Aaron is pushing him backwards.

Nik braces himself up on his arms, flushed, his skin pebbling where his sweat evaporates in the air conditioning. His cock is *beautiful*—dark and so hard, and already a little wet from Aaron's mouth. There's no time for romance, now—Aaron needs him, needs the smell of him in his nose, so he digs his fingers into Nik's thighs to pull him closer to the edge of the bed, reaches for Nik's dick and pulls him into his mouth.

Nik whimpers above him and slides a hand into Aaron's hair to hold on. It's fast and wet. Aaron pulls off to lick down to Nik's balls, then sucks them into his mouth while Nik moans and flops back against the bed. Aaron slides his hands beneath Nik for a double handful of his ass and licks down to where his thumbs have pulled Nik's cheeks apart and his scent is the strongest so he can lap at his hole. Nik swears and groans above him. They've never done this—this level of want is *way* beyond even their ill-advised summer tryst—but Aaron likes it, likes how Nik throws his legs up to grasp behind his own knees, likes how he grinds his ass back against Aaron's face, how he gasps and swears when Aaron pulls his tongue back into his mouth to get it wet, taking in the strong taste of Nik and pressing it against the roof of his mouth. Nik's legs are strong above his head and Aaron slides his hands up to *feel* them, to dig his fingers into the muscle and hold on.

Nik sounds desperate, so Aaron licks back up and uses both his hands and mouth on Nik's dick, pulling and sucking and sliding. Nik lets out one huge groan before he comes, silently, in a full-body spasm. Aaron holds him through it, sliding his arms around his hips in a gentle squeeze, before standing and starting to work on his pants. Nik blinks and watches with hazy eyes as Aaron undresses and then Nik pulls his legs up again, ready to be fucked, and God, Aaron wants to take him, wants to watch him squirm and pant underneath him.

Just not yet.

He pushes Nik's knees down with a small shake of his head and straddles him. Aaron has left his shirt on, desperate to get down to the essentials. Nik watches him as he licks his own hand and starts jerking off. He can't stop staring at Nik's face and Nik is watching him back; his hands come up to pet and stroke Aaron's thighs. "Yeah, Aaron, come the fuck *on,*" he says, his hands ghosting up and over Aaron's ass, and that's it—Aaron is coming, spilling over Nik's chest *hard,* and whining through it all.

Aaron falls to the side, wrecked, but Nik is right there, using his discarded T–shirt to wipe most of the mess from his chest and then kissing him, crowding into his space and wrapping him up; Aaron is devastated, destroyed.

Nik kisses him through that feeling and then pulls away, his eyes drifting across Aaron's face with a bemused look. Aaron looks back.

"I missed you," he says.

Nik brushes some hair from Aaron's face, strokes his cheek and says nothing.

"No, listen. I *missed* you."

Nik wraps him in his arms and says, "Oh, Aaron. I still love you, too."

And that's it—that simply, Aaron gives up all over again and buys in. He clings to Nik and he lies very still until he's sure he won't cry.

WHILE NIK IS IN THE shower, Aaron stares at the ceiling. Then he grabs his tablet and scrolls through his email. Everything looks fine with his grants for the fall, and everything looks ready for his new job in his new department—he's got a few more emails about paperwork he needs to fill out for tax purposes, but nothing that can't wait. A few new comments on his old blog entries awaiting approval, so he clicks them through. His personal email is a shitshow; there's been another minor roommate dustup—Tara's back to gallivanting about the apartment without pants again, now that it's summer, and Jamie's had it—but Aaron has enough egos to deal with, so he sends back a strongly-worded email about leaving him out of it when he's not there. He ignores the handful of emails he's received from people he sometimes goes out with; they seem especially unappealing.

The water's still running in the shower, so Aaron clicks to his secret personal blog, the one that he only very rarely updates and is *really* personal, strictly anonymous, and has nothing to do with any of his other work. It still doesn't have a title, and he likes that. From the first post it's been a place for working out ideas he doesn't want to attach his name to, things he needs to find a place for if only to get them out of his brain so they don't end up in something he's going to try to publish. It's the only way he knows to keep things private, to force that kind of discipline on himself, and so far it's worked; he's never wanted to use any of this material because everything on the Internet lasts forever, and he would die if even *some* of this stuff ever became attached to his real name. He pauses for a moment, and then starts typing.

I don't think it surprises anybody who knows me at all that I will probably make my living on the strength of my words, one way or another. It makes some sense, I think—I've always had plenty to say, and have always had to work hard to edit my thoughts before they come out of my sarcastic mouth. And the voice I write in here is a version of authentic—I really am this mean-spirited and cynical and scared of everything. Live in fear, live in horror.

The irony, of course, is that when there are gentle and tender things I really need to say, I often find myself coming up short.

Which is to say that there's a man—The Boy, in fact. We've reunited after a long time apart, and he's sweet and beautiful and he's grown into himself. And he's changing his whole life to try to be with me, and I want it—I want **him,** *all of him.*

Once upon a time, in a land just up the interstate, he helped me learn exactly the right words to say to him, back when I was falling in love for the very first time, back when we were still kids. It was so easy, then, to tell him everything, to just peel myself open and give him everything: in whispers, in letters, in more emails and text messages than I care to remember. I have never had this problem before, ever: but as I've developed my professional voice and some of my other skills of expression (you're all filthy, filthy people; you're also not wrong), I think I've lost the ability to **live** *through my words, to let them express who I am and what I'm feeling. Or maybe it's more than that; maybe it's simply that he's one of the few people I've known who I want to give everything to. I would be willing to share with him the scary secrets inside of me that can be expressed in the very simplest words: my fears, my hopes,* **everything,** *and all of it I would happily lay out before him with no thought of how pretty it sounded. And that's a lot of power to give somebody when you usually care so much about how the message is put together.*

*What I **really** mean to say is: I'm in love with him, I have **always** been in love with him, and it really is just that simple. I am for him. I told him that once, I told him one thousand times, and I thought he hadn't heard me.*

Turns out he did. And now I need to learn to say it again.

He hits post, watches the page update and then stares at it for a long time.

ONCE NIK IS OUT OF the shower and they're back in the kitchen, they find that everybody has cleared out except Alex and David, who are sitting at the table holding hands and talking quietly. When Aaron and Nik walk into the kitchen, Alex and David stare at them until Alex bursts out laughing and comes to hug Nik.

"Oh, you're both just so—can we talk about this *now?*" she says, squeezing Nik's shoulders.

Aaron hasn't really blushed much since high school, but he can feel heat rising in his cheeks. Nik rests a hand on his back and steers him to the table, where they sit while Alex gets them cups of coffee.

Nik tips his chair back. "What's up? I feel like I'm facing down the Broussard women all over again," he jokes, but there's tension in his voice.

David clears his throat. "So this is happening now? No more long looks, no more worries and 'he saids'?"

"David, man, I thought you'd be happy for me. You've been telling me for *years* that I—"

"I know I did. And you decided to listen to me the week that you're my best man and Alex is counting on Aaron to pull everything together?"

Nik is staring at David, and Alex has drifted over to put a hand on David's shoulder.

"Are you actually *angry* at me? I'm sorry, David, I didn't realize I had to have your approval for our timetable, but it's the first time we've been in the same place since I—"

"Nik! Relax. Nobody's angry," Alex says, putting both hands on David's shoulders for a squeeze. "I think he's just anxious, and that's probably my fault. He's... well, Aaron knows. We both want this wedding to be *perfect*—we've pissed off both of our mothers to do it on our own, and I think we're both... tenser than we've been letting on." David looks up at her, his brow furrowed with a sweet, private look, and covers one of her hands with one of his. Aaron hates that this conversation is happening, but part of him that loves watching them work through their anxiety together.

"Nik, man, I want you to be happy. It's just that there's been... okay, look, there's been a lot of unhappiness between the two of you, and the look on your face when Aaron left the room and the way you took off after him—I can't deal with the pining and the puppy-dog eyes this week. Were you two somewhere sniping at each other all this time, *already*?" His face is drawn, concerned, and Aaron can barely hold in a wave of affection for him.

Aaron looks at Nik, who stares back at him with a bemused grin. Then he turns to look at Alex, who is grinning and then bursts out laughing. Aaron and Nik both join her, and David groans and tips his face into his hands.

David groans. "Man, I can't believe my best man is going to get more action this week than I am."

Alex slaps him on the shoulder and says, "David!"

"What?" Nik and Aaron both blurt.

"Shut up, it's *romantic*," she says defensively and her face colors as she crosses her arms across her chest.

"It's *insane*," Aaron retorts. "God, no wonder he's snapping at people; the man needs stress relief, Alex!"

"I relieve his stress plenty, thank you very much—"

Nik holds his hands up and mouths, "TMI."

"And I'll have you know that it's supposed to deepen the marital bond, to come to your wedding day... newly chaste. Well. Sort of," Alex says as her voice trails off. It's clear that she's not even kidding herself.

Aaron smirks. "Whatever makes you feel better, Carrie Underwood. I'm just glad I'm not on that regimen, because my very good friend has been possessed by the spirit of Bridezilla, and my stress levels have never been higher."

David recovers enough to say, "Thank you! Exactly! That's my point! It hardly seems fair that this week I'm going to be suffering while you guys are... doing whatever it is you're doing. Finally. God *damn* it, Alex—are you sure this is a good idea?" He looks up at her, pleading, but Aaron could have told him that ganging up on Alex is a sure way to shut her down; it's probably worth taking the time to try to have that talk with him sometime in the next three days. Alex folds her arms and raises her chin and yeah, Aaron already knows how this is going to end.

Nik pipes up. "Well... I guess we could—"

"Nik!" Aaron interjects. "What are you doing?"

David and Nik lock eyes and assess each other as only two brothers can.

"No fucking?" David holds out his fist to bump, and Nik gives him a level look and a nod and bumps it.

"No fucking." They stand for a ridiculous bro-hug that leaves Alex beaming.

Aaron puts his heads in his hands and moans, "Oh my God, I hate you all."

"Ease up, man. It's already Wednesday; you can wait until Saturday."

Nik leans over to Aaron and whispers in his ear, "Don't hate me; I'm going to be a teacher. I can find a creative way around *anything.*"

Wednesday is the day the entire house starts to feel the wedding bearing down on them—there's so much to be done. Aaron sends Mia and Nicole off with the shopping list for the food and liquor and finally entrusts Stephanie with the keys to his car after it becomes clear that the alterations to Jasmine's dress will take longer than he thought and he isn't going *anywhere* until they're finished. It takes until two that afternoon before everybody is satisfied with the final result, and then he sits down with Alex and Jasmine to finish their hair and makeup negotiations over salads they throw together from last night's leftovers.

He recruits them to help with the cake decorations after lunch; they've agreed to use violets from the Baxter's flower flats—Stephanie swore her mother wouldn't care, and with luck he'll be back on the East Coast before she notices. But Alex also likes the look of jeweled cake picks and a fantastic—gaudy, but definitely fun—rhinestone monogram for the top of the cake. He gets them started making picks with crystals, wire and some needle-nosed pliers, then sits at the other end of the long dining room table with stencils, glue and rhinestones to make the monogram.

He's engrossed in his work until he reaches for his glue bottle only to find it missing. When he looks up, Nik is sitting on the edge of the table, cradling the bottle in his hands and looking back at him.

"You still know how to make everything?" Nik asks in a low voice, and Aaron recognizes that quirk in his brow—Nik actually picked it up from him sometime in their last year of high school. Stephanie said it was a sign that they were simpatico, Jasmine found it vaguely creepy and Aaron thought it was adorable. He still does.

"You know what my mom says about idle hands. Besides, it's like Alex designed this wedding pretty much for me to come in and take over." He slants a look at her, and she sticks the tip of her tongue out at him and grins.

Nik is smiling. "I wouldn't be surprised if she did. She thinks the world of you, you know. She talks about you all the time. "

"Lies, these are all terrible, slanderous lies. Cool it, Warren," Alex sing-songs from the other side of the table.

Aaron snorts. "We're all lucky that my mother believes in doing things herself. And that she believes practical isn't good enough; everything also has to be *pretty*. I have been well trained."

"Well, she's really good at making very pretty things," Nik says.

Aaron stares at him as an incredulous smile grows on his face. *Jesus Christ,* is he laying it on thick. It's reminiscent of what Nik was like a thousand years ago, when a "romantic" night out meant going to dinner and a movie at the mall but also getting to hear things like this. Nik has *always* been like this, relentlessly and unflinchingly romantic, without a single embarrassed bone in his body, and if Aaron had thought the part of him that could appreciate that was dead... well, he's wrong all the time, so that's hardly news.

The moment is broken when Alex starts to giggle and Jasmine says. "Oh my God, *Nik*. Get it together, son. Did you actually forget we were *in the room*?"

Nik closes his eyes and makes a face. "Yeah. Thanks for reminding me so graciously, though." He steps around Aaron, puts his hands on his shoulders and bends down to kiss Aaron's hair. "Anything else you want to say, while we're already completely embarrassed?"

Jasmine gives him her very best bitch look and holds eye contact for a long few seconds before she smiles. "I think I need to talk to Aaron first, but I said everything I needed to say to you about Aaron years ago, Nik. Don't tell me you don't remember."

"Understood."

She looks at him for a few beats longer, then turns her bitch face to Aaron. "This time I'm saying it to you too, though—don't fuck it up again."

"Message received, princess, but let me ask: Are you looking forward to seeing Joe this weekend?"

The expression on her face is priceless, but just then Tu sweeps into the dining room with his camera, eager to get a few snaps of wedding preparations, and Aaron files the tiny revelation of that moment away as something to be revisited.

That night at dinner, Nik slides into the seat next to him and pours him a glass of wine. Conversation is animated, excited, and when it's his turn to check in, Aaron tells the group about the shopping trip and shows off the completed cake-toppers. Nik rests his hand on Aaron's shoulder as he leans over to take a closer look at the curl of the letters, and Aaron catches Stephanie's eye across the table. She's smirking into her glass of wine, and he only cocks his head and shrugs; and then she smiles, radiant and happy. When he stands to clear the table, Jasmine grabs his hand as he reaches for her plate, and when she slides their fingers together to tickle his fingertips, he grins at the old, familiar handshake and winks at her.

After dinner, Aaron slips into the kitchen to bake the cakes, eager to get them in the refrigerator before bed so he can do most of the work tomorrow. He brings the timer to the living room and perches on the edge of the sofa closest to the kitchen with Nik sitting on the floor and leaning back against his legs. Between his runs to the kitchen, they get their asses handed to them in Trivial Pursuit; their pairing is strong in the cultural categories but utterly hopeless in Science & Nature, and Aaron's kitchen chemistry and Nik's jokes about that *other* kind of chemistry don't do much to help their cause. Later, though, Nik helps Aaron wrap the cakes and place them in the refrigerator, and then drops out of the game so he can drag Aaron to bed early—it's all Aaron can do not to stick out his tongue at David's raised eyebrows as they go— and quietly make bad jokes about friction and conservation of energy as they rock against each other slowly and insistently and so, so carefully.

Nik falls asleep in the middle of a kiss, and Aaron laughs at the symbolism and then lies awake and thinks of what he remembers from his physics class in college about inertia and momentum, potential energy and bodies in motion, until he drifts off with his front plastered to Nik's back.

In Their Own Words

*A*n email dated February 14, 2011:

I can't sleep. Mom was so tired she fell asleep in front of the news again, and I finished my homework in a panic by seven because I was SURE your mom was going to call here and I wanted it done before we got into it. So there is really nothing to do right now except freak out. You should be sleeping or I would text you, but knowing your dad he took your phone, and the last thing I want to do right now is make anybody in your house angrier at me. Or you.

I am SO SORRY, Nik. I know it's not anything I did, really, but I feel guilty, like I got you into trouble you were trying so hard to avoid. I swear I didn't hear anything either—for what it's worth, when I left, I did notice that your dad hadn't pulled into the garage, so that's why we didn't hear the door going up. I hope it wasn't too bad when I left, and I hope your mom didn't cry. I know you hate that.

Also: okay, so I know what we had just finished doing, but I don't know what HE knows. We were dressed, everything was covered. Does he know?

One last thing: Until he came home, until he opened your door, until your eyes got wider than I have ever seen them, this was the best, sweetest afternoon of my life. I'm sorry you're sick, and I'm sorry that it ended like it did, but I liked making special grilled cheese for you and I liked feeling like I had a place to be after school, that I was needed. I liked pretending that I was coming home to you, and I like what it means about what New York can be. I'm sorry your dad was there, but I'm not sorry that I was, or that you were. I'm not sorry for all the ways I can find to take care of you, and all I can really think about right now are other ways to make you feel better and better. Only some of them require you to have a fever. None of them require it to be Valentine's Day.

Okay. I'm going to send this now. Let me know how it's going over there as soon as you can. I can't stand this. Happy Valentine's Day, Nik.

Thursday

Aaron slips out of bed early with one last kiss to Nik's shoulder and, after a quick shower, he grabs his phone and sneaks out to the front porch. The morning is sticky, overcast and still, and even the Gulf seems lazy as uninspired waves collapse slowly over the gray of the sand. He woke up with someone on his mind, and he needs to make a call.

It's just after seven, so he calls the work number. He paces while the phone rings, anxious when it rings more than three times and then he's more tightly-wound when he hears, "Brenda's Baby and Kid Care, this is Karen, how may I help you?"

"Aunt Karen, it's Aaron."

"Aaron! Oh, there you are, it's showing up now—we got a new phone system for this side of the house and it is *so* laggy on the caller ID, I'm sorry. How you doin', honey?"

"I'm good. Everything's going fine here."

"Alex isn't working you too hard, is she?"

"Oh, you know. It's Alex. She's freaking out, obviously, but it's not like I'm not used to her when she's in an absolute panic."

"Are you having fun, at least?"

He kicks the side of the house and pictures his aunt, standing there with a baby on her hip. "You know I am. How are things there?"

"*Busy.* The teachers go back to work next week, so we've got a lot of theirs here so they can have a few days to themselves before it all gets started again, and there's a whole crop of little bitty ones, and you know what they're like."

Does he ever. "Totally unreasonable, but absolutely adorable. I bet she's in love with all of them and can't stop bitching about it."

"You got it, honey, and between us, I'm sure the money's nice."

He smiles; it's nice to know that this is in no way about him and how much he costs, because there was a time when he wasn't so sure. "No doubt. Is she busy, then?"

"I think she's probably not too busy to talk to you. Did you need to…"

"Yeah, Aunt Karen, please, if you don't mind." He winces.

"It's not a problem, honey—you never are. We'll see you Sunday?"

"Um… yeah, I think so. I'll let you know as it gets closer. Is that okay?"

"Perfectly fine. Hang on a second, and if I disconnect you, just call back, okay?"

The line goes dead before he can respond, and after almost two minutes of silence his mom picks up with a fumble and a thud.

"Aaron?"

There's tinkly music in the background, and he can picture his mom, surrounded by cribs and toys and sticky hands, standing in the addition she paid for in barter and years of savings. She's been watching kids since he was little, but once his dad was gone for good she'd become serious about making a living at it, and the business she's built is the culmination of over a decade of careful planning and smart decisions. Their lives are completely different, but he is so damn proud of her, and suddenly he misses her desperately even though it's only been a few days. He leans against the wall of the house and slides down until he's seated.

"Yeah, Mom. Hi."

"How you doing? Getting ready to get Alex all married up?"

"I think so. She's… do you remember how excited she was when we got tickets to see Janet Jackson at the rodeo our senior year? Give her five years to grow up a little bit, then multiply by one thousand. She's *that*."

Brenda chuckles. "That must be a picture; she always was so pretty when she was excited—her face gets all full of life and it's like she's a whole new girl. Give her a big hug for me, will you, and tell her I'm so sorry to miss her big day. It's such a busy time, honey, and I'm pretty sure I'll just want to rest this weekend. Josh'll be bringing a gift, though, and it looks like Megan is going to have to work, so it'll be just him and Joe."

"I'll tell her." He's quiet for a few seconds, and then he says, "Mom, do you... I mean, I know you've got work and all, but can you talk for a minute?"

He can hear her office chair creak as she sits down, and it wrings the knot in his belly a little tighter to know what he must sound like if she had already headed for the office.

"Any time, Aaron, *any* time, you know that. Just hang on a second." Her voice is muffled by the hand he knows she's pressed over the phone as she calls out to one of the girls she sometimes hires. It's morning, so they're maneuvering around drop-off and breakfast; this is a rhythm he knows in his bones after helping out himself during so many school holidays. He leans against the side of the house and lets his head thump against the concrete siding and his eyes slide closed while he listens to her muffled vowels and the misshapen pitch contour of her voice. He thinks about her hand over the mouthpiece—her hands are where her age is showing up first, but they're still so *strong*.

"Okay," she finally says, and he's startled by the clarity of her voice. "Tell me what's going on."

It seems as if he has no time to waste, so he launches directly into it. "It's Nik."

"I figured. Is Ollie there?"

He laughs, just a little, and tears up at the same time. "No. No, not at all. They broke up." He pauses, and then dives in. "He's moving to New York in the fall. For grad school. And... also for me. He's coming to New York."

She's silent, the only sound the faint drone of NPR she always has running on the clock radio perched on top of her desk shelf; she says she keeps it on to remind her that there are adults somewhere out in the world, because sometimes she can forget by lunchtime. Then, all at once, Aaron hears a quick intake of breath and the rustle of fabric and creak of ancient springs as his mom leans back in her chair.

"Oh, *Aaron*. Oh my *God*."

"I *know*. I know, okay." Her hush has settled over him, too. "It's... we... he's still in love with me."

"Did he *say* that? In those words?"

"He did. And he is, Mom. I'm absolutely sure of it."

"Tell me the whole thing."

He smiles, then, because of course that's what she wants, so he does— sort of. He tells her an edited version, a sanitized story about how Nik chased him and about how incredibly easy he was to catch.

There's another pause on the phone, and then she asks, laughter in her voice, "So exactly how back together are you?"

"Mom."

"Oh come on, honey. I'm trying to figure out how I can help. All I mean is, how much of a done deal is this?"

Aaron takes a chance, screws up his face and says, "I left him in my bed to make this phone call."

Brenda gasps. "Aaron Joseph Wilkinson!"

"I'm sorry, but you asked! And it's true, and I'm not gonna act like it isn't once we're back there, so you might as well know."

"Oh, *Aaron*. That doesn't... honey, I *hate* saying this to you. But that doesn't necessarily mean anything. You know that, right?"

"Mother. Believe me, I *know*. But this time it does. I really think it does."

"So you're saying you both jumped into it feet first, without really thinking about it."

He thinks about that and tries to figure out how to say what's been lurking in the back of his mind. "Actually, I don't think so. It feels more like we've picked up exactly where we would have been if we had never broken up."

"But you *did*, honey, is my point. You broke up a long time ago, and it was hard and messy and awful. Did he ever explain exactly why?"

"His dad, basically. His dad's worst side, and then money stuff."

His mom is silent while, he's sure, she works through the mental puzzle, slotting the players together in the right configurations, and then she sighs. "Well, that sounds just about right. His mom was such a nice lady, but his dad could be a *real* hard-ass. Poor kid. And he didn't tell you any of this then?"

He winces. "Yeah, I think a lot of that might be on me." His mother snorts. "I know. I was *such* a jackass, and I don't think I was in any position to listen. And he was completely freaked out, and didn't know how to tell me without shouting it in my face, which I don't think he could have done. It was just too much, and we blew it."

His mother's voice is soft and sympathetic. "You were both so damn *young,* honey."

"We were. We aren't any more."

"You're younger than you think you are."

"But not as young as *you* think I am."

Brenda chuckles. "Now *that* is probably true." She pauses, and then she finally asks the right question. "So why're you calling me?"

"Mmm, that's a good question. I'm not exactly sure." He pleats the hem of his shorts, lets it go and then does it all over again. "I think because… it feels important? To my life, I mean. It feels like a big deal. And you should know about those things. I *need* you to know about those things."

He can tell she is choking up when she finally speaks. "Okay. Baby, I'm so proud of you. Thank you."

"Mom," he says, his voice level.

She sniffs, just once, before she comes back with her voice a little more in control. "I know. Okay. Okay." She blows out a long breath and then says, one more time, "Okay. But—let me ask you something else. Why haven't I gotten this phone call before? You're a good-looking kid and I'm sure you've been dating, and I haven't heard one single, solitary word about a boy since Nik."

He takes a second to feel surprised that he never told his mother about Michael. Now that he thinks about it, nobody back home knows about *anybody* at school; his mom has visited enough times to meet his roommates and put faces to names, but that's about it. "I guess that's because he's the one that really matters." How easily he says it; it's so stark and simple it makes him smile and want to beat his head against the wall, and his eyes fill with tears again.

"My *goodness*, Aaron. Okay, so there you go. You really happy?"

"I'm... I think I am, underneath being absolutely fucking *terrified*. Sorry, language, I'm sorry."

She chuckles, low and easily, and says, "No, yeah, that sounds about right. I think it is terrifying. But one more thing: You said he was in love with you. You feel the same way?"

He's quiet, because saying this out loud is a new thing, and he doesn't know how to say it without sounding pathetic and he hates himself a little for that. "For a very long time, and... without any real interruption."

"Oh. So there you go," his mom says, this time in a soft whisper, like she used to use the few times he remembers going to church with her. She blows out a big breath and laughs her way through the tail end of it, and when she speaks again her voice is back to normal. "Well. It's like I've always said: You are *stubborn* like a damn mule. I should have known it would always end up back here."

"You could have told me!" he says, wiping away tears.

"Like you woulda listened if I had said so then."

"Yeah. Mama, I—thank you."

"Like I said, baby boy, any time. Is he coming back this way with you after the wedding?"

"I think so. He's spending the summer at home, so he'll be around when I am."

"Get him over here. I want to see him."

He rolls his eyes, seventeen all over again. "Mama, tell me you're not going all protective again."

"I think I've earned it—he wasn't the only one you were an ass to that last semester of high school—but no. He was always such a good boy, real respectful, and I'd like to see how he turned out. And he can remind me why I don't drive over and tear a strip off of his old man —shoulda done that a long time ago."

Aaron grins. "We should put together a posse."

"And, you know... your aunt Karen will want to see you two together. She always thought he was a handsome boy. It'll help her feel a lot better about this whole thing."

"Karen, huh?"

"Honey, you know exactly how nosy my sister is."

"Uh huh. It's fine—I'm sure he'll want to see you, too. I'll call you with the schedule once we figure it out."

He can hear the grin in her voice. "That sounds great, baby." After a pause she says, "When we get off the phone you're going back to bed, aren't you?"

He grins back. "It's a distinct possibility, yes."

"So, look, Aaron, honey, I've been wanting to talk to you for a long time about, uh, about your new graduate program! Tell me more about that, why don't you."

He laughs down the phone, "I love you, Mama."

"Love you too, Aaron. Tell Nik I said hello."

"I will. I'll talk to you soon."

And just as he's getting ready to hang up, his mom says, "Hey, Aaron? I'm so happy for you both, baby."

"Thank you."

After he hangs up, he sits on the porch for a few minutes longer and then slips into the house, creeps up the stairs and lies, fully clothed, on his bed, watching Nik sleep. Eventually Nik stirs, his eyes twitch and his head turns toward Aaron before he fully wakes. His eyes are still sleepy and content when he cracks them open and says, sleep clouding his voice, "'Morning."

And it's on Aaron's lips to tell him, to say everything he's been carrying around that is roaring up in him like a untapped well, but then Nik rolls against him and he smells so *good,* and he's warm and pliable and his mouth is wet and morning-sour, and the words are lost in just one more slip of the tongue.

They'll keep. He wraps an arm around Nik and holds him there.

AARON LINGERS IN BED WHILE Nik goes on his run, staring at the ceiling. Nik left the door ajar when he went back to the room he shares with Tu to change, and, already anticipating Alex's arrival, Aaron lets it stay that way.

He thinks about his conversation with his mom and lets his mind wander back to that spring, to overhearing his mom talking to Aunt Karen in the kitchen late at night. At the time he felt vindicated, a little victorious, to hear the anger at Nik that was buried in her voice. He was *so* hurt, dumped and jilted and abandoned after they'd shared so much, and hearing his mom rage on his behalf threw him right back to the day, years before, when his mom had finally told his dad to get lost. He gloried in it, wallowed in his righteous anger and the fact that, no matter what, his mother was always on his side. He had stayed angry for a long time, and he hadn't allowed himself to tip over into melancholy and mourning until sometime in his sophomore year in college, long weeks after he and Nik had tipped into bed after too many drinks and savagely taken advantage of each other. That episode had changed the way he thought about their relationship so much, and, even though he still hates that it happened, he also thinks now that maybe it *had* to, that that closeness, that flip side to their intimacy, had burned off much of the rage and let him carry on.

He's thinking about that morning after, how he finally gave in and cried in the shower after he made it home, how free he finally felt once the weeping was over, when Alex pushes open his door after a soft knock.

"'Morning. Nik already gone?" She stands in the doorway in a green tank top and plaid boxers with her hair loose around her shoulders.

"He's running." He gives her a grin that's all teeth. "Come stare at the ceiling with me."

She flops down on the bed, mirroring his loose and easy position. She rolls against him, bumps him with her shoulder and asks, "What are we looking at? Is it like the clouds?"

"We're looking for answers, Alex. Don't be silly." They lie there for another minute, just resting together quietly, and then Aaron says, "I called my mom this morning."

"About Nik?" He keeps his eyes on the ceiling, but he nods, and the big breath she exhales out lets him know that yeah, she saw. "Whoa, so that's intense. How did that go?"

"Better than I expected, really. I went in expecting to have to defend him, but she seems to be willing to go with it." After a second he asks, "When did you know the reasons he didn't come to New York?"

She sighs. "God, Aaron. That was… *years* ago. Right after that party where you guys hooked up again." She pauses and then rolls toward him, resting on her side. "David and I had an argument about it—it was our first really big fight. The next morning Nik was super quiet, but it was pretty obvious what had happened—you marked him up pretty good." He winces, thinking about Nik spread across navy blue sheets, bruises on his throat and hips.

"I was pissed, because I couldn't believe that after everything, the two of you had just rolled back into this fucked up *thing,* and I took it out on David—God, I was *such* a bitch that morning," she continues. "After everybody left, he dragged me into the living room and we had it *out,* and he told me everything then. About what a mess Nik was after you broke it off at his prom, how he called that night, feeling like he'd given up like two years of his life and gone deep into all this conflict with his parents and just had it all thrown back in his face at the last minute. Do you know he spent the rest of that weekend at David's?"

Aaron shakes his head and keeps his eyes fixed on the ceiling.

"Okay, so David went to prom with some girl he wasn't really into—"

"Livvy," Aaron supplies. "They were math club friends. Nice girl, pretty hair, boring dress."

"Right, fine, whatever. Anyway, so Nik called David right after he left your house and David ditched her because Nik didn't want to go home. He slept on David's bedroom floor for the rest of the weekend because he was so pissed at his parents, and by the end David called in Tu to sit with them and bring them food and stuff, because Nik was a *disaster* and he didn't want to leave him even to go down to the kitchen or whatever. He makes it sound like it was a hell of a weekend. It's part of why they're all still so close, I think. Kind of like us and how we had to put you back together."

He remembers; he remembers crying, screaming—so much drama. He finally turns toward her. "Why didn't you ever tell me any of that?"

She shrugs one shoulder. "What was the point? Did you not *know* that Nik probably hadn't had an easy time of it? And besides, by the time I knew all *that* it was like months later and the damage had been done. I told David that I would, if you ever brought it up—that was the end of the fight, when we just decided that we needed to stay out of it. Well—when David convinced me that we needed to stay out of it. He was right, though—it wasn't up to us. And God, you were... you were a mess, anyway. And then there was Ollie, so." She shrugs again.

"But what about now? Like when we were shopping? You couldn't have told me *then*?"

She just stares at him with her face going stormier by the second, and he starts to feel regret before she even starts speaking. "Aaron, your relationship with Nik is not my job. I have had enough of the bullshit between the two of you to last me forever, and besides: I think I have enough going on right now, don't you?" He kicks her, just a little, tangling their feet. "And to be honest? It really pisses me off that this has been going on for so long and that David and I are just supposed to be graceful around it all the time. It's been forever, and it's too much to ask. I have *never* asked you not to mention Andy, have I? So I thought, okay, they want to do this? Then *they* have to fucking well do it."

Aaron quirks an eyebrow at her. "We're doing it now."

The furrow in her brow smooths and her face melts into a smile, still a little bit sad. "I know you are. I'm happy for you, even if you're both idiots."

"Well, I say that—we're not doing *it*, now are we?"

She rolls her eyes and flops over onto her back. "Look, those two are *ridiculous*, especially when you get them together. I swear they regress to high school instantly. I don't care *what* you do, just keep it down."

"Nik and his absurd sense of honor, and you know how he is about David. It won't happen until Saturday night, because David said he couldn't."

"Glad I'm going to be out of the house, then. I have plans of my own for that night." Her grin is lurid, lascivious, and he rolls his eyes.

"Yeah, so, about that. What on *earth* made you think that was a good idea?"

She laughs a little and looks down at the mattress between them. "He proposed in bed, did I tell you?" He shakes his head. "Yep. And you know that it started with David way before it ended with Andy. I've always felt a little weird about that—not that it happened like it did, because holy shit it was romantic and so fucking hot." Her smile is all filth and mischief, only for a flash. "But this is the beginning of something, and this is my *husband*. Someday I'm going to have this man's children; we are going to get old together, and I just… I don't know. I think that part of me wants to wipe the slate clean, to start over, to put some kind of really clear before and after there." She always has talked with her hands, and this time she punctuates her sentence by bringing down the side of her hand, as if she can carve her life into pieces by the power of her will.

He frowns at her. "Don't tell me you're going all wife and mother here, Alex. It's disturbing."

At that, her face is suddenly brightly beatific. "Aaron, I *am* going to be somebody's wife and mother. It doesn't mean I'm a different person than I was when I was sneaking off to fuck David on a Thursday afternoon," she says, giving him a savage grin. "But this turned into something much more important than sex a long time ago."

"But why does it have to be one or the other?"

"What do you mean?"

He thinks for a second. "I mean, you *like* having sex with David—I think we're all pretty clear on that much, at least." They smirk at each other. "I don't get why suddenly not doing it is a good thing."

She sighs and rolls back to look at the ceiling. "I don't know, maybe it's a girl thing. Or a Latina thing. A feminist thing, even." She pauses and then says, "For as much as it's some kind of norm, it gets strangely complicated, you know, being a woman who *likes* sleeping with men. It gets weird—there are all these expectations about what you're supposed to do and how you're supposed to feel, and sometimes the one thing I can't quite figure out is how much of all of that is about me and how much of that is about what, like, the *culture* is expecting me to do."

He's missed this, he realizes with a tiny grin—Alex and her sharp and critical mind, her insistence that she is important and worth understanding. It's not that he's not used to these conversations; he's a memoirist at heart, and so conversations like this with his colleagues and with himself are his bread and butter. But Alex is the person he learned to do this with, back when they were just kids in middle school who were trying to figure out what could ever be special about them—they were so sure they were, and all they needed to do was figure out why—and her voice is sometimes the one he hears inside his head. He feels lazy, out of practice and so eager to dive back in.

He grins at the ceiling and says, "So, wait, before, you were sleeping with David while you were still dating Andy, which is a bad thing—"

"Total slut," she interjects, lazily. "And also, I mean, besides all that: just kind of mean? And I am not mean."

Her kindness has always been something he could rely on. "No, you're not mean, that's fair. But now you're not doing that anymore, obviously, so you're going to be a good girl and have some kind of... white wedding?"

She laughs, sounding a little bitter but mostly tired. "Right. *Or,* before I decided to do this waiting-for-the-wedding thing I was giving David exactly what he needed, which is what a woman is supposed to do, and now I'm taking a little space and control over my own body and my own pleasure, which makes me a frigid bitch."

He looks at her and then breathes, "Oh my God, I have never been so glad to be a gay man."

She elbows him in the ribs. "Thank you for your support."

He thinks about it before he speaks again. "Hmmm. Still. Do you want to sleep with him?"

"You mean right now?"

"Not, I mean, not really at"—he cranes his head to look at the time on his phone—"eight forty-seven on a Thursday morning, but just, you know, in general."

She stretches and gives him a naughty little smirk. "I actually like it in the mornings."

He grimaces. "Don't *tell* me these things."

"You asked. No," she says upon his reaction, "you didn't, I know, I get it. But that's kind of the point. Like, I can't always tell what's me and what's everything else?" Her hands juggle an unseen weight, tossing it back and forth, and right then he knows exactly what she means. "So that's part of why I was just like, let's wait and see what happens after, like, three weeks. And what I *can* tell you is that I have never been so hot for him, *ever*, even back when I had to throw over all of my morals to get him into bed, so." She shrugs. "I mean, there is *that*."

"*Nice.*"

"I know, right? So it's weird, but. We'll see."

It takes a second to take this in, to figure out what it might mean. Aaron finally chimes in with, "You're sort of doing it all backwards, you realize."

She grins at him and says, "You're one to talk. Look at yourself."

He flops onto his back and groans at the ceiling. "I know. I keep trying to figure out how to write about it, and all I can think is: God, we are *all* so fucked up."

"I blame high school. Think about where we were and the shining examples we had when we were learning how to be in relationships. Everybody we went to school with is basically a disaster—we're the only ones getting it close to right, and you only figured it out *this week*. I must be a *genius*."

He pulls a face and means to argue, and then there's another knock on the door. Stephanie's there, wearing a tank top and boxers too—although hers are color-coordinated and involve rhinestones.

"Hey, Stephanie," Alex says. "We were just talking about you." Aaron pinches her leg and she kicks him softly.

"Forget *me*—for once, I think I'm the really boring one. Let's talk about Aaron and Nik," she says with way too much energy in her voice for this early, and jumps onto the bed. Aaron groans and rolls over to press his face into his pillow.

She drums on his back, one-two-three-four, utterly relentless. "Don't be like that! Tell me *everything*."

WHEN AARON MAKES IT DOWN to breakfast, Nik is leaning against the kitchen counter drinking a glass of water. Aaron goes to him, leans against him and kisses him. It's not until he feels the glass, cool against the back of his neck, that he realizes Nik didn't even take a moment to empty his hands before he wrapped his arms around Aaron. Aaron loves it. He whispers, "Good morning again," against Nik's mouth when they part. Nik's smile is radiant.

When Aaron turns back to the table, Jasmine is the only one watching, and for once he can't read what's on her face.

After breakfast, Nik stands behind Alex and puts his hands on her shoulders. Before, Aaron resented how close they seemed to be becoming. For years he pushed down that jealousy, and now that everything is changing around him it feels different; he's suddenly so grateful that they're close, now that he knows that there's plenty of space for him. He smiles into his coffee cup.

"Okay, lady—your playlist is done. You ready to check it out?"

Alex grins, bouncing a little in her seat while he smiles behind her. "Now?"

Tu pipes up from the other end of the table. "I have you at eleven, Alex. Don't forget."

"Right, and you need to do makeup and hair for you and Jasmine before that," Aaron adds.

"But I thought you were working on the cake this morning," Nik says, frowning a little.

"Oh, shit, the jam—" Alex is on her feet and slipping out the door, and they can hear her pounding her way up the stairs.

Stress gathers in Aaron's shoulders and he sighs. "Okay, here's what needs to happen. Nik, you can hang out with Jasmine and Alex and me while I'm getting them ready, and you can go over the playlist while we're doing that. Nicole? Nicole!" She looks up from where she has been blearily staring into her cornflakes; her brown eyes are hazy through a cloud of frizzy red curls. "Are you *actually* awake?" At her nod, he continues. "You're not going to be in the kitchen today, are you?"

"Not really? We need to do some prep work, but you finally made your point about the cake, and we won't take up too much space, I promise."

"Thank you. Actually, though, I need your help. If I put something on to reduce, can you keep an eye on it?"

She looks slightly more aware. "How far do you want the reduction?"

"Just about halfway. I'll walk you through it, but it needs some time to cool before it goes on the cake."

She stands, taking her bowl with her to the sink. "Yeah, I can do that. Let me get showered, see if it'll wake me up."

"Okay. And Tu," Aaron says, turning to find Tu watching him, "you… go do whatever you need to do. Take Stephanie with you; you guys walk around and find the best spots for portraits." They both nod. "And that leaves David and Mia. David, can you call the florist and confirm that everything is still on track for Saturday?" David salutes. "And Mia, assuming she ever gets out of bed and drags down here, can help Nicole with their prep work." He looks at the ceiling, counts things off on his fingers and nods. "There. No problem."

Alex runs back in with a plastic bag from the grocery store H-E-B, which contains clinking jars of jam that weighing it heavily. "Here!" She thrusts the bag at Aaron. "Six jars of David's grandmother's strawberry jam, from last year's garden."

"Perfect." Aaron takes the bag and turns into the walk-in pantry to rummage for supplies.

Alex looks around the room at the bemused faces and settles on Nik's, on his gentle smile. "What happened?"

"Just… Aaron. He was channeling his mom for a minute there. You know how she is."

Aaron breezes past toward the stove. The jam is gone but two bottles of champagne dangle from one hand and he holds a box of powdered sugar in the other. "I was amazing. You missed it."

Alex sighs and sits back down, then pulls her coffee cup toward her. "Damn it. Sometimes being the bride *sucks.*"

AARON GETS THE CHAMPAGNE SYRUP to a boil just as Nicole and Mia make it to the kitchen, and he walks them through what he wants for the reduction. Mia gets it quickly—as it turns out, she was a bar-back for a cocktail bar for a while during college, and the bar manager had insisted on a proper, rich simple syrup, so the concept is clear. Aaron has to reiterate that it should be way more reduced than simple syrup, and then she's got it.

He sets out butter to soften, takes one last peek at the wrapped cakes in the refrigerator and heads up to Alex and David's room.

Jasmine has already put on her dress. The alterations really are perfect. Bringing up the hem a little bit more makes her legs look fantastic. She's touching up her toenail polish, and her hair is already twisted up and back on the sides and falling in gentle waves.

Nik and Alex are sitting on the bed, poring over iTunes and checking out what Nik has put together for the reception music. Alex is silent, concentrating, and when Nik looks up and winks, Aaron just smiles and crosses to Jasmine.

"Hey there. Want me to do your eyes?"

She beams up at him, waving her hands over her toes to get the polish to dry faster. "I've gotten better, but it's still a pain in the ass. You don't mind?"

"Not at all, if you're willing to trust yourself to my hands."

"You still know how?"

Aaron shrugs. "How hard is it? Hell, it might be the only thing I actually learned in high school. Theater had to be good for something." He looks at her. "Natural colors, big lashes?"

"And like a deep pink lipstick—something natural-looking?"

"Yeah, I think so," he says, nodding. "Okay, get to work!"

Jasmine sets up her makeup on the little table between the wing chairs by the fireplace, while he opens the blinds and drags the other chair over so that he's sitting right in front of her. And then, as on so many other days, he gets started.

She's already put on foundation, so he goes straight for the eyes. He's beginning with a simple highlight to her brow bone when Alex says, "Oh,

God, this song! That was such an amazing album," and the opening notes to Adele's "Rolling in the Deep" start.

Aaron sings as he works; he can't help it. This song was in heavy rotation with him and Nik during their senior year of high school, and for long weeks it seemed as if every time they made out in one of their cars it was the soundtrack. So *many* songs were important to them, songs that remind him of being young and in love and so wrapped up in Nik, audio snapshots of moments he'll never forget. But this one always reminds him of Nik's mouth, hot and fervent against his throat, of wandering hands on steamy afternoons and the sound of his own broken gasp loud in his ears. Years later, he heard it in a cab on the way home from a late night, and as he sat on somebody's lap in the too-crowded back seat and listened to the heartbroken lyrics while he stared out at a cold and wet New York October, he suddenly understood the song all over again—he'd never realized how sad it was, that it had been strangely prophetic and perfectly fitting the whole time.

Aaron pulls back to switch to a pencil and casts a glance over at the bed; Alex sings along and Jasmine takes advantage of the break to join in, but Nik stares at him, a cryptic smile on his face. Aaron tilts his head and raises his brow, and Nik shakes his head and looks down.

He looks back at Jasmine as he picks up the pencil, and she's a little drawn-looking; her eyes are downcast.

Aaron leans closer to do Jasmine's eyeliner. "Look up," he says, drawing a faint line with a steady hand. Quietly, he says, "You gonna tell me what's wrong?"

Her eyes fill with tears and he quickly whispers, "Oh God, fuck, no crying! Jasmine, your eyes!"

Jasmine dabs at her eyes with her middle fingers, and then quickly presses both to the inner corners of her eyes and takes a deep breath. "Right, okay. Sorry." She opens both eyes. They're glassy, but the threat seems to have passed. "Mitchell sent me an email. He's not going to make it to the wedding."

He squeezes her knee and then bends to do the opposite eye. "I'm sorry. Do you miss him?"

She exhales, still gazing up at the ceiling and trying to keep her face still. "It's not that. I think—I think there's somebody else."

He pulls back and looks at her. "That is such bullshit. Honey, I will just remind you again—if you are not his top priority, then he should not be yours."

"It's not that easy, Aaron. And besides, two days ago you *finally* put together a relationship that you let stay broken for four years—you're really gonna give me advice?"

He's stung—that was sharp, even for Jasmine. "We're not talking about me, though, are we? We're talking about *you.*"

"I keep telling you: It is *not* that easy. Besides, tell it to somebody who hasn't known you for fifteen years. I read your blog, Aaron, and even if I didn't, I know you're not *nearly* that together. You and Nik found each other again: Congratulations. How long were you just jumping into bed with whomever seemed like a good idea?" He hates how she fixates on that; he always has. *She* might have grown up religious and conservative, but he didn't.

Aaron puts down the pencil and thinks while he opens a package of false eyelashes. Big dramatic eyes are standard for photos and performances, and he learned to apply eyelashes on this very set of eyes, so long ago, back when Jasmine was sure that her future was in disappearing into characters on the stage and he was trying to pad his college applications in his own desperate attempt to escape. He readies his tweezers and looks up at her. "First of all: You know that's your baggage, not mine, so please stop trying to share. We have *had* that conversation." She rolls her eyes and frowns at him, but she nods—the hardest thing they ever had to get over was what it meant to her when he came out of the closet; one fight about God was enough to last a lifetime, and at this point he's pretty sure nagging him about his sex life and his lack of shame about it is only habit for her. "Also, though, ma'am. It is not that I think this is easy. It's that I like you *way* too much to watch him do this to you, and I don't think he's making you happy, and I hope you find a way to get off of his hook soon."

She sighs and watches his hands. "You know, I don't even think I really care. It's not about *him.* I'm just *bored,* and I miss college already, and I'm nervous about what comes next. I still haven't found a job I really *want*, and I *sure* as hell don't want to actually go to grad school, and I'm moving back in with my *parents*, for God's sake. Whatever else Mitchell is, he's been one hell of a distraction."

Aaron tilts his head to the side in one sharp motion, and says, "Okay, *that*? That I understand, better than you realize." He thinks of the distractions he's pursued over the years and then he gives her a sad smile and says, "Close your eyes, and when you open them, at least you'll have the eyelashes of your dreams."

Just as Aaron is finishing the second set of lashes, Alex says, "Nik, this is pretty much perfect. I can't think of a single thing I want added or taken away. Thank you so much!"

Aaron hides a smile at the relief he hears in Nik's voice. "You're so welcome—I'm just really glad you're happy with it. David would give me endless shit if you weren't."

"I do have a favor to ask you, though," Alex asks, her voice hesitant and wheedling.

"Watch this," Jasmine whispers as she opens her eyes to watch. "She's about to totally play him."

He turns, and yeah, it's going to be brutal. Alex knots her hands together, the very picture of a distraught bride, and Nik looks so worried and... yep, there it is, his hand is on her shoulder. He wants to help, and it's going to end in blood.

"It's just... this is so awesome," Alex says, "and I realized that I really want to have something *great* to send home with the guests. Do you think it would be possible for you to collect, like, fifteen or so of the songs and make some CDs for people to take home with them?" Alex, drama queen that she is, has clenched both of her hands together in front of her in some parody of prayer.

Nik's face is growing more and more uncomfortable—it's a big ask, over one hundred and fifty CDs to burn and label in under forty-eight hours, and it's not as if there aren't a million other things to do. Alex can't know how Nik's been worrying about the performance they're meant to pull together tomorrow afternoon, and it's that thought that makes Aaron say, "I can help," because he has an idea that will probably be impossible, but would make the CDs *amazing* if they can pull it off.

Nik looks at him as if he is a lifeline and asks, "Are you sure? You have so much to do."

"It's fine—I'm not terrible with graphic design, and this is something we can do in fits and starts over the next couple of days. Really—say yes, Nik."

Nik grins, looks back at Alex and says, "You heard the man—I'm saying yes."

Alex throws her arms around him and Jasmine murmurs, "Damn, she got *you*, too? I *have* to figure out how she does that."

"I'll tell you later. Now. Mascara, and then Alex is up."

AARON STEPS OUT INTO THE hallway with Nik while Alex gets her dress on, and after he whispers his questions and plans, Nik kisses him hard and says, "God, I love you and your ideas."

"You think we can make it work?"

Nik bounces on the balls of his feet. "I think I know who can. Let me get started on that. I'll find you later?"

"Please do." Nik gives him a quick kiss and turns to go.

Aaron grabs his hand and says, "Wait, just a second," and then he kisses Nik one more time, long and slow, dragging Nik into it with him so that Nik backs into the wall for support, pulling Aaron along with his hands in the small of Aaron's back. Aaron keeps him there, falling into the kiss and letting it linger, and when he pulls his face away with a hint of teeth to Nik's bottom lip and plasters himself against Nik's body, they're both breathless.

"Aaron," Nik whispers, his voice breaking and desperate. His hands don't let go.

"Just… *thank you*," Aaron whispers back fiercely.

Nik looks at him, lost in a haze of want and confusion, and says, "Whatever it is, you're welcome to it."

An hour later, Nik strolls into the kitchen, hands tucked in his pockets, looking exceptionally pleased with himself.

"Well?"

"Taken care of—my friend Nathan is running up with the equipment tomorrow night, and he'll do the recording at the rehearsal session. David thinks you're a genius, by the way."

"Of course he does," Aaron responds automatically. "And we'll see, tomorrow."

"When are we going to manage putting the CDs together?"

Aaron lifts the first bowl of buttercream out of the stand mixer and starts packing it into piping bags. He's helped his mother with this so many times that he barely even thinks about it; she paid for every single school trip he ever went on by baking cakes from her kitchen. "That will be the easy part—software will help with that, and I want to ask Tu if he has a good shot of Alex and David to use as the cover, and we can hit a Kinko's or something and abuse their largesse with the paper cutters. No, the *hard* part will be keeping Alex's grabby hands off of them once they're done."

Nik leans against the kitchen counter and makes a move for the frosting bowl. Aaron slaps his hand away and then pulls out a spoon. "No double-dipping."

"Okay, so *when*?"

"Tomorrow morning I'll put the layout together on my laptop, and you can run out and get the discs. You'll transfer the playlist to my machine on Friday night, and then we'll crank them out. It'll take a while, but it's not impossible."

Nik digs into the icing bowl, bringing out a glob of rich white buttercream almost too big for the spoon. "Aren't you supposed to be icing the cakes tomorrow? And won't you be busy on Saturday morning?"

He shrugs. "So you might have to man both machines for a while. I'm not saying it'll be *fun*, but it'll be manageable, and then it'll be perfect."

Nik frowns a little. "What is that face?" Aaron asks.

Nik looks up, smile a little chagrined. "It's nothing." Aaron gives him a brow, and he shrugs. "I'm just starting to get why David thought this was a bad time for us to get back together."

Aaron is taken aback, and his face must show it, because Nik hurries to add, "No, it's—I want some more time with you."

"So stay here with me while I make the cakes." Aaron is shaken, but he knows his voice sounds cool. Good.

"I will, but that's not exactly what I was wishing for." Aaron can't believe there was *ever* a time when he found Nik inscrutable; the uncomfortably hungry look on his face isn't difficult to interpret.

"*You're* the one who made that agreement with David. Besides the obvious, what do you want that you're not getting?"

Nik smiles at him, a little predatory, and then sticks the almost empty spoon back in his mouth and hollows his cheeks around it, raising one brow at Aaron, who laughs and says, "Oh, I *see.*"

Nik pulls the spoon out with an audible pop and licks it. "There's a walk-in pantry right behind you. I bet I can still make it so, so quick."

Aaron's hands slow in spooning the frosting into bags. He remembers racing against the clock, against curfew, against his mom's regular half-hour checks that his bedroom door stayed open, and he remembers one particularly ill-advised race against the alarm on Nik's phone telling him he had to leave *now* or be late getting back to school at the end of his lunch period. He also remembers the anxiety that came with every single one of those experiences, especially that last one, and as much as he wants Nik's mouth—hot, wet, beautiful, wrapped around his dick, lips rosy and shining where they pull tight and wet, God, so wet and *warm*, and it's ridiculous that after all the blowjobs he's had, that that image is still so clear in his mind—he says, "God. Later? Later, I *promise.*"

Aaron puts the spoon back in the bowl and, kisses Nik quickly and rests their foreheads together, and he lets his fingers push against Nik's mouth until Nik pulls two fingertips into his mouth and presses against them with his tongue. Nik always had loved giving him head, and *God.*

He doesn't quite whimper, but he knows he makes a noise close to it when Nik inhales tightly.

Aaron pulls away, letting his fingers trail wetly over Nik's mouth. "David really was right," he says, the remorse clear in his voice as he washes his hands and goes back to the buttercream.

Nik wraps his arms around him from behind, presses a kiss to his neck and whispers, "I'm holding you to your promise," before he lets him go.

They pass the next three hours in work and quiet conversation. While Aaron carefully cuts each layer in half, Nik asks about Aaron's writing, about how he turned one blog to document his move to New York into four blogs and came to think of himself as a developing memoirist. And as Aaron drizzles the cooled syrup over the surfaces of the cakes, he tells Nik what a surprise it had been to be valued for his ability to write about experiences he always saw as so uninteresting, even worthy of some degree of shame, after so much time thinking it would be journalism and his ability to find distance that would actually get him somewhere. He pipes dams of frosting around the edges of the cut surfaces, neat and steady circles, while he tells Nik what it had been like to let go of that old perspective and take small freelance writing opportunities, what it had felt like the first time he submitted to a literary journal, and what he thinks about his chances as a critic. And while he spreads the jam inside those circles, he tries to find words for the sweetness of how each comment and quote and citation and reference leaves him feeling full, appreciated and understood in a way he hadn't even been able to hope for when he was just a poor kid from the Texas Gulf Coast.

Nik listens and watches and asks pointed, interested questions. He brings Aaron new jars of jam when he drops the spoon with a clank into an empty jar, and when they're finished, when Aaron has three layers of unfrosted white cake with champagne syrup and strawberry filling sitting on the counter, he realizes that he's *never* talked this long and this openly about his work, about what it *means* to him. For a while he's forgotten, forgotten everything that had hurt about this relationship, and fallen back into a place where Nik is his best friend, his confidant, the person who understands him better than anybody else ever could.

Aaron wipes his hands on a kitchen towel and says, "I'm sorry. I've rambled on so much."

Nik wraps him in his arms and says, "I loved it. I've missed you, too, you know."

Just for a moment Aaron forgets about the cakes, forgets about how they need their crumb coat before they go into the refrigerator, forgets again about his hurt and clings back.

AT AROUND SIX, AFTER THE cakes are back in the refrigerator and the group has long returned from Alex's adventures in portraiture, a party bus pulls into the long driveway. Jasmine drags Alex out to the porch, "Surprise! And you thought we wouldn't have time for a stag party!"

Alex squeals and runs back into the house to rouse the masses and quickly throw on a short skirt and her favorite party shoes. David looks flummoxed until Nik laughs and hustles him up the stairs to change into something more appropriate. Aaron is glad that he and the rest of the house pitched in for the bus, because trying to coordinate transport would have been too much.

Twenty minutes later Jasmine is dragging Alex to the bus, telling her she can fix her makeup on the way, and they all stop milling in the yard and pile in. It's ridiculous to turn on the dance-floor lights when it's still daylight outside, but the drinks start flowing immediately and as soon as they're halfway to Houston, nobody seems to care about the lights. David has a grip on Alex's bare knee, Nik is leaning against Aaron, Mia and Nicole have pulled Tu, Jasmine and Stephanie into some kind of drinking game, and fuck it—they're young and they're supposed to be ridiculous.

Jasmine has clearly given the driver thorough previous instruction, because the bus pulls to a stop in the valet circle of a strip club lit up in harsh neon. Nik says, "Okay, gentlemen, this is where we get off."

"Not likely," Aaron snipes under his breath, and Nik kisses his temple and squeezes his knee.

"No, that's more your end of the deal tonight, I think. No dancing with strippers, unless you send me a picture." He pauses for a moment, and then says, "No, wait. Don't do that. That would suck."

Aaron raises a brow and says, "We'll see."

Nik grins at Aaron and then he and Tu disentangle David from Alex and sweep him out of the bus. They flank him and march him into the club, where some of David's friends are waiting. Aaron grins as they go.

Then the bus is rolling again, just a few blocks down to the oldest male strip club in town. Once they're inside, they're met by a wave of Alex's friends including Shelby and Bianca, with whom he hasn't spent time in far too long and greets with hugs and hellos. Shelby seems excited to be out of the house, and she looks as gorgeous as she ever did. She was closer to Alex at the beginning of high school, before she joined the drill team and got scarily gorgeous; now she's a real estate agent and the mom of a two-year-old, with a sensible haircut and the hungry look in her eyes to go with it. Bianca he knew better, because like will always find itself.

As she lets him out of the hug, Bianca says to him, "Okay, this is unfair. How did you end up with the girls tonight, and where are the boys?"

Bianca had come out not six months after he did and never looked back. Facebook tells him that she's still in Houston, living in The Heights, working in an insurance office and making her way through a string of girlfriends, the very picture of stereotypical lesbian serial monogamy, bless her heart.

He smiles. "Maid of honor's prerogative—Jasmine insisted, and I *really* didn't argue. I'm sure you'd be welcome to join them, but I think the fun is going to be in watching what happens to Stephanie's face when there's a gyrating cock shoved in front of it."

Bianca chokes on her drink and her eyes go wide, then she sighs and says, "Dammit, I can't miss that."

From: Aaron

Alex is marking things off her Single Bucket List at an alarming pace. Please tell me that things are a little calmer over there.

From: Nik

Now I'm *really* sorry I'm here. This is nothing you haven't seen before. David's sitting here like he's in the middle of a board meeting, Tu is beginning to unwind a little (which is terrifying) and most of the other guys are acting about like you would expect.

From: Aaron

Classy to the end?

From: Nik

Something like that, although I'm shocked by what a horndog Richard has turned out to be. What did Alex do, anyway?

From: Aaron

Among other things, she kissed a girl and she liked it. At least her Babycakes stock rose a little bit higher, even if she will never have that hair.

From: Nik

Damn. Jasmine?

From: Aaron

Stephanie, actually. Bianca and Shelby are here—you should have seen the looks on their faces. Totally opposite, both completely hilarious.

From: Nik

I bet Stephanie is a good kisser. She looks like she would be.

From: Aaron

This is how much I hate you right now (he attaches a picture of his own hand tucking a five-dollar bill into a loaded g-string).

THE DRIVE HOME IS A whole new kind of absurd.

Nik is pleasantly drunk, greeting Aaron with "I missed you" breathed hot against his ear, and he's handsy, indulgently affectionate. The bus seems bigger, somehow, with everybody else crowded around the bar at the other end, still drinking and swapping stories about the night they've had. Aaron reels Nik in close and tells him about their time at the bar, about Alex's friend Jennifer making eyes at Bianca, about Alex's friend Camille's obvious distaste for the surroundings. Nik rests against his shoulder and lets his hand slide over Aaron's chest, then presses it to Aaron's cheek and turns his face for a kiss that starts out needy.

Twenty minutes later, Nik has Aaron pushed into a the corner at the back of the bus, one hand shoved into his hair and the other worming its way under his shirt, blindly groping for skin. Aaron lets his head fall back against the glass of the window a little harder than he'd meant to, and he stutters out a gasp and stares at the flashing lights and swirling colors of the ceiling of the bus as Nik mouths at his neck, sucking a kiss to the tendon beneath his ear while he rolls one of Aaron's nipples between his fingers. Aaron feels drunker than he actually is.

Nik shifts suddenly, making Aaron's hands fall away from his back, and then suddenly Nik is looming over him and stuffing his knee between Aaron and the wall so that Aaron has to shift his ass to the side to make room for Nik, who falls gracelessly so that he's perched across Aaron's lap, straddling him. Laughter erupts, one of the girls yelling, "Damn, get it, Nik," loud enough to be heard over the thump of the bass. The others seem far enough away that Aaron can use both hands to send the same obscene message before they laugh again and he has to stop flipping them off so he can tangle both hands in Nik's hair.

The world narrows sharply; the seat beneath him is perched directly over a subwoofer, and it shakes and vibrates just right. Nik is warm and heavier than he looks, the press of his hips insistent. Aaron slides a hand down the convex curve of Nik's back to tuck up under his ass, pulling his hips in tight while his torso bows away so he can keep his hands up Aaron's shirt, so his fingertips can drag and press.

"Gonna suck you, can't wait to taste you again," Nik mumbles against his neck, and Aaron has to grab at his hips to keep Nik from rutting against him.

For one small, dark second he thinks about it, imagines Nik on his knees in the back of this bus. He's done it before, held a head between his palms while he locked eyes with somebody else, and it's heady, intoxicating—it's so *good* to be so wanted, and for the world to see it.

Nik keeps mumbling, though, pressing words to his skin between kisses, and as Nik slides his hands around Aaron's torso and pulls him away from the seat so that their bellies and chests press together, so that

Aaron's own spine is a concave mirror of his own, Nik says, "Want you, God I *love* you, never want to stop touching you, *Aaron.*"

Aaron takes Nik's face between his hands; Nik's eyes are glassy, the pupils blown, and his cheeks are flushed. "Just wait, sweetheart. Wait until I have you alone." The endearment falls from Aaron's tongue, rising up as if it's simply been waiting there all this time, ready to be used again when Aaron feels tender and protective. Maybe it has—he can't tell—but when Nik collapses against him, buries his face in Aaron's neck and goes still, Aaron whispers it into his hair. "Shhh, my sweetheart." Nik shakes against him and clutches him tighter.

Later, when they've tripped up the stairs and Nik has locked the door behind them, Nik gently maneuvers Aaron into the narrow shower. After they've rinsed away the last of the soap, he eases Aaron up against the cold tiles and then drops to his knees. He takes a long time, tracing his fingertip over the crown and down the long purple vein and then following with his tongue, and he's quiet while he does; just the rush of warm water and the stutter of his own breath fill Aaron's ears. Nik lingers over the slit, squeezing out tiny beads of salty slickness so he can rub them over his lips and then lick the taste away. Nik looks up through eyelashes dark and spiky with water while he does this, while his mouth is glossy with Aaron's pre-come. Aaron's body is wrecked with fatigue and desire; maybe that's why he feels as if he wants to roar and cry and shake until he falls apart. When he holds Nik's head between his palms, though, and pushes his dick between those lips (his *mouth*, it's like sense memory but it's real again, *God*), he can't look away, locked there by Nik's gaze, in this moment that's theirs, only theirs, with no clocks and no observers and no expectations but their own.

In Their Own Words

post from an untitled, anonymous, deeply confessional blog, Wednesday, October 29, 2014:

Once upon a time, I was a little gay boy growing up in a world hostile to me. I was poor and kind of gawky and probably too smart and definitely way too interested in making sure everybody knew it. I was immature and too mature all at once; my dad had run out on us and I had way too close a relationship to my mother, a woman who worked so hard to make sure I never wanted for anything, and who I still think is a saint. So far, so clichéd.

But I was really lucky. I had good friends, really surprisingly good friends in retrospect, and then I had the enormous good fortune to fall in love with one of them. And, even more improbably, he loved me back. It seemed, at the time, like I was set for life: I had the people I needed, I had him next to me and I had convinced people who had never even met me that I was smart. Life was going to be glorious. As a boy I churned through fantasy novels from the library as quickly as I could get them, so I knew that I had gathered my party and was ready for the adventure to begin.

And then he left me—all it took was the loss of one person, and suddenly it was apparent that I had never had anything; it only *seemed* like I did. The circumstances changed, somehow I didn't know myself at all, and my adventures turned into a simple struggle for survival.

A year later I was in a new city and a new life. I had a new boyfriend. He liked to kick his roommates out and cook dinner for me. He had money; he talked about whisking me away to Europe, something that seemed impossibly exotic to me and frankly still does. I never told him that I thought he overcooked the pasta; I never told him that I was a much better cook than he was; I never told him that I didn't like the way he dressed; I never told him that I couldn't imagine all those places he dreamed about, not when I barely had my feet under me; I never told him that I didn't love him. And then, one day, I looked at him and it was like looking at everything I hated about myself, and I told him everything, and I burned it to the ground. I have never felt so powerful; I was glorious in my destruction and I was thorough. But after I was left there in the middle of the ashes, I didn't feel proud. I felt alone, still barely surviving.

Since then I've been doing something new with myself: I've been fucking around like it's 1976, a celebration of freedom, only with every barrier known to young gay men. My best friends, who knew me when I was just a boy—the people who probably still know *me*—would be horrified, religious by default as they are. Sex without strings is their only real taboo; alcohol is fine, drugs are probably fine (not the good stuff, don't get crazy, it can't be *too* good), and sex is okay if you're in love. But the kind of pleasure that I've been after is something they just wouldn't understand, and so I don't really talk about it. They wouldn't understand the release that I find in it, the way that I find it something just shy of sacred but definitely holy. There are so many different kinds of pleasure, and I think some of them can be sacred; but sacred is rare, isn't it? You can seek for a lifetime; it's a quest, not an everyday pursuit, and certainly not the kind of thing you can go after while you're just trying to survive.

In just under a year, I'll hit a major milestone in my life—I'll finish one chapter, and so far the rest remain unwritten. They aren't even outlined, and that's a scary place for a writer. I really have no idea what I'm going to do with myself. Lately, though, I've been thinking about those old novels that I loved so much as a boy. They start with a quest, a simple question, and it always looks the same: Something has been lost, and somehow a simple boy from the middle of the sticks (a poor boy, usually—that's probably part of why I loved the books so much) is, improbably, the only person alive who can find it.

I'm not a big thinker; I'm self-absorbed and self-obsessed and my life begins and ends with me, standing alone in a crowd. And I can think of a lot of things that I've lost: my father, my first love, my virtue. I'm not sure any of them are worth questing after; I can't help but think that if those things were so damn important in the first place, they never could have been lost. But lately I feel that same old disquiet, that yearning for adventure, and I think: Maybe I survived, and maybe it's time to start thinking about adventure again.

I have one year left to assemble my party and gather supplies before I am required to set forth. I have one year left to bask in the comfort of my new routine and my new home; one year left to try to survive and make my mother proud. And then it's all on me, and the place I take that first step will decide the fate of my quest. Stand by while I gather my weapons: the power of the pen, the tatters of what was once an iron will, the love of a mother who will wait by the door forever and an unlikely collection of loving buffoons.

Hell's bells, being an adult is hard. My mother would finally be proud.

Friday

From the moment Aaron opens his eyes his mind is full, busy with everything that needs to be done. He disentangles himself from Nik with one soft kiss to his bronzed shoulder, strokes his hair and whispers until he settles back down, and then sits in the chair by the window.

He pulls his tablet from the table, and the first thing he sees is the personal blog entry he made on Wednesday, still up on the screen once he unlocks it. He rereads it quickly and smiles at himself, shaking his head.

He shifts into his list-making app, noting everything that needs to be done. It's going to be a busy day, full of things to take care of, and half of them have to be done while keeping Alex at least partly in the dark. He envies Nik his morning run, the chance to think without anybody interrupting or asking questions.

Nik shifts on the bed, rolls onto his back and reaches for Aaron. Aaron drops his tablet on the table and goes to sit at the edge of the bed, waiting for Nik to wake up enough to talk to him. Nik's hand hits his leg and clings, and Aaron strokes some hair away from his face.

"I see you're joining us this morning," Aaron says, watching Nik's eyes flutter.

"Mmmm, hey," Nik says, voice still sleepy. "I was dreaming about you."

"Good things, I hope."

"No, it was—" Nik clears his throat and opens his eyes. "It was bad. We were back on your front porch, and we were like we are now, like, we looked like we do now, I mean, but you were telling me that you hated me, that it was a mistake. And then Alex was there, and she was wearing her high school clothes but her hair was like it is now, and she was all mad at me, too. And then we were at my high school for my prom, only it was—I mean, I *knew* it was high school, but it looked like my dorm building at school, and my parents were there and—"

Aaron strokes Nik's face. "Oh, gross, I hate dreams like that."

Nik grabs his hand and pulls. "Just—come here for a minute."

He lets Nik pull him down, and Nik curls up on his shoulder and rests his head there, running his hand over Aaron's other shoulder.

"I'm right here, sweetheart," Aaron coos as he strokes Nik's hair; for an instant he feels like an ass, but Nik cranes his neck to look up at him, beaming.

"I still love that," he whispers.

"I'm glad, because I don't appear to be able to stop saying it." Aaron reddens a little and raises a hand to run through his hair.

Nik intercepts it and presses a kiss to Aaron's palm. "No complaints from me. Say it all you want."

"I think I'm done for now, thanks."

"Ah, the romance is dead," Nik says, grinning.

"The *romance* is still getting its feet under it, so go easy on it. And on me, please. I'm a little distracted at the moment."

"Right, busy day." Nik rolls over to lie flat on the bed next to Aaron. He stares up at the ceiling, finds Aaron's hand and laces his fingers through it.

"It is. We both have a lot to do today."

"And then it'll be tomorrow."

Aaron turns to look, and Nik is already watching him. "It will."

"I'm looking forward to it, Aaron." The look on Nik's face and the tone of his voice make it pretty damn clear he's not talking about the wedding.

"So am I. I have been for days."

"Me too."

"Then why on *earth* did you make that agreement with David?"

"It seemed like the right thing to do at the time. And also..." Aaron watches him and waits for him to finish. "Well. I know it's probably stupid. I just wanted to give you a little more time. I know it's not much, just a few days, but I could tell you were having some trouble with all of this, and I wanted you to be able to really *decide,* without jumping right back into bed. Because no takebacks, not this time."

"You mean this bed? The bed we're lying in right now?"

Nik rolls his eyes. "I know, I *know.* Still. I feel like… there's a difference, I think, between what we've been doing so far and what I hope will happen tomorrow night."

"You mean, just—" Aaron makes an incredibly vague hand gesture.

"Well. Not *just* that, not really. But I want… I want time. I want to take all night with you, if we want to, without worrying about what needs to be done, or worrying about Alex walking in the next morning. I want to spread you out and get to know you again, *all* of you, and I thought… well. Give it a few days."

It's a heady thought. Aaron says, "You want epic, dirty, newlywed sex. Well, it's a good thing you waited a few days."

Nik smiles back. After so long, he's unfazed by Aaron's sarcasm. "Yeah. Something like that. And look, we didn't even have to get married!"

Aaron pushes at his hair gently and says, "That might be a lot to ask for a first time back together."

"After the other morning?" Nik chuckles and wipes a hand over his face. "God, I *really* don't think that's a concern. I am *never* giving up running, if that's what it inspires."

Aaron smiles and quirks a brow. "No complaints here." They're quiet for almost a minute, and then he says, as gently as he can, "Why weren't *you* having trouble with all of this?" He waves a hand between them to clarify. "It's been a long time."

Nik grins at him, his smile bright and a little impish. "It has. It's also been a long time coming. I've been ready for this for months, mostly just thinking about it. I've been pretty sure I wanted to try since last summer, and then when I saw you at Christmas… yeah." He stretches. "I'm prepared for you, Aaron Wilkinson. Gimme your worst."

Aaron quirks a brow at him and Nik rolls his eyes and says, "Sure, why not, that too," and then he waggles his brows at Aaron and Aaron has to climb on top of him and crush him into a kiss. Nik is still smiling against his mouth when he gets there.

After they're up and breakfasted and showered, Nik runs in to the business end of town to raid Wal-Mart for blank CDs, jewel cases and liner inserts, and Aaron drags Tu upstairs with him to get photos for the inserts and then finishes the layout. By the time Nik is back, breathless from running around and then up the stairs, Aaron has transferred everything to a thumb drive and closed up his laptop, and then he feels guilty about handing Nik his keys and asking him to run everything back down to the car so Alex doesn't find it and they don't forget it when they head out later. Nik presses a kiss against his temple and then goes off again. Aaron shakes his head and smiles and starts packing up his sewing supplies—they'll need the table space later tonight.

Aaron hears the cars from the window, and he looks out to see Nik meeting both the rental truck *and* the minivan full of musicians pulling up in the driveway. Nik throws his arms around his friends, smiling and joyful to see them again. He's gone all out for this wedding, calling in every favor he's amassed at UT to get people to play for this event. It won't be long, just some of the ceremony music, but Alex will be walking down the aisle to one of Houston's finest string quartets because somebody's dad is the violist. Nik always does manage to know everybody, and remembering Alex's squeal of joy when Nik told her about it and Nik's grin in return leaves Aaron smiling all over again.

He heads downstairs to work on the cakes, meeting David and Stephanie on the stairs; they are running outside to work with the people from the rental company. In the kitchen, Mia is frying pounds of bacon and Nicole is sniffling while she chops her way through a pile of onions, eager to get most of the prep work out of the way before noon. The menu is simple and designed to be stable in the summer heat, but as elegant as possible considering the entire dinner service will be buffet style—Alex and David hadn't wanted either the stuffiness or the expense of hiring servers—still, they have a lot of work to get through today and tomorrow morning. Aaron rolls up his sleeves and washes his hands, pulls the cakes out of the refrigerator and gets to work.

THE SCREEN DOOR SLAMS AND Jasmine, Alex, David, Tu and Stephanie spill into the kitchen, faces stormy. Alex is *pissed*. It turns out that, among other things, the rental company misunderstood something about the electricity on the house and can't provide the table lighting they ordered. Aaron sags against the sink and takes a moment to be grateful that the weather's going to hold out and they can cancel the tent—they would have lost the moonlight, then, and would have been in even more trouble.

"Okay. Look. Go back into town. It's summer, so canning jars should be cheap and they should be *everywhere*."

"Like jam jars?"

"Yes, exactly. In fact, we'll reuse the ones from David's grandmother— the labels are still on them, with her handwriting—it'll add charm. Get… a lot. Get maybe one-fifty—no, two hundred—of those, and enough tea lights to fill them twice. We'll just use candles on the tables, lots of candles, and with the lighting from the arbor it'll be fine. And they'll go with the wildflowers—it'll be very country relaxed, very summertime casual. And it'll be cheap. Alex, are you fine with that?"

"You don't think that's tacky?"

"It's very *casual*, maybe, but look," Aaron says, reaching for one of the empty, washed jars sitting by the sink. "See? It's meant to look like cut crystal. Only, *obviously*, not. We're not using them for glasses—it's not a *hoedown*, for God's sake"—Alex grins at him—"but you're the one who wanted a relaxed summer wedding. And again, the wildflowers. Get the tiniest jars you can find, and I think it'll work." He looks at the jam jar, turning it in his hand. "And get a bag of sand while you're there. We'll put sand in the bottom, so the candles sort of nestle down in there."

"Got it—jars, candles, sand." Alex looks up from her phone, where she is typing all of this in. "Can't we use beach sand?"

"It's Gulf beach sand—you wanna think about what's in it?"

"Right," Alex says, turning back to her phone. "A bag of sand. Where do you buy sand?"

He shakes his head when he thinks about how many bags of sand he's bought for use at his mother's house. "Landscaping department, definitely. Oh, and lemons!" Alex narrows her eyes at him and he smiles and says,

"For the *cooks,* Alex." Aaron nods toward where Mia and Nicole are still actively ignoring them. "They're losing it about lemonade. Get lemons, a *lot* of lemons, bags and bags, and another few bags of sugar, and some more club soda, and if you see a cheap electric juicer, get that, too. And then I think you're done."

Jasmine rolls her eyes and Alex chants the list under her breath while she keeps typing and then they're off. Tu and Stephanie are arguing about the placement of tables on the lawn and Stephanie's waving her hands *everywhere,* and that's *enough.* "Stephanie, your life will not be worth living if you stick your hand in Alex's wedding cake just to prove you're right. Out! Get out of the kitchen!"

WHEN ALEX WALKS BACK INTO the kitchen, arms filled with plastic bags, Aaron is frowning at the cakes and muttering to himself. He smooths the buttercream, trying to get it as perfect as possible, mentally cursing Alex's distaste for fondant and yes, fine, it tastes like the sugary paste it is, but at least it's *beautiful.* This is a mess. If he could only—

"Aaron!" He looks up, and Alex is scowling at Mia and Nicole. "Has he been like this all afternoon?"

They look at each other and refuse to say anything, and Alex rolls her eyes.

"For fuck's sake, Aaron, come sit down and have a glass of lemonade."

"I don't have time for that—I have to finish these cakes. And then I need to—"

"No you don't—I'm the bride and I *say* that you don't. Come on, Aaron, don't care more about my wedding than I do—you'll just make me look bad."

Aaron looks at Alex and then follows her into the dining room, slumping into the chair next to her. "How are you not a wreck right now?"

"I don't have to be—you're doing it for me." Alex runs her finger through the ring of condensation the glass is already leaving on the table, and ice clinks in her glass as she puts it down. "You know, the whole point of a wedding is to celebrate. I didn't mean to make you crazy."

Aaron looks at her—she's completely serious. "You might have thought about that before you asked us to burn one hundred and fifty CDs *yesterday*."

She winces. "Yeah—sorry about that. It just… it seemed like a good idea at the time?"

He grins at her. "Ah, yes. One of those."

"I have a lot of them—like asking my friends to do this for me. I'm sorry."

"Don't be sorry—it's been an honor. I want it to be perfect."

"It will be—I'll marry David and you'll all be there to see. That's enough, it really is."

"As long as we finish the CDs in time."

"*God*, yes." Alex's smile is bright and sarcastic, and he loves her so much. "Really, Aaron—is it going to be okay?"

He thinks about it. "I have to finish with the cakes—I want them done so in the morning all we have to do is move them. You and Jasmine can get the candles ready for the tables, and then after the rehearsal I have to run into Houston with the boys to make sure their clothes are sorted."

"You guys can't do that here?"

"No, there's… God, you don't want to know the details, but no. And that's okay, really, because I have to pick up the programs anyway, and now we have to print jewel case liners," he says, glaring at her, "and so I'd have to be out of the house anyway. So then tonight Nik and I will be burning midnight oil and roughly a *thousand* CDs. It's fine—we'll figure it out. When are your parents getting here?"

"God," she groans. "They're actually already down here—my mom called while Jasmine and I were running errands and so we stopped by the hotel. David's parents are there, too, so all four of them were hanging out in my parents' suite, getting busy with what looked like *several* bottles of wine. The rehearsal is going to be interesting."

Aaron grins at her. "This is what happens when you let the parents be idle—you should have given them work to do."

"And let them call the shots? No way."

"Still. They have nothing to do but sit around and think, and you know how that always ends." He looks at her. "You know, you should have *them* deal with the candles and the jars. After rehearsal, when I'm gone with the boys. Set them up here at the table and make them work for it. Make them do the lemonade, too."

She stares into her glass. "God, my mom would *love* it. You should have seen how David's mother teared up when I told her what the jam was for, last week. Is it terrible that I didn't even think of getting them to help?"

He shrugs. "You've always liked doing things on your own—no reason to stop now. And after your mom's reaction when you broke up with Andy—well, it makes sense. It sounds like they've come to really like David's parents, though?"

"It's still awkward, but they're trying. Our dads this afternoon, especially—they were sitting there talking about football like either of them gives a damn, and they're *so* much alike, and someday I think they're going to be real friends. It's just been weird—my parents really know David now, they like him, but we should have had our parents get together more often."

The screen door slams, and Alex's mother's voice cries out, "Hello?"

Alex sighs and mutters, "Here we go," before she calls out, "In here!"

Alex's mom comes in first, and squeals, "Oh, Aaron, *m'ijo!*" and then he's being gathered up and smothered again. Maria Martinez Garcia is a force of nature—Alex comes by it honestly—and since Alex is her only kid, she's been trying to mother Aaron since he and Alex were in middle school and he came to her house after school for help fixing two buttons ripped off his shirt and a cut on his forearm before he went home. It's not worth the trouble of trying to stop her now, and he's not even sure he wants to. That long-ago afternoon, the woman he still called Mrs. Garcia gave him a needle and thread without a word, and then washed the cut and avoided meeting his eyes while Alex stuck cinnamon toast in the oven. They were quiet while the water ran pink and then clear, and just as she smoothed the Band-Aid over the cut she tried to tell him how much easier his life would be if only he could butch up a little—what she had actually said was, "How about football, maybe?" That was enough to inspire him to avoid her for three years.

And then one morning, toward the end of their sophomore year in high school, Alex was taking forever to get dressed for school. He was trapped in the kitchen with her mom, and over the sound of Alex trying to outshout Sara Bareilles in her bedroom—"You mean well/ but you make this hard on me"—he took a long drink of Diet Coke, looked at the floor and said, "I'm gay," mostly to see what would happen. He'd already told his mother and his aunt, his girlfriends all knew and had been sworn to secrecy, and things were just starting to heat up a little bit with Nik; maybe that was why he wanted to say it out loud to somebody who wasn't family and wasn't a stranger but something in between. Adrenaline pumped through his body, and he was finally ready—he was ready to flee and he was ready to fight. And instead, she put her arms around him and said, "Of course you are, you brave boy."

And that's why, even now, Alex's mom can hug him and call him *m'ijo* and baby him whenever she wants. It's not *only* because she still scares him a little bit.

He hugs her back, he smiles for Alex's dad and David's parents, and then he gets the hell out of there and back to his kitchen, begging Nicole to let him take over for a little bit while she takes lemonade out for the group.

THE REHEARSAL IS A WELCOME break—everybody is out in the yard except Mia, Nicole and Aaron, and they put their heads down and work. Before the screen door is slamming to let them all back in again, he has finished the cakes—at least as finished as they're going to get tonight—they're back in the refrigerator and he's filling up two more piping bags with buttercream for disasters and repairs tomorrow.

Stephanie laughs all the way into the kitchen and says, "We're ordering pizza again. Totally appropriate for a rehearsal dinner, am I right?"

Mia and Nicole are lavish and a little pathetic in their thanks to her, and Aaron hums to himself as he washes a bowl—he's so glad somebody else is doing most of the cooking, and he's just as glad that he is getting out of here for the night.

After Nik comes in, sweaty and happy from talking music with his friends, and drags him out of the kitchen for a shower and a slice, they stand in the living room and say their goodbyes. David's dad is coming along, telling Alex that he wants to see his boy all decked out before the big day. They take two cars so that Tu and David and David's dad can head straight back, and the drive to Clear Lake, so close to where they all grew up, is easy, relaxed, almost reflexive. Aaron keeps glancing at Nik, who is watching this nondescript patch of highway fly by. Right after they cross the bridge to the mainland, Aaron asks: "Why grad school?"

Nik shrugs. "It seemed like the right thing to do; they threw some money my way and since I didn't pay for anything as an undergrad, I can afford to do it." He's quiet for longer than Aaron expects, and when he glances at Nik again, he's back to staring out the window. "God, I *loved* my student teaching—it was a weird semester, being single again and being in the classroom all the time—but it was amazing. It's better, though, for me to get a little more experience under my belt, get a little older, before I'm in a classroom full-time."

"Did something go wrong?"

Nik takes a deep breath, blows it out, and then takes another. "No, not at all. It's just... I thought about my own time in high school *so much*. Everything with the music programs is so ordered, you know—the state organizations run everything so carefully—and it was even more intense because, I mean—you know what our school was like." Aaron nods; he'd always been so jealous of the opportunities Nik had simply by virtue of where his parents could afford to live.

"So, you know, we had this long tradition of excellence and the whole vibe was so *defensive*, so competitive about everything. And I thought a lot about your experience, too, about how hard you worked to get out, and how different it was for you—I mean, just how different the schools were, and the demographics and the *money* and what that meant for both of us. I don't think I had really taken it all in, not until I got into a classroom of my own, about how different it was for us because of that one thing. So, yeah, I think a little more space, being somewhere else, and having a little more distance from my own experience can only help with that."

Nik pauses for a long time and Aaron waits until he continues in a voice soft, reflective voice. "The school where I was teaching was kind of a mess—it was mostly working-class kids, so the music programs were really pretty hit-or-miss. And there was a boy in the orchestra where I was teaching, a freshman cellist named Ryan. He reminded me *so much* of you—not physically, but his mannerisms, and God, his smarts. He was fourteen, and I'm not even sure he was out to *himself* yet, but it was coming. I wanted to wrap him up, keep him safe, protect him from everything he was up against. And it would have been the absolute worst thing for him, because even in the time that I was there he grew so much, really came into his own—kids are remarkable, you know?"

"Did he come out while you were there?"

"Not that I heard about. But he stopped being so timid about speaking up for himself, found some good friends. Just… his *body* was looser, he smiled more, he was even a better cellist—he was easier in himself somehow. If I'd tried to make a pet project of him, he never would have learned to do that for himself, and God knows he'll need it."

Aaron drums a non-rhythm on the steering wheel. "Sounds familiar."

"Yeah. I told you, he reminded me of you. I thought about it a lot, what you must have been like before I knew you, what you might be doing while you were so far away." Nik reaches across the car and puts a gentle hand on Aaron's knee. "It… this sounds ridiculous, but I am so far from done with you. I think I'll always want to know more about you."

Nik's hand is warm and soft on Aaron's knee, but mostly what he feels is this incredible *tug* between them, like a line straight between him and Nik that quivers and shakes and pulls, always pulls, and he wants *so badly* to hurl himself across the few feet that separate them. Instead he says, "And so that's why New York."

Nik watches him and says, "Well, yeah. That's a part of it."

"What's the other part?"

"Well shit, Aaron, *New York*!" Aaron laughs. "It's not like I didn't *want* to go there—there's no place quite like it for a musician. And, I mean—Columbia's program is amazing, it really is."

"Oh, Nik, you are gonna *love it* there. I can't *wait* to show you *everything*."
He glances at Nik, whose head is rocking back against the headrest, turned
toward him with an eager smile.

"Are you still living in the East Village?"

"God, no—the rent was too steep, and two years of that pretty much
cleaned me out. At the beginning of junior year I moved to Brooklyn, and
ended up with two of the worst roommates known to man."

Nik grins. "Tell me about them."

So he tells Nik about Tara, with her phallic art and her disturbing
habit of asking her male friends to model for her; and about Joseph, who
seems to need to fry everything he eats and is still deep in the middle of
a seafood craze; and his partner Jamie, who basically lives in Joey's room
and spent all spring smoking her way through her student loan money.

"So, in short, the whole apartment reeks of fried fish, turpentine and
pot smoke *all the time*—when I pulled things out of my suitcase at home
the first Christmas after living with them, my mother actually sat me
down for a Very Special Chat. We live in a cold climate and wool holds
on to every scent that comes near it; my sweaters are now living in *plastic
bags* because of that. Plus I have to be *very* careful to be fully dressed at
all times in case Tara ambushes me again! It's ridiculous."

Nik laughs. "So why don't you move?"

Aaron shrugs. "It's a hassle to find a new place, and I've settled in
there. Manhattan is so expensive, and I've just gotten used to Brooklyn.
And the commute's not terrible, so." He shrugs. "I'm used to it, I guess."

Nik gets quiet, looking out the window, and then he says, "And what's
the commute like between Brooklyn and Morningside Heights?"

Aaron shrugs. "It depends on the time of day, but probably at least
an hour."

Nik's head whips around. "An *hour*?" he says, distress clear in his voice.

Aaron grins. "Nik, between walking and train schedules, it takes an
hour to get *anywhere*—you've gotten used to Austin. New York is like
Houston, only much worse."

"I'm never going to see you!"

Aaron smiles. "Oh, it'll be fine. We'll have all weekend, and during the week you'll be busy with school and performances, and God knows I'll have enough to figure out with the new program and whatever they have me doing. But we can meet for dinner, or I can come up to you on some nights and just... stay for breakfast."

"You mean booty calls." Nik is grinning again, and Aaron is glad for it.

"I mean crashing at a friend's place."

"You mean spending the night with your boyfriend."

Aaron startles a little—it's been a long time since that word fit anything he was involved in, but it still feels good. "Well. I guess I do."

THE HOTEL ROOM WHERE THEY meet to practice and record is full of empty beer bottles and friendly faces, some of them half-remembered from long ago, when Nik and David were in high school together. Aaron spent so much time with Nik then, when they shuttled back and forth between their schools and their groups of friends, that the names come back easily. He's not surprised that David has managed to keep so many friends from high school; people don't often go far away for college here. Some of them had headed up the road to A&M with him, and he's spent years seeing them around campus. Even so, it's heartwarming how many friends dropped what they were doing and traveled to be here, and although a lot of these guys were at the party last night, they still seem to be enjoying their reunion. The handful of men from David's chorus are friendly, polite and mingling well—it's a pleasant room, warm and filled with excitement.

The rehearsal goes surprisingly smoothly, and Aaron revels in watching Nik manage it. He's come so far, he's *grown* so much. Nik has always been a leader, a voice that people turned to when they needed direction. At first, it had been natural—Aaron had always done the same, after all—but the more he'd come to know Nik, the sillier it had seemed. Nik wasn't perfect; he was an attention whore; he was too easily hurt and reactive because of his own experiences. This Nik, though, is *different*—he's still likely to use humor to get what he needs out of people, but he wears his authority better, with more assurance that it's owed him, and he's not the same perfect little prince he was in high school.

During the second pass through the recording, Aaron watches David's dad sit on the edge of a bed as David sings a ballad for Alex, surrounded and backed up by his old friends. David is his usual calm self, but even he is starting to crack a little, overwhelmed by everything that's going on, and when he sinks back on the bed while Nathan fiddles with the equipment for one last take, his dad puts his hand on his shoulder and they turn to each other and smile tightly. It's like watching two halves of one whole hold each other up; Aaron has to look away, and he meets Nik's eyes, which are sad and a little mournful, and moves a little closer.

The final recording session goes well, and after they've all shared a beer and caught up a little, they walk down to the parking lot with Nathan so Nik can give him a little something for gas and thank him profusely. Then they sit in the car and listen to the master. It sounds *good*—whatever Nathan did to minimize echo worked, and their voices sound clear, sharp, but not tinny.

"You're still in good voice," Nik says.

"God, I'm so out of practice—I'm glad I was able to pull it off."

"You really don't make music at all anymore, then." Nik looks sad, disappointed.

"I sometimes sing in the shower? It's just… it's not part of my life. I told you."

"I know. But don't you miss it? I can't imagine."

"Well that's why you do what you do, and I do what I do."

Nik grins at him, raises a brow and nods in recognition.

Aaron looks at his hands for a second and then says, "Honestly, no, I haven't missed it. Not at all. But right now? I do, a little. That was fun, being part of the group. I forgot that part of it."

"Mmmm." Nik's voice is smug. "We should find you an orchestra. Or a chorus—I told you, you have a better voice than you think you do."

Aaron laughs and shakes his head. "There's no way I'd make it through an audition now—in either. I haven't played my sax in… well, since high school." He shrugs. "I don't do music… that's not really part of who I am anymore."

Nik leans against the car door and looks at him, his eyes soft. "So where are you?" Aaron looks at him, his head cocked to the side, his brow up. "Because I've read some of your blogs, and I'm not sure you're there, either."

Aaron smiles at him even as he bristles a bit on the inside. "You think so, huh?"

Nik holds up his hands, instantly a bit defensive himself; maybe Aaron is just far too obvious to somebody who's known him for so long. "Hey, wait. Don't get mad. I didn't say it was *bad*; you know you're good at what you do, Aaron. Shit, you're the smartest person I've ever known, and you know I love your writing." He pauses and takes Aaron's hand. "I still have every word you've ever written to me."

"Oh, God," Aaron groans, and Nik laughs at him and squeezes his hand.

"I do! I… I'm not even going to tell you where I keep all of it—it's too embarrassing."

"Tell me you didn't print them," Aaron begs. "Oh God, I would be horrified to know that some of that stuff made it past pixels."

"No, of course not. But it was important to me—I was keeping it. I am still keeping it, and I'm not telling you where. It's mine."

Aaron looks at Nik, studies his face. *His mouth is still so beautiful.* He's always liked Nik's mouth, the curve of his top lip and the sweet fullness of the bottom, and the way they press together and curl up at the edges so that it looks as if he always has a little smile trying to grow. Thinking about the little dip just above Nik's top lip, he's startled when Nik speaks again.

"But that's what I mean. Those blogs don't sound like you, and I still consider myself something of an expert."

Maybe—*maybe* that's true. Aaron thinks that there was a time when Nik knew him better than anyone; they had grown together and dreamed together. The life he's living now is according to a blueprint he drew with Nik, and not everything has worked out the way they planned it, but he doesn't feel like a different person, not really, not while they are here together. At the same time, though, he can't help thinking of everything his mother said on the phone, and everything that Nik still doesn't quite understand about what it's like to live in New York, and wonder what they don't know about each other. It probably should to scare him; right now it feels like nothing so much as an adventure.

Still. That's not really what Nik asked, and so he just says, "My voice is a work in progress. I might have lots of them before it's all said and done—one for everybody who's willing to pay me for the privilege. It doesn't mean I didn't make them all and that they aren't all me." Aaron starts the engine of his car and turns to reverse out of his parking space; he braces his hand on the back of Nik's seat as he does and gives him a grin. "Besides, you haven't read *everything* I've ever written. I can guarantee it."

Nik watches him, gives him a little smile: those corners of his mouth curl high and tight and threaten to give way to dimples. "Fair enough. Keep the mystery alive."

At Kinko's, Nik heads straight for the color printers to start cranking out jewel case liners while Aaron goes to the counter to pick up the programs he emailed over for printing and assembly the day before. Everything looks fine, so while the guy boxes them up he joins Nik by the printers and starts ripping apart the inserts and filling jewel cases as fast as he can.

Aaron has finished not even a third of them by the time Nik is through with printing, and they gather everything into bags and set off for the car, eager to get home and finish up. The night has started to wear on now, and, when Nik offers to drive, Aaron is happy to let him so he can just sit in the passenger seat and be still for the hour it'll take to get back to Galveston.

He means to go over his mental list, to straighten out how tomorrow will go, but instead he watches Nik drive. His face is filled with expression and energy as he sings along to the radio, which is turned down low, and his thumbs occasionally tap along in rhythm on the steering wheel. It's so familiar, Nik driving his old car—even as Nik is this different, mature, wonderful person.

Aaron sags back into the door and stops fighting it and says, "I love you."

Nik's eyes dart toward him and then back to the road, but he smiles, bright and open. "Say that again."

"I love you?" Aaron can't help smiling back, and he feels dumb, silly, like they could get stuck here grinning at each other forever.

"Oh, now it's a question?"

"Nik."

"I'm sorry. Here, let me—" Nik slows and pulls off the freeway, then turns into the crushed-shell parking lot of a ramshackle bar, throwing the truck into park while they're still close to the road. He leaves the car running but turns to Aaron, leans back against the driver's side door, and says, "Okay, now: hit me." Semis continue to barrel down the highway; their lights stream behind Nik's head in the semi-darkness.

Aaron rolls his eyes. "Well, now I just feel ridiculous."

"I can sit here all night." Nik pauses, and then says, with a smile in his voice, "I could go in, have a beer, make friends with the locals, and you could text me whenever you're ready."

Aaron looks at him, at his cheeky smile and the affection in his eyes. He looks past him at the parking lot and the brightly blinking sign, at the freeway and its Friday night traffic. None of it is remotely romantic; none of it is how he thought this might happen again. Except for one thing. "Nik, for reasons that escape me at the moment, I love you."

Aaron feels as though he might burst with joy, and he wants to laugh.

Nik's smile shrinks until it's small and private. His voice is quiet and so sincere, as if he's making every word fresh for just this moment. "And I love you, Aaron, for too many reasons to mention. Now get over here," he says, holding out his arms.

Aaron slides across the seat, leans across the console and kisses him, long and sweet and soft. When he pulls back, he says it again and again; his mouth slides against Nik's, as if maybe, if he spills the words out right here in the small space between them, they'll be safe, protected. "God, I *love* you. I always did and I still do. Stay with me this time, *please*, just stay."

"Shhh, shhh, I love you, I'm right here. It's not so hard to say to me, is it?" Nik strokes his hair and down along his neck, so tenderly.

Aaron shakes his head and buries it against Nik's neck. "You have no idea." He breathes Nik in while Nik holds him—one long, shaky breath—and after he breathes out, he holds on tight until the urge to shake apart passes.

IT'S ELEVEN BEFORE THEY GET back to the house, and they stop in the living room to say their goodnights. Alex's and David's parents are interspersed among the more familiar faces, chatting and drinking and nibbling at pizza crusts. Alex's mom is talking to Stephanie and Jasmine about the day tomorrow, and her dad is nodding along with Mia and Nicole, talking about A&M's chances for next football season. David's parents are on the long sofa with Tu sitting at the other end, trying to keep up a conversation while Alex and David sprawl on the floor at their feet, holding hands and looking at each other. Maria gives Aaron a long look and a fond smile, and he feels the weight of Nik's hand at the small of his back and winks back at her before they excuse themselves. They clamber up the stairs, plastic carrier bags bulging and bumping along the walls, and dump everything into a heap next to Aaron's bed. And then they get to work.

By two a.m., they've finished burning two-thirds of the discs and have stuffed all the jewel cases. They've been peeling off clothes since everybody else turned in, and Aaron has given up and stretched out on his belly in his underwear, watching iTunes burn each CD as if his life depends on the completion indicator crawling across the screen. Nik brewed coffee an hour ago, and Aaron wants another cup but he can't get up—he's just too tired. He gives up, pillows his head on his arms and watches Nik.

Nik is in the desk chair with his bare legs sprawled out in front of him. He's lost his pants and is sitting there in boxers and a T-shirt, illuminated by the glow of his laptop and the bedside lamp. The light bounces off his hair where his head is bent to the guitar in his lap. The window is cracked open so he can hear the water and the cicadas singing into the night over the hum of the ceiling fan. Nik plays soft and low, nothing Aaron recognizes, but a more technically complicated piece than he remembers hearing him play before.

"You've gotten better," Aaron mumbles drowsily.

Nik looks up at him with sleepy eyes as his fingers continue to work the strings. "Yeah. There was no piano in the dorms, and the guitar always went over better than singing. I played a lot."

"It's nice. What is that?"

Nik glances up through long lashes and tosses off a casual shrug. "Something I've been working on a little bit. Just playing around."

"I like it—it's pretty."

"I'm glad." Nik looks up, gives him a gentle smile and keeps playing. Aaron keeps watching, and the light is soft and the night is quiet and Nik is right there, so beautiful.

"Baby, wake up a little."

Everything is fuzzy, darker, quiet, and Nik's hand is sweeping up and down his bare back. When Aaron opens his eyes, his laptop has disappeared and Nik is perched next to him on the bed. He startles, lifts his head and says, "No, wait, I need to—"

"Shhh, don't worry about it. You can do it in the morning. Come to bed with me now."

Nik shoves him gently and he rolls over a little so that Nik can strip the bed of its blankets, down to only a sheet and a light summer quilt. Then Aaron flips around and crawls under. Nik curls up behind him, sliding one arm around his waist and pulling him close.

"Did you finish the CDs?" Aaron asks, rubbing his eyes.

"Just a handful left—it's fine. I'll take care of it in the morning. Now shhh, we have a big day tomorrow."

Nik's broad hand is stretched across Aaron's belly, and the fan spins on high, leaving the cool, sweet air washing across his face. He just lies there for a few seconds as Nik shifts against him, settling in and tucking his feet between Aaron's ankles, and Aaron hangs suspended and ready to slip back into sleep until, suddenly, he knows he won't. He still feels lazy, cozily tucked away from the aggressive air conditioning that is a feature of Texas summers, but Nik feels warm against him, and the delicious contrast of textures and temperatures reminds him that there's something he wants a little bit more.

"Roll over," he whispers, and when Nik does he follows, ready to be the big spoon. Nik cuddles into it, sliding his ass back to wiggle into Aaron's lap like he's made to fit there. If Aaron had more energy, if tonight weren't just so easy and comfortable, he might take it as a hint. Instead, he nuzzles into Nik's hair until he can kiss the back of his neck and slides his hand into Nik's boxers.

Nik hums his satisfaction when Aaron curls his hand around him, and Aaron hums back when he finds Nik's cock soft, lying against his thigh, his balls loose and low and so warm. "Hi," Aaron whispers, and hears a huff of a snorted laugh from Nik. He buries his own lazy smile in Nik's hair, thrilling with the intimacy of this perfect, perfect moment.

He rolls the whole package in one gentle hand, and Nik sighs and yawns, tipping his head so Aaron can get to his neck more easily. "God, that feels good. I wish I weren't so tired."

Aaron tastes his skin, presses kisses against the side of his throat and around to the back of his ear. "You wanna try anyway?"

Nik hums one more time and then says, "Will you be upset if I say no?"

Aaron considers it. "No, not really. I had a nap; have you been up all this time?"

"Yeah."

"So get some sleep. Sleep is good—so good." Aaron starts to withdraw his hand to give Nik a little bit more space to drift off to sleep, but Nik makes a noise in his throat and puts his hand on Aaron's wrist.

"No, it's... do you mind? Just leaving your hand there?"

Aaron grins, because he gets it immediately. "You want me to play with you until you fall asleep?"

"Oh, *God* yes," Nik says, his speech already thin and slurred as he starts to drift, just a little.

"Okay," Aaron whispers. He peppers kisses across Nik's neck, just at the bottom of his hairline, and rolls Nik's balls in his hand and just holds them there, soft and tender. The house is so quiet, and his heart is so full; this might be the most calmly intimate moment of his life so far, timing his breathing with Nik's and listening to the fan rustle a few papers across the room. Nik jerks just one time as he falls asleep; his whole body shocks awake for a second, and when he wakes up enough to whisper, "Aaron, love you," his voice is almost gone. For one sleepy, half-awake moment, all the joy and responsibility of taking care of Nik, of being careful with him and loving him the way he deserves, sweeps over Aaron, a wave of tenderness that he might find suspect in the daytime.

And then it's gone. It slips away between one breath and the next as Aaron murmurs "Love you too" into Nik's hair and follows him into sleep.

In Their Own Words

An email from Aaron sent Saturday, June 12, 2010:

Dear Nik,

I'm putting this into words because I need to. The journalist in me needs to report on it, because this is a story the world needs to know about. And important requests should always be made in writing.

I've been home for two hours. I've unpacked, I've taken another shower, I've checked in on my mom and I've pulled some ground venison out of the freezer to thaw. I feel unfocused and unsettled. I feel strange in my body. It took me two hours to realize that I feel lonely.

We spent the night together last night, a whole night, just the two of us. You were there, but the facts still require reporting: We enlisted our friends and we lied to our families and we got a hotel room. You took me to eat oysters and then you made me laugh so hard I choked on them and then you took me to bed. I brought the necessary supplies and you brought an endless supply of patience. You told me you loved me and I told you to prove it, and you did. It hasn't even been a year, and I'm surer of you than just about anybody. You are part of my family.

Here is a thing I want you to think about: What if we didn't have to lie to make nights like last night happen? What if we spent this last year in high school as our last year in Texas? You know how badly I want to get out of here, and you know how badly I want to go everywhere with you. Come with me. In three months we'll start school and suffer through one more sweaty Texas autumn. By next year, let us be somewhere where the leaves change colors, where we don't have to worry about our parents knowing everybody in a twenty-mile radius, where we can be on our own. Dorms in big cities can cover a multitude of sins, and I want to commit every one of them with you.

I love you,
Aaron

Saturday

Aaron had set his alarm for early, but when he wakes half an hour past the time he'd meant to get up, he sees that it's been turned off and Nik is gone. He lies in bed for just a moment and thinks about everything he has to do today, about Alex's wedding, about tonight. He thinks about telling Nik that he loves him. It had felt right so very suddenly, without space for planning or an actual agenda, and for a moment he lets himself worry about that. But then he thinks about last night, about how quiet the room had been, about falling asleep holding Nik, about how *easy* it all still is between them. And he thinks about how hard the last four years have been, and stretches and smiles.

His bedroom door opens, and Nik peeks in. "Oh. You're awake," he says. He pushes the door open and pads in on stocking feet to sit on the edge of the bed. He wears a T-shirt and running shorts, and he's sweaty and his hair has started to go a little frizzy around his face. His eyes are bright, though, and he looks happy, alive.

"Just barely. I assume you're the person who turned off my alarm?"

Nik smiles sheepishly. "Guilty. But you were sleeping pretty hard, and I thought I could buy you another thirty minutes. Is that okay?"

Aaron stretches, and says, "It's fine. I have a lot to do, but it was nice to wake up on my own." He looks at Nik, stretches out a hand and says, "Did you get enough sleep? C'mere."

Nik says, "I'm fine. I'm all sweaty, though," but he leans down anyway.

"Don't care," Aaron mumbles against Nik's lips, sliding a hand into Nik's hair and tangling it there. He wants to pull Nik back to bed, wants a do-over for last night and a simpler, more joyous reenactment of the other morning; but he can't shake the lists running through his head, and when Nik pulls back to rest his forehead against Aaron's and run his hand down Aaron's side, Aaron shivers and then throws back the blankets.

"You're getting up already?" Nik pouts, hovering over Aaron and looking adorable.

"No rest for the wickedly fantastic. How many more CDs do we have to finish?"

Nik pulls a face. "About forty?"

"Forty?" Aaron pushes out of bed and stands, running his hands through his hair. "You said we were almost done!"

"I know, I just didn't want you trying to stay up to finish them."

"Nik!" Aaron is frazzled now. He looks for his laptop, which he can't find anywhere.

"Hey, relax." Nik stands and grabs Aaron's shoulders. "Relax, okay? We'll get them done. I put a pair on when I left on my run, and two more when I got back. In a minute I'll go do two more, and then we're down to almost thirty. It's fine, okay? It'll be fine."

Aaron looks at him and breathes. "I need to make a list."

"That's fine. Hey—" Nik squeezes Aaron's shoulders. "We'll get it done, okay? We don't really need to start getting ready until like four, and it's only eight. We have *tons* of time."

By noon, Aaron begins to think Nik was right. At ten the screen door had slammed and the house was suddenly filled with a sea of old friends, eager to pitch in. Aaron and Nik pressed Bianca and Shelby into service keeping an eye on the laptops while they burned the last of the CDs. They both threatened Bianca with some future, unknown repayment to keep her from rummaging in their hard drives, but Shelby lifted her chin and said she'd keep Bianca in line. God help them all. Josh and Joe drove together and were glad to take some time to lounge on the sofa and catch up with everybody.

They still present as the funny-looking pair they always have: Josh the shorter, solid working-class white guy in jeans and steel-toed boots, and Joe… well. Joe has *always* looked good, and before they really knew him,

Jasmine code-named him "Mario" for his resemblance to Mario Lopez so she could gossip about him with impunity. The comparison still holds, unfortunately; Aaron despises Mario Lopez, but he's never had anything bad to say about Joe.

Josh and Joe's friendship has amazed Aaron over the last couple of years; there was a time when he envied it, because even if he and Josh are as different as two blood relatives could possibly be, Josh is still the closest thing he'll ever have to a sibling, and when Joe showed up, he basically became Josh's brother.

Joe Harper, his four brothers and sisters and his mom had moved back to San Antonio the summer before senior year, breaking Jasmine's heart and leaving a surprising hole in Aaron's life. Aaron remembers thinking at the time that none of his friends had understood how much they appreciated Joe and his quiet strength until he was gone. There had been one last party at Josh's house while Aunt Karen was working nights, a spirited going-away that turned weepier as the night went on and everybody got drunker, and then that had been it, except for Facebook.

In the spring of their first year out of high school, Joe mentioned on Facebook that he was thinking about going to Alaska to work for the summer. He was still in school at one of the community colleges, but even with the little scholarships he'd picked up, paying for it was rough and he thought he needed to earn a little cash, to be physical for a few months, and besides that he was looking for a place to be far away from everything going on with his family. Aaron wasn't surprised to see the post, had thought it was probably a good move for Joe, and hadn't thought much more about it.

Two days after Aaron got back to Texas the summer after his freshman year in college, Josh had shown up at his house for dinner with Joe trailing him sheepishly, his crooked white grin familiar and welcome. Aaron still doesn't know all the details of how it happened, particularly what Josh said to convince his mom to let it happen, but Joe spent the rest of the summer sleeping on the floor of Josh's room. He was apparently a dream houseguest, up every morning to make breakfast before heading out to work for the day, and Aunt Karen was ready to adopt him by the time the summer was over. Mom told him that Karen cried when Joe left to go back to San Antonio because his mom sprained her foot and needed help.

It's always a bit awkward for the first hour or so, integrating Joe back into even this increasingly loose-knit group. Most of them share so many things that Joe just doesn't get, especially related to the events of senior year, and when they're together there's always a tendency to fall back on those jokes and memories. And, too, there's the Jasmine issue; she'd been hurt by the way he left, by how sudden his departure was, and the last few times Joe was around she'd been quiet.

But Joe and Alex and David had bonded during that summer Joe spent back in Houston and had even gone to San Antonio to visit once or twice, and the joy on Alex's face when he walks in now, sweeps her up and twirls her in a circle makes Aaron smile.

So Josh and Joe sprawl across one of the sofas and the girls cluster around them, perched on the arms and, in Alex's case, draping across the guys themselves, and they all flip through photos on Joe's phone as he talks about what he's been doing since he dropped out of school, about working down in Corpus Christi fixing boat engines and the sagging porches of summer houses. Alex pokes his cheek and tells him that he looks just like her favorite stripper from the night before, "Fabian," all tanned skin and shiny hair and white teeth.

The CD project is finally completed, and Shelby and Bianca drift in right after Aaron finishes cutting garnishes for Mia. Nik and David finish walking over the property, making sure they're ready for last details. One by one they all reconvene in the living room, ready for one last quiet moment together.

Eventually Stephanie orders more pizza—so much pizza this week, it's ridiculous, but it's cheap and fast and Mia and Nicole have been glaring at people who set foot in the kitchen after ten a.m. and pizza can come to *them*, which is really the important point—and suddenly it's two p.m. During a lull in the conversation, Aaron looks at Alex, and when she makes eye contact she gives him a nervous smile, and then a nod.

"Okay, people," Aaron says, raising his voice both in volume and pitch. "I think it's time to handle the last-minute details, and then we have to start getting ready. Alex and David are getting married today."

They're all quiet for a second, stalling while that settles in, and then the whole room breaks out into grins and they start hauling themselves off the sofas. The florists are coming in an hour so the flowers don't just wilt in the afternoon sun, and the last thing they need to do is put out the candles. While Stephanie and Nicole gather the pizza boxes and paper plates into trash bags and Tu fiddles with his camera, Aaron hauls David, Nik, Josh and Joe over to the boxes of impromptu lanterns.

Aaron stacks a couple of boxes in each of their arms, and everything is going *fine* until Josh stumbles over an invisible seam in the carpets and plows into David's back, who in turn tips forward, dropping his boxes on the ground. Josh, *being Josh,* immediately drops his boxes as well and rushes to David's aid to help him up, all while Aaron looks on in growing horror.

Alex rushes over, pulls David to his feet and brushes him off. David's "I'm fine, no, seriously, I'm *fine,"* rises over the general mayhem of the room, and all Aaron can see for one moment is how wide Shelby's eyes are over the hand she's raised to cover her mouth in horror. And then everything is moving again.

David *is* fine, just a little red at the knees where he slid forward across the carpet, but both his and Josh's boxes have fallen upside down, spilling jars and tea lights and oh, God, sand is *everywhere,* all over the carpet.

"Stephanie! We need a vacuum cleaner!" Aaron calls out, his hands on his hips as he surveys the damage.

She runs in from the kitchen and stands agape while a horrified silence falls over the room again, and then she says, "Oh, damn. Well. Actually, I think glitter was preferable."

TWO HOURS LATER, THEY'VE SET up outside and cleaned up the mess in the living room and everybody has rushed off to shower and dress. It's still only four, but they have to be prepared for guests, and the florists have just left, Tu has snapped pictures and Aaron has declared the space on the lawn ready. They'd played around there for a few minutes once the candles and flowers were in place; David swept Alex into a dance without music while everybody else looked on and murmured happily.

Aaron and Nik move around each other gracefully as they shower and change. Aaron, always concerned about creases, is waiting until the last possible minute to slip into his linen trousers, and Nik waits to put on his tie and jacket until he's shaved and finished his hair.

While they jockey for mirror space, Nik finishes patting on his aftershave and says, "So you're leaving tomorrow?"

Aaron freezes, hand halfway to his hair. "Yes. I am." He shakes his head and goes back to fiddling with that last recalcitrant strand. "I can't believe I forgot."

"What are you going back to?"

"Well, like I said—I'll be in Texas until next Saturday morning. I don't think there's anything planned for that week, just spending time with my mom. And then I have to get back to New York, because I'm starting another new job the Monday after—I'm going to be an office assistant for the new department for the summer. Part of my package."

Nik grins while he squeezes a dollop of product into his hand and leaves the obvious joke unuttered; Aaron *loves* him for it. "Are you nervous about it?"

"Of course. I mean, not *really*," Aaron says with a shrug. "I barely know anybody there, but I know the type and I worked at NYU the whole time I was there. And the first week will likely be more of the same, just with new faces." He finishes with his hair and leans forward to look at his face a little more closely, trying to decide if the situation on his chin is likely to go critical; the humidity here is great for skin long-term because it helps prevent aging, but in the short-term it can be a disaster. "If anything, I'm scared of the new program. I don't want to give them anything to regret before classes start. I don't... I know I'm fine, I do. It's just the newness of it." He rinses his hands and dries them on a towel.

Nik runs the last bit of product through his hair and starts to arrange his curls, wrapping them around his fingers. "Who would have thought that's where you'd be? Back when we met, I mean."

"Well. I mean: Me, for one. Not necessarily THERE, but I was never going to stay here. That was the whole point." He leans back, turns to look at Nik and then puts his hand on Nik's shoulder, nods to his hair and says, "Can I?"

Nik shuffles over in front of him. "What does your mom think about that?" he says, lowering his head a little.

Aaron gets his hands in Nik's hair and twists the curls. "Oh, you know my mom. She doesn't quite understand how I came from her, and she still tells everybody all about it. Mostly what she tells them is how hard I work, because *that* is something she sure as hell understands." Aaron smiles at Nik's hair, at how newly familiar it still feels, slipping through his fingers. "I will tell you, though, just between us?" He leans forward and whispers, "Sometimes I still feel like such a fraud."

Nik closes his eyes and leans his head into Aaron's hands, his breath against Aaron's cheek, and murmurs, "Mmm, Texas boy in New York City?" Nik's voice is quiet and low, gravelly and intimate. Aaron has so many memories of it like this, and he wants to keep them forever.

"Something like that. My family isn't like yours; it's not like I was born into a long line of intellectuals." It's so easy to say this to Nik. He should have known how valuable that was, how much that meant.

"Do you miss the kids? Or the cooking? Or all of the… other stuff?" Nik's eyes are still closed, and his voice has gone a little dreamy and faraway.

"Not really, no. I have enough of a hustle trying to keep my rent paid. I do miss working with my hands, though. Sometimes I think about getting a job tending bar just to keep my body busier. And sometimes I think I need a hobby. Maybe I'll take up knitting or something, something that will use my hands but let my brain wander."

"You have such *good* hands." Nik sighs, and he opens his eyes and looks at Aaron dreamily. Aaron grins at him, finishes with his hair and kisses his nose, and moves away to wash his hands again.

"I'm glad you like them. You have any ideas for keeping them busy?"

Nik smirks at him and says, "Oh, now you're just teasing."

Nik digs his hands into Aaron's hips, sliding them against the smooth fabric of his boxer briefs, and pulls him into a kiss. Aaron kisses him there in the steamy bathroom, and lets one hand rest against Nik's smooth cheek, still the tiniest bit tacky from his aftershave gel. Nik smells so *good*, clean and herbal and woodsy and just right, and he tastes like toothpaste— and it's love, God, this is love, and it's his.

"Okay, ladies, it's time," Aaron says, finally knocking at Jasmine's bedroom door. He pushes it open.

Alex is standing in front of the mirror. She's perfectly still and silent, and if that's not alarming enough, she's just staring at her reflection. "Alex, are you okay?"

She blinks. "I'm fine. God, Aaron, I am… I'm completely fine. Totally. Fine, I mean."

He watches her, watches the reflection of himself watching her. "You've said that three times, so I'm starting to doubt you."

She meets his eyes in the mirror and forces a smile, saying, "No. Really. I just… maybe I'm a little freaked out that I'm so fine?"

He looks at her; her eyes are wide, but he can't tell—is this what "shocky" looks like? "Okay, you've lost me here." She picks up a brush and runs it through her hair, watching her reflection. "Can you, like, give me a signal? Blink your eyes three times if I need to go have a really awkward conversation with David, or something?"

She blinks at him once, twice, and then laughs at him. "Really, Aaron. I'm fine. I think I expected maybe not to be? You see so many movies, you know—those romantic comedies really get in your head." She turns and rests her butt on the ledge of the dressing table, smacking the hairbrush against her hand. "But I feel like…. this is just what happens now. We've been talking about this for so long, and we've been planning and… it's David. He won't hurt me, he would *never* hurt me. So today, I'm going to marry him. It's that simple."

"Really?" Aaron knows he sounds a bit skeptical, but the look on her face is twitching between manic and serene and he can't tell what's going on with her. It's something in her eyes, something new.

"Really. Let's do this!" she cries, hairbrush held aloft, and then she's unbuttoning her shirt.

"Damn, Alex! Okay, let me get into the bathroom."

"Aaron, how many times have you seen me getting dressed?"

But he's already slipping into the other room, hissing at her. "Shut up, we should pretend to have some decorum—your mother could walk in at any moment, and I don't need the Maria Martinez-Garcia stink-eye all day."

She laughs as Aaron closes the door and leans his head against it. He catches his breath—he'll never tell her, but she'd had him going with that blinking thing. He was already halfway through imagining how on earth he was going to tell David that Alex had put him through this for no good reason before she finally broke. *She can be such a bitch,* one of his very favorites. He smiles.

"Okay, princess, all essential parts covered."

He walks back out and zips her back into her dress. "Where's Jasmine? I can't believe she's shirking her duties again."

"She was talking to Joe—I didn't want to bother her."

"Alex! It's her job, to be bothered by you!" He finishes the hooks at the top and then stoops to fluff her crinolines, reaching under her skirt and thank God her mother *isn't* here. "And her and Joe? We're really going there again?"

"Mm hmm, I think so," she says, conspiratorially.

"You think they're interested?" he asks absently, looking over the line of her dress with a critical eye. There's nothing to see, though—it's perfect.

"Oh, who could ever tell with Joe. And Jasmine—I don't know. She's still so fucked up over Mitchell, but maybe? Maybe it could be just the thing she needs."

He looks at her, at her sly smile, and says, "Hmmm. I think it's good that you're going to be somewhere else for a little while. You've turned into a vicious matchmaker."

"Says the man who was reunited with his high school sweetheart by my machinations."

"I very clearly remember a conversation where you said you were staying out of that."

"All part of my brilliant plan." Aaron rolls his eyes, but she says, "Hey, it worked, didn't it?"

"I think it just might have."

"Exactly."

There's a knock on the door, and Alex's mom and Jasmine spill in, eager to help Alex with the rest of her preparations. Aaron waits for a minute to see if they need him, and then he meets Alex's eyes in the mirror, winks and blows her a kiss, and slips out the door.

She's ready.

AARON AND STEPHANIE SIT TOGETHER on the aisle, right behind Alex's parents. Nik's smile for Aaron, just as the strings pick up into a processional, is small and private, and Stephanie squeezes his hand and then squeezes tighter when Jasmine steps from behind the crowd and walks slowly down the aisle.

And then there's Alex, and oh God, this is actually happening: one of them is getting married.

Aaron watches Alex marry David and remembers. His first memory of her is from elementary school; there was a schoolyard fight, and she was fierce in it, and he remembers thinking, *Oh yeah, that girl lives down the street.* He remembers sharing the back seat of her mom's car; mocking her for her great and earnest love of O-Town; dragging her to their first newspaper meeting at the beginning of freshman year so he wouldn't have to go alone; laughing with her while they finished Jasmine's Magenta makeup for her first—and last—go at *Rocky Horror*; checking his phone in a Hot Topic so he could pretend he was *anywhere* else while she bought another six sets of multicolored hair extensions; hearing her laugh at the graduation after-party, where she sat drunk and loose and draped over Andy's lap. He remembers the summer afternoon they drove to Montrose in Houston to get her hair cut off; her grimace as she got her first tattoo;

the way she smiled when David laughed at her and pulled her across his lap for a spanking, and how she raised her brows at Aaron when he was done; her serious face just days ago, when they stared at the ceiling together in his bed and talked about love and sex and commitment.

Stephanie is already crying, and so is Alex's mother, so what the hell—he might as well join in. The three of them can cry, because Alex's face is radiant, joyful and she's moving on.

LAYING HIS HAND ACROSS HER jaw and turning her face toward him, David draws Alex into a kiss, and Aaron takes just a moment to join in the cheering before he stands and moves to the middle of the aisle. People close in around him, jostling to fit into the spaces as quietly as possible as David kisses Alex, bending her back just a little as she clutches to his shoulders. When the kiss is wrapping up, while they're pulling back to stare at each other, a guy next to Aaron quietly hums a note and starts counting off.

The middle voices come in with the rhythm, steady and slow, and then he soars above them, la-la-ing and grinning because Alex has turned to face them, her eyes wide and surprised. David takes Alex's hands in his own, his face so serious, and Nik moves to join the group, preparing to back him up in tempo. The doo-wop guys continue to rock the falsetto, woo-ing like a choir of the silliest, most wonderful angels, and then David launches into his part.

David sings a gently romantic song about second chances, about all of the things he might not have managed to get right in the past. The lyrics tell the story of a lifetime of mistakes, the misdirection you don't recognize until you're already three steps down the wrong road. The chorus, though, is a reminder that sometimes you get lucky and find the right thing after a long time getting it wrong, and a celebration of that moment when you finally recognize it.

Nik takes his hand, and Aaron floats within a sea of high voices singing in unison, flying above the rest of the voices holding them up. It's a beautiful moment—Aaron doesn't sing and he doesn't even really like doing readings, but he likes *this*, likes being part of something so much bigger than himself. The wind is in his hair, the sun on his skin, and he can't stop watching Alex, who is quietly and beautifully crumbling. He's seen her like this before—in high school she'd been so easily overwhelmed by how deeply she could feel, and he had been embarrassed for her then, ashamed that she didn't know how to conceal the things that were most precious to her. Now he watches her eyes fill with tears, watches the tears streak her face—not a hint of black among them, he's delighted to see—and he loves her for it, appreciates her tender heart for the gift it is.

He squeezes Nik's hand and moves a little closer to him, and he sings, for Alex, for David, for himself and for Nik. He sings.

"WHAT I NEED YOU ALL to understand is that I spent the better part of three days making this thing. Do you remember how I behaved when we had to scrap the newspaper layout the week before the start of senior year?" Everybody winces. "Exactly. And that was ridiculous to begin with. This, however," and he gestures with a flourish to the three layers of cake sitting on the countertop before them, "is not. This is a beautiful, handmade white cake with heirloom strawberry filling and champagne syrup and meticulously applied buttercream icing. Do not—Josh, I'm looking at you, make eye contact, please—do *not* fuck this up."

Joe looks serious, Josh looks like he needs a bathroom and Nik is clearly trying not to laugh. Aaron throws up his hands. "Oh, forget it. Let's just... okay, let's do it. Just... for fuck's sake, *please* be careful."

Nobody moves.

"Well! Don't just stand there! Pick up the damn cakes!"

Josh stumbles toward the counter, and Aaron grabs his arm. "Josh Broussard, I know where you live. I will... I'll *tell your mother* if you destroy Alex's cake, do you hear me?" When Josh blanches, he knows he's got him.

Nik moves up behind Aaron and lays a hand on his arm. "Aaron. Aaron, honey, come on. Go easy on him. If he starts shaking, he's useless to you."

Aaron gives Josh one more glare and then says, "Fine. *Fine.* Josh, I mean it though. Please just... be as careful as you know how to be." Aaron mutters under his breath as he opens the back door. "Oh my God, why did I think Josh would be useful for this? Bianca—I should have gotten Bianca and Shelby. Flexible, *graceful* former dancers."

They parade out the door—Joe in the lead with the bottom layer, smiling at Aaron as he clears the threshold; Josh right behind him, his eyes trained on the middle layer; and Nik bringing up the rear with the top, jewels already in place. Aaron pulls the door shut and walks behind them, and when he hears Josh say, "Dude, I'm *so glad* you're back with Aaron. Does this mean you're going to be coming home with him all the time? Because that would be *awesome*," he allows himself one vicious smile before he hurries ahead of them to ready the table.

THE CAKE HAS BEEN CUT, most of the food has been eaten and God knows the bar has been busy—Mia has finally just grabbed a chair so she can rest between takers and shaken her long, dark, wavy hair into a cloud around her shoulders. Aaron leans against the bar, ready to help her out, while Nik chats with the last of the musicians, who are still lingering and enjoying the free food and last drinks before they get back on the road.

Jasmine swings by the bar and steals a bottle of wine to take back to her table, and Aaron grabs her by the waist before she can go. "You okay?" he says under the music.

"I'm better than okay," she says with a giggle. "Joe brought a blunt. It's just like old times." He snorts into her hair and she slaps at him before she hugs him, and for a moment it's like it used to be, just the two of them who will always find a way to understand each other. The older they get, the less they seem to have in common—she seems to get less serious as she becomes an adult, while Aaron has never been anything but directed—and, when you've known somebody for a long time, it sometimes doesn't matter how different you are. Jasmine is drifting a little, but Aaron knows she'll make her way to somewhere wonderful eventually; and right now, under these lights and with these people, that is its own kind of beautiful.

"Can you believe one of us got married?" he says.

She looks straight at him and shakes her head. "And you know what's worse? You're totally next."

He scoffs, but he can feel himself blushing, and she points at him and laughs while she twists and dances away, wine bottle dangling from her fingers.

The playlist swings into "Make Me Better" and the energy takes a jump—the music pours into the open air, but it still feels as if the chairs are vibrating from the bass. Everybody with a willing dance partner hits the floor, some of them even dragging unwilling partners along and under the gentle twinkling lights all over the arbor. A gaggle of Alex's girlfriends pass in front of Aaron, heading in to do one of their girl group dances, and then the crowd clears and he can see his people.

David is singing to Alex, being adorable and silly, and she's laughing, always laughing. Jasmine has abandoned the bottle, and now she and Joe are dancing together, Joe looking dumbstruck while Jasmine manages to look both shy and smug through her smile. Bianca has grabbed Shelby and is grinding against her ridiculously, crowing into her ear while Shelby laughs hysterically and holds onto her shoulders for the ride. Josh and Stephanie and Tu and Nicole are all at a table together, laughing and chatting like old friends. Josh and Nicole are locked into some kind of epic argument about sports, he thinks—Josh slaps the table a lot when he talks about sports and yep, there he goes again. Stephanie and Tu lean against each other, while Tu fiddles with his camera and halfheartedly scans the area for photo opportunities. Even the parents seem a little drunk sitting at their table and smiling indulgently at the young people, and the grandmothers are chair-dancing next to them.

Aaron relaxes; this is exactly what Alex wanted: the best night, the most fun, just simple and joyous and *happy*. They nailed it, and it's done.

THE NIGHT IS WINDING DOWN—THE tea lights flicker in their jars, most of the women have lost their shoes and dance in bare feet or stockings in the grass and the casual guests have left for hotel rooms or inns or home. Nik's playlist sets the tone for this part of the night perfectly: it's quiet, contemplative and softly romantic, and a man's voice gently sings about finding love and giving it away.

Aaron is back by the bar, toasting an exhausted Mia with a glass of champagne, when arms surround him from behind and Nik's chin rests on his shoulder.

"Don't drink too much. I think you and Beyoncé just made me a promise," Nik whispers in his ear.

Nik had built in a whole block of songs from their middle school and early high school years, and Alex and Jasmine and Stephanie had done a choreographed dance from memory while he had laughed from the side, meeting Nik's eyes just once. "Yeah? You planning on putting a ring on it?"

"You planning on finding somebody else if I don't?"

Aaron grins over his shoulder and says, "Not this week. Come on, come dance with me."

Nik takes Aaron's hand and leads him to the arbor as the song changes to George Jones, one of those classic, hard luck country songs his mother has always loved. This song is special, though, because it was another one of theirs, and Aaron smiles when he thinks about Nik making the choice to include it—this one could only be for them. Nik wraps his arms around Aaron's shoulders and tucks his cheek against Aaron's. Aaron smiles sadly against him, remembering the last time they danced together, just hours before it had finally fallen apart for the last time.

He thinks about what Nik just asked, whether he would find somebody else right away if it fell apart, and he asks, "Were you in love with Ollie?"

Nik goes rigid against him and then pulls back to look at him, stunned. "Oh. Oh, wow. Are we having this conversation now?"

"I think so. If... I mean, I do want to know. Can you?"

Nik is quiet, looking over Aaron's shoulder as they turn and move together, and Aaron says, "Nik, you were with Ollie longer than you were with *me*, and you were older—it was important. It *is* important. I think..."

Nik holds him close and rests his chin against Aaron's shoulder; he sighs and speaks quietly in Aaron's ear. "I was... I was not as in love with Ollie as I should have been, I think. I spent a lot of time wishing I were. But he was... God, Aaron, he was *so good* to me. He was good *for* me—he taught me so much about relationships. He would have done *anything* for me, and it's... that feeling, it's kind of terrifying. Knowing that you have that kind of power over somebody, I mean. By the end, well—it had become obvious I wasn't ever going to love him like he loved me." Nik pauses for a moment. "It's part of why I went home with him last summer—we were in trouble, and we needed some space from everything else to see if it could actually work or if it had just burned out. And then, when we got back to school, I ended it. It was awful—I should never have let it go on so long."

Aaron slides his hand up Nik's back and anchors it between his shoulder blades, pressing him closer. He thinks about Nik and Ollie together, about Ollie's bright smile, about the way he looked at Nik. He'd always hated it.

In a quiet, small voice, Nik continues. "I think he felt about me the way I still feel about you—hopelessly besotted. There's a lesson there, I think." They are quiet for a minute more, and then Nik says, "So, you know, you think I was with Ollie for a long time and that it's important, and that's true, I guess. But it's also true that I was yours the whole time I was with him. It's never been a competition."

Nik's voice washes over Aaron's neck, and he shivers.

It's a lot to take in. Aaron holds Nik against him and keeps moving them around the dance floor, Nik's body and breath warm and familiar against his own. This connection, this *thing* between them—it's been so much a part of his emotional landscape for so long that waking it up has been as easy as breathing and as scary as walking off a cliff. But what Nik's talking about now, *that* kind of fear—" I don't feel terrified. By your feelings, I mean."

"You don't?"

"No. It feels… it's good. Knowing I'm not alone in it. Anymore, I mean." Nik's hand presses firmly against the back of his neck, and his fingers curl into Aaron's hair, and Aaron wants to kiss him but Nik keeps dancing.

"Ollie told me, you know. After we broke up, one day we met to exchange stuff, just… I don't know, finishing it up, I guess. He was still so pissed—he had a right to be—but he told me to come after you. It… how I felt, about you and about what we had, it wasn't a secret. We never

talked about it, not really—it might have been better if we had. But...
he knew."

Aaron imagines it, imagines sitting across from Nik in a coffee shop
and knowing that he is in love with somebody else. It's gutting, brutal.
But it's also a strange kind of gift to know that somebody as kind as Nik
could *be* so cruel, that a heart as large as Nik's is so full of Aaron that
there isn't room for one more person. They've wasted so much time. "I
wish *I* had known."

"So do I."

Nik does kiss him now, sweetly and with such longing. His lips are
soft and wet, his tongue gentle, and his hands tug at Aaron's hair. Aaron
thinks about how they must look, what the parents and the friends must
think—and then he kisses Nik back, because he's not seventeen anymore
and this is a place he spent all week building, and if he can't show Nik that
he loves him at their best friends' wedding, then he's not sure where he can.

Nik pulls back before the kiss can become too intense and props his
forehead against Aaron's. "God, I want to get out of here."

"Do you think we need to wait until they leave?"

Nik pulls back and glances toward the spot where Alex and David
have spent most of their evening, and Aaron follows the glance. Alex is
hugging some of her friends goodbye, and she looks tired—he's not sure
she'll be here much longer as it is.

"Probably, but let's go see."

Aaron takes Nik's hand and leads him over to Alex, who is watching
her friends walk away. She turns to them, smiles at Aaron and says, "Go."

Aaron blinks at her for a second until she says, "I saw you—David
and I were watching you. It's—you're so *romantic,* it's ridiculous. But it
was a beautiful wedding gift, watching the two of you together again, so
thank you, and now get the hell out of here." She grins at him and then
pulls him into a hug; Nik lets go of his hand to shake hands with David.
"Really, *thank you,* for everything," she whispers in his ear. "This day was
perfect, and I couldn't have done it without you."

Aaron pulls back to grin at her. "Did you like the cake?"

"Oh my God, it was amazing. And the flowers, and Nik's playlist, and the *song*—just, everything. It was perfect. Thank you, so much."

Aaron squeezes her hands. "You're leaving for Vegas on Thursday?"

"Yep, and we'll be back in town on Tuesday for one last dinner with my grandma before she goes home, so let's get together so you can tell me *all about it.*"

Aaron gives her his best big-eyed stare and she laughs, and then he pulls her toward him and plants a kiss on her hair and whispers, "I'm so happy for you. Congratulations."

She squeezes him back and says, "You too, baby."

Nik and Aaron are quiet on their way up the lawn back to the house, their hands laced together. About the time they hit the back of the house, the first trumpet call of the Aggie War Hymn sounds, the fight song of the university where Alex and David fell in love—and the rival to the school that Nik spent four years learning to love. Aaron snorts with laughter, and Nik slants a grin over toward him. "Well. You weren't the *only* reason I wanted to leave the reception." Alex and David and Jasmine and all of their friends from school are just coming together in a circle to whoop and yell when two girls in sleeveless dresses and bare feet dash out the door and push past them to join the party, their hair streaming behind them as they giggle and run and try to sing, all at once. Aaron smiles and lets the door slam behind him on the way in.

NIK NABS A BOTTLE OF champagne as they make their way past the bar, and when they get back to Aaron's room he puts the bottle on the table and runs a hand over his head. "Do you mind if we shower first? I have all this stuff in my hair, and I feel a little gross."

While Nik showers, Aaron straightens the room and locks the bedroom door. He opens the champagne and looks for glasses or mugs or *something* before he gives it up for a lost cause and takes a drink straight from the bottle. Mostly, he tries not to be nervous. It's silly, really, how important tonight feels. He reminds himself of who he is, where he's been, everything he's done and everything they've done together, but still, when Nik opens the bedroom door to a billow of steam and his towel-wrapped silhouette, Aaron can't help feeling like a teenager all over again.

Aaron slips past him, wordless, and thinks about it during his own shower. Years ago, he and Nik took that first last step together, in a room not so different from this one, one weekend while Nik's parents were out of town. It should be easier now, now that the mechanics are clearer. When they were young, they were scared of all the wrong things. Then, it had been physical pain, and the idea of what it meant to do *that,* to cross that invisible line that signified one of the last things they thought was still childlike about them.

Aaron remembers Nik diving for his iPod that day, rolling off of him once they were finally together there, naked and excited, because a Disney ballad had come up on his "Romance Primer" playlist. Nik was flustered, saying, "God, I used to watch that movie with my babysitter, what was I *thinking?*"

As Aaron dries off and wraps the towel around his waist, he thinks about the stakes tonight. They shouldn't seem so high—he and Nik both know what they're getting into, after all; they both know what this entails and what's expected. But—and maybe it was the conscious waiting, maybe that's why this feels so important—sex tonight seems like more than sex, as though they are signing a contract, as if it's the start of something big, life-shifting, not the same as the last time they took this step together. It feels… fuck, it still just feels adult, only completely differently than last time. Aaron makes a face to himself in the mirror as he finger-styles his damp hair; it would be great if he could start feeling like a real adult anytime now, thanks.

He walks out of the bathroom. Nik has just one of the bedside lamps on and has already crawled into bed; the white sheets cover him up to the middle of his chest. It seems like a cliché, suddenly, as if Aaron has become a nervous virgin on his wedding night. If it were any other moment he'd laugh at the layers of irony.

It's not any other moment, though. And then Nik says, "Come to bed, Aaron," his voice low and gravelly, another thing that's not helping—Nik is so serious tonight, so *solemn*. All week they've played in bed, laughed together, and the change in tone puts a knot in Aaron's belly.

Aaron goes, though; he walks to the bed, drops his towel and stares down at Nik. Just for this moment, when Nik's look changes to one of hunger and the kind of desperate want that isn't sure it will get what it hopes for, Aaron feels powerful, back on his feet. And then Nik controls his expression and lifts the sheet for him and it's back, the sense that this is harder than it has to be.

Nik hovers over Aaron and kisses him, long and deep, and Aaron throws himself into it, drifts into the taste of Nik's mouth and the smooth slide of his skin. Nik moves closer, leaving kisses along Aaron's neck and nuzzling his throat, his collarbones. "What do you like now?" he says, his breath puffing hot against Aaron's damp skin.

Aaron closes his eyes against his view of the ceiling and curls his hands back into Nik's hair. "God, it's been so long since we were really *together.*"

"Since we fucked," Nik corrects. Well. "It has. So tell me. Tell me what it's been like for you." Nik leaves kisses across his chest, never going lower than his nipples, not even really paying them any attention—he's either stalled out or buying time, but either way, Aaron is suddenly sure that Nik is listening very carefully for his answer.

And he doesn't know what to say. He doesn't *want* that here. He's not ashamed of asking for something he wants, but this isn't the time or the place for it—he'll tell Nik later, pull it out as a spicy story one night to turn him on and make him pay attention. Instead he says, "I've learned a lot."

"Aaron." Nik has pulled back to watch him now, his brow creased, a sweet, confused smile on his face.

"I like... I like everything."

"I can't believe you're being so shy!"

"I'm not! These questions are just so *general.*"

Nik rolls his eyes at him and then softens this by coming back to kiss his neck again. "Fine. Do you still like topping?"

He lifts his chin toward the ceiling and thinks about it, about how badly he wants to fuck Nik, to feel him around his dick. "Oh, yeah. Yes, I do."

"And how about bottoming?"

There, *now* Nik is moving this along a little, sliding his hand across Aaron's torso, shoving the sheet back with his wrist and letting his mouth drift down to follow. He peppers Aaron's chest with small kisses, pausing to lick-suck-bite-pull at a nipple.

"Mmm, sometimes."

"You were never that comfortable before."

"It's still not my favorite. It's…. well. You know."

Nik kisses back up his chest until he's whispering in Aaron's ear again. "I know how it is for me. Tell me how it is for you."

He can't think with Nik's tongue there—Nik knows that spot just behind his ear, and this is so unfair—so he answers. "It's messy, and it's so close. I get hot and stuffy and overwhelmed and… it's a lot. I like my space."

"Yeah." Nik straddles and crouches down over him, slowly, gently sinking his teeth into the curve of Aaron's neck and licking it, and God, that spot, too—Aaron sinks his hand into Nik's damp hair, holding his head there and moaning, low and steady.

"I like it best when I'm bottoming from the top—riding somebody is just… God, fuck, that's so good." He's not sure if he means Nik's mouth on him or what he's remembering. Both, maybe.

Nik blows over the place he's just left wet. "Mmm. I bet you like that—being over him, him looking up at you while you have all the control." Aaron remembers, remembers riding Nik like that the few times he'd bottomed when they were together. It had been easier then, they both thought, easier for Aaron to set the pace and go with his comfort level.

"Yeah."

"Yeah." Nik has pulled back to look at him, and for once Aaron can't read him at all.

So he says, "What about you?" Now he can reach up to run his hands over Nik's chest—as much as he loves the smooth skin of Nik's back, he loves this too, the soft scratch of Nik's hair, the patterns it grows and swirls into.

"Ah. Well. A little of everything—I still like bottoming, I love it, but right now… mostly I just want you," Nik says.

Aaron smiles up at him, his face soft and fond. "So where does that leave us for tonight?"

Nik watches him for a moment and says, "I want to try something. Something that's still somehow new, for you and for us together and... in some ways, for me, too."

Nik leans down again, lowering himself so that he's right back in Aaron's space, nuzzling their noses and faces together and speaking low, every breath a gust across Aaron's cheek, every slow blink a brush of his eyelashes against Aaron's skin. "I want to spend some time with you, with your body. I want to touch you and taste you everywhere. And then I want to stretch you out underneath me, and I want you to taste my skin and smell *me* with every breath and I want you to watch me while I fuck you. That's what I want—I want to fuck you, and I want to be in your space and I want to overwhelm you, and I want you to try not to forget, even for a second, that that's exactly what's happening."

Aaron's breath comes out in a rush. Now he knows; now he knows why this is so scary, why Nik is so solemn. It's because Nik doesn't just want sex; he wants *everything*. Nik is pushing again, he's upping the ante, and Aaron pants, "Oh," and takes a moment to try to think about what *he* wants, beyond Nik's mouth back on his.

Nik is so close right now, so incredibly physically *present*. Aaron wants to go back in time and take Nik to New York with him; wants to rage at his younger self and make him listen to what Nik was trying to tell him; wants to have never let him go.

But he also wants to have had these years, these years on his own in the city when he learned so much about himself, when he fearlessly explored some parts of himself and hid from some others. He wants to stop regretting their breakup and regretting his last hookup, and he wants to find a way to be as bold and fearless here, right now, as he is in so many other places. And he wants *this,* he wants it too, every bit of Nik that he can get, right here, and the best way to reach out and take him is to let himself go, let Nik take him wherever he wants to. It's not at all what he's used to, but maybe that's the point.

Nik is still just rubbing their cheeks together, maybe waiting for him, and it shouldn't feel so sensuous but his words still ring in Aaron's ears and Aaron is so turned on by the thought, by the images that Nik has planted in him. He reaches up and frames Nik's face in his hands, pushing him gently back and taking a moment to look at him, serious and so, so loved, God, before he pulls him down into a kiss. "Yes," he says against Nik's mouth, nodding. "Yes, I want that."

Nik lets his torso fall against Aaron, pinning him to the bed, and slides his tongue into Aaron's mouth with a heady moan. He kisses him wetly for a long time, and then pulls away breathless. "I thought you wouldn't."

"Then why did you ask?"

"Because I wanted you to say yes."

Aaron laughs, *finally* lets the tension crack a little and breathes out heavily through his nose with a wide smile. Nik grins against him, forehead to forehead, and says, "Yeah, I know."

"No. I just... I think the likelihood of me saying no to you right now is pretty slim."

Nik pulls away and sits up tall, beaming down at him. "Well, in *that* case—" Aaron grabs at him, pulling him back down.

"No, that I *will* complain about. Don't go anywhere—stay here with me. I want you close." Aaron pulls Nik into a kiss and slides his tongue into Nik's mouth, tangling his hands in his hair again. Then he pulls back, pressing his head into the pillow. "What you said—I want that. I want you to fuck me."

Nik groans and grinds against him, once. "Say that again."

Aaron grins. "You have me repeating myself a lot this week."

"You keep catching me off guard, and some things are worth committing to memory." Nik suckles Aaron's earlobe and slides against him, his cock dragging against Aaron's balls, and Aaron moans into the movement. "Say it again, Aaron," he whispers against his ear. "Ask me again."

"I want you all the way inside of me. Stay close to me, wrap me up in you and fuck me, Nik."

Nik groans, and Aaron shakes. "Do you like it hard? Slow? Tell me what you want."

"Let's find out," Aaron whispers as he pulls Nik's head back toward his for a kiss.

Nik was serious about taking his time; Aaron watches him slowly, slowly kiss from Aaron's chest to his belly. He sucks Aaron's balls into his mouth, tender and slow, bathing them in broad, soft strokes, and then has to drop his head back and pant at the ceiling. He teases the back of Aaron's knees with his tongue, holding Aaron's legs so he can draw designs there. Aaron finally hands down a pillow for Nik to shove under his ass and slides his hands behind his knees, still slick from Nik's mouth, and holds himself open. Nik moans against him while he rims him open, sliding his wet tongue and fingers wet insistently over Aaron's hole. When Aaron's fingers start to shake, Nik tugs on his knees, pulls his legs down and turns him over.

Nik fingers him for a long time, raining kisses across his ass and adding more lube when he needs to. Aaron breathes through the stretch.

"God, look at you," Nik says. "This ass is a fucking crime, so damn sweet."

Aaron is open, vulnerable and bare, and Nik presses two fingers inside him and curves them to press there, *just* there. He slides his tongue down to flick around Aaron's opening again.

Aaron breathes through it and thinks about how Nik must look right now, thinks about his eyes closed and his forehead wrinkled in a moan, about his tongue extended and the look on his face. It *is* overwhelming, and he's ready before Nik is. He cries out, "Please, Nik, *please.*"

Through the haze he laughs at the irony: begging to be fucked! He's heard it plenty of times and never understood it, but now he's so full and not full enough, feeling strangely *alone*, stimulated but incomplete.

Nik pulls his fingers away and Aaron whines with the loss, and then Nik is turning him and crawling up his body. Aaron grabs at his head and pulls him down—he needs him, needs him close, connected, and Nik groans into the kiss and presses himself against Aaron, pushing his tongue closer into Aaron's mouth to sweep through and take him.

Nik pulls back to roll on a condom and lube it up. He is flushed, sweaty, his hair is askew and his hands are shaking, his body trembling.

"I love you," Aaron says, desperate to keep Nik close even when he's so far away, to let his words tie them back together.

Nik glances up from where he fiddles with the condom. "God, Aaron." He shoves the pillow under Aaron's hips again and tips him up. Then Nik pushes into him, hot and wide, and Aaron gasps from the stretch and the slide.

He panics for a second, clutching at Nik's hip and his hair, and then Nik is kissing him again. He smells like sex, tastes like Aaron's body and the salt of his sweat, and he's thick, so thick inside of him. Aaron flushes with the heat of their connection and their bodies so close together, and Nik is right there, familiar green eyes blown wide and staring into his. The push and drag of Nik's cock aches, so sweet and so right, and Aaron wants to close his eyes against it but Nik is so present, watching him, so he can't, he *can't*. Nik moves slowly, steadily, his gaze a brand while he drags it out even longer, staggering his perfect rhythm with sudden, syncopated, strong thrusts so that Aaron cries out for him every time, his breath pooling hot between them. Nik watches, taking him in as he comes apart over and over in between kisses that linger, lips clinging as Aaron gasps into Nik's mouth with each sharp push and reaches down to grab Nik's thighs high, right below his ass, to anchor him there, inside of him, hot and so thick and *God*.

Nik moans, "Aaron, Aaron, I *want* you," into his mouth.

Aaron says, "I'm here, yeah," but he knows it's not enough, it can't be enough, because the sex will end, and it's just their bodies, not their *selves*, and he can't stop *wanting*. He wants to swallow Nik whole so he can keep him, wants to absorb him through his skin so he'll always be here, close, close, just like this.

"Please, *please*," Nik gasps. Aaron pulls him closer, gives up on kissing and watching so their faces are pressed together, sharing breath between them. They're both sweating; their foreheads slide while Nik pumps into him, back to steady and slow, and Aaron breaks apart and winds tighter and tighter with each shove of Nik's belly against his cock. Aaron gasps against Nik with each push in and slow drag back out. He winds his legs around Nik to keep him close and wraps his arms around Nik's shoulders and buries his hands in his hair and keeps him.

Nik moans his name, "Aaron, God, *Aaron*—" and suddenly his hips stutter and he's groaning out his orgasm against Aaron's mouth. Aaron *feels* him, feels him swell and their rhythm fall, irregular and broken, and he's so close he wants to tip over, to come with him but it's not enough, he's not there yet. So while Nik presses into him in long, shuddering, desperate strokes, Aaron shoves a hand between them to curl over his own dick, to strip and pull at it.

"Yeah, yeah," Nik groans, and before Nik is finished riding out his climax, Aaron roars and spills between them, clenching around Nik's barely softening cock and God, there, *yes*. Nik's breath catches once, twice, and then he's kissing Aaron through it, licking into his open mouth to get that little bit closer. Aaron can't breathe, because everything is *Nik*—the weight on top of him, the air in his lungs, the taste in his mouth—and every time he catches a breath it's Nik, *Nik,* stealing it right out of him again.

Aaron shoves at Nik's shoulders, starting to panic again, and Nik shifts his weight to his knees so Aaron's lungs can expand but he doesn't stop kissing him, doesn't pull his mouth or his body away. He keeps his hands firmly in Aaron's hair and presses his tongue, sloppy and wet, against Aaron's. Aaron breathes in deeply through his nose and smells sex, bleachy spunk and clean sweat. His fingertips tingle where they slide against the sweaty skin of Nik's back, and Nik's rapid breath is hot against his cheek and loud over the roaring in his ears. Nik is everywhere, *everywhere,* and the same thing that left him panicking is now what calms him, because he isn't alone, Nik is here, still hard within him and around him and a part of him.

And then Nik's hips shift and he pulls back just far enough to look Aaron in the eye, intent and so goddamn *predatory,* and he presses into Aaron again and says, his voice rough, "I'm not done with you yet," and it's long and slow, a thick, stinging pull that's God, yes, please, God, *yes.*

In Their Own Words

A post from the blog A Lone Star in Manhattan, *Sunday, December 28, 2014:*

I'm back in my apartment after a week at my mom's place for the holidays. It was, as always, great to be there at Christmas. My mother continues to be a breathtakingly good cook and an outstanding host, and the bar will forever be set by how lovely she can make a holiday. I ate too much, surprising nobody; we watched a lot of movies and cleaned out more than one closet; I saw a lot of my friends from high school; and I spent a lot of time outside. That last is unusual for me, but at the holidays the warm weather is such a novelty that it drives me outside. We walked over to the churchyard where my grandparents are buried, and I spent some time walking the path the county just built next to the bayou at the end of our street. My cousin even drove me out to his deer lease, where I sat for whole minutes before the stillness of it made me a little bit crazy. It was good.

One of the things I did while I was home was go to a Christmas light display with some old friends of mine. Every year this park near my house goes all out and has a walk-through light display and it's a very big deal where I grew up—tour buses come and the whole thing. When I was in high school we used to man the concession stand to raise money for the school newspaper, and it was with some of the same friends I used to sling popcorn with—and the group we've gathered around us—that I went this year.

One point of tradition is to take comfort in the familiar, and so it's appropriate that this visit to this park reminded me of how little people really change. Besides my mom and my aunt, there are three constant women in my life: let's call them A, J and S. They have seen me through everything. Latina, white and African-American, they are my muses and my confidantes and my competitors and my very own Three Wise Women.

There was a moment last week, standing in a clutch of trees, surrounded by millions of white twinkling lights, when A was laughing with her boyfriend at some running joke that is just between them and J and S were squabbling over competing memories of who was elected homecoming queen our sophomore year of high school. All three of them were eating from the same bucket of popcorn, timing their handfuls as if they eat together every day, as if it was still four years ago when we were the ones filling the popcorn buckets and living in each others' backpack pockets. It was the simplest passing moment, and there is no way they remember it happening, but I saw them there, just as I had seen the three of them so many times years ago, and it hit something inside of me. That "something" is the same thing that makes mothers cry at graduations, I think; it's the same thing that makes us walk over to my grandparents' place in the cemetery every Christmas. It's tradition, and growth, and how, even as we change and everything changes around us, little artifacts of who we are and those we have loved stay with us and take root within us, shaping us forever. And it's a really trivial thing that these three beloved women know how to share a bucket of popcorn without any awkwardness or hesitation—and let me be clear: They were going at it; these women like to eat— but it's also kind of beautiful, at least to me, at least right now.

We all graduate from college in just a few months. I don't know exactly what happens to all of us then—I don't even know exactly what happens to ME then. I don't know how many more evenings like that one the four of us will have together, and I'm not sure when the next one will be.

But I've loved the ones we have had, and as we get ready to move into 2015 (it's the future!), I want to be more aware of all of these little moments. My resolution for 2015 is to pay more attention, to try to see better and hear better and slow down enough to maybe even savor my life. If nothing else, I'm sure it will make me a better writer. It has to, doesn't it?

We'll see. For now I have a weekend full of parties ahead of me, and 2015 and everything it might bring can wait just a few more days.

Sunday

When Aaron wakes the next morning, the sun is already high in the sky, and he can hear noises from outdoors and from elsewhere in the house. He wakes slowly, and Nik is there, right there, pressed against his side where they've shifted in their sleep.

Last night they disentangled themselves, finally, and Nik wordlessly cleaned them up and then collapsed back into him. This morning, with the sun up and the night over, he's almost embarrassed to remember what it was like, especially the second time. He hasn't been that close to somebody—that exposed and *intimate*—in such a long time, and he forgot how vulnerable and shaken it leaves him, how hard it is to live with when he's become so used to keeping more distance.

But lying there with Nik, the second time and then, God... afterward, they just quietly watched each other. Nik settled on his back and Aaron pillowed his head on his shoulder and watched his hand move over Nik's chest in aimless circles simply for the satisfaction of touching a different part of his skin. Nik breathed deeply and hummed his satisfaction, and Aaron laid his hand over Nik's heart to feel it beat. It felt so calm and so... simple, really.

Aaron thought, then, *He's real*—and it's so silly, Aaron knows it's silly, but this morning he still feels the same—Nik is real, he's right here, he's breathing right next to me and soon he'll open his eyes and he'll look at me and he'll *still* be real. Years of knowing Nik, of sometimes understanding him so well and sometimes not at *all*, don't make this seem any less likely.

Aaron lies there, warm and loose and naked, enveloped in sheets that smell like them, and he stares at the ceiling and makes himself think about going home today, having to peel himself away and go back to his mother's house and then New York, go back to his life just as he left it, with one hell of an exception. Some things will change—he has a lot of people he'll be cutting out, for one thing, and the fact that he doesn't feel that as a bigger loss makes him wince and stop to breathe for a minute. But the thing is, he can *see* it.

He can see how it's going to work, can imagine Nik there with him. Maybe it's easier because he's had so much practice picturing Nik in New York—so many years of it. But he also thinks about what it will be like *now*, about the difference that four years of adulthood make, about the difference between playing in the city as a new undergrad and making a real go of it as a writer and grad student. If Nik had come then, it would have been play, one grand adventure. Now it feels like the beginning of something very different, a whole new phase of his life, his adulthood, and now Nik will be with him for it. Aaron will straighten Nik's tie, fix his hair, steal his kisses. It's a funny thing, to shift your life to fit around somebody with so little warning, but Aaron has already done the less-fun version of this, the rewrite that suddenly strips all those little things *out*, so this… this could be easy. Happy, anyway.

Nik shifts and sighs and wraps an arm around Aaron's waist, hums into his shoulder and says in a sleepy voice, "I'm going to miss this, waking up with you."

Aaron turns to Nik and studies his face, his sleepy eyes and the small, unconscious smile bending his mouth. "Not for long, you won't. You'll be in New York in a couple of months." His eyes trail down Nik's jawline, and he lets his fingers follow as he says, a little unsure, "You should come out early if you can. You've heard all about my apartment so I realize it's not that tempting an offer, but I *do* have my own bedroom and you'd be welcome there. If you want to."

Nik sighs into the caress, and closes his eyes and clears his throat. "I will. Still. Even once I'm moved there, it won't be like this every day."

"No. It won't." Aaron brushes some hair away from Nik's eyes. "We still have lives to lead, you know. Not every day is part of your best friend's hellish wedding week."

Nik opens his eyes, smiles at him and says, "No, we can't be that lucky."

"Still." He finally meets Nik's eyes. "We're pretty lucky, I'd say."

"The luckiest," Nik whispers as he pulls Aaron into a kiss.

They kiss for long minutes, sweet and soft. Aaron still feels overwhelmed by Nik—in such a different way from last night, but just as wonderful. He slides closer and pushes one thigh between Nik's, tangling their bodies together again and letting himself fall back into the closeness, overwarm and sticky and perfect.

Eventually Nik slides out of bed after a lingering kiss and returns to his room to grab another change of clothes. Aaron rolls over and pulls his tablet from the nightstand to check his email—as much as part of him wants to stay here forever, he's already starting to get his head in the game for what comes next.

There in his personal email is a comment from CityDan, a stranger who has been sporadically commenting on Aaron's personal blog for almost as long as he's been posting there. Aaron has no idea who he or she is—he imagines CityDan as a wiry man in middle age, quiet and contemplative, because his advice is always very thoughtful and reasonable and *kind,* so sensitive for a person who somehow manages to read full, unfiltered Aaron and keeps coming back. Aaron has Google-searched the username before, but the hits are very thin and he doesn't seem to be able to put together a consistent sense of a user. Over time, he's come to think of CityDan as his fairy godfather; he's not real, not *really,* but Aaron would still miss him if he disappeared, and he'd like to think CityDan would miss him, too.

As always, CityDan's comment is short. And, as always, it takes his breath away.

I'm happy for you. It's hard, sometimes, to let ourselves go with people who have hurt us. But I think that finding your way back to somebody who has known you for a long time and can still love you is a precious thing. It's even more precious to know somebody for a long time and to love them—*most of us can spend a lifetime looking for somebody we feel that way about.*

Good luck to you both. I'll be pulling for you. Just remember that falling in love isn't the point. Living in love is.

Nik comes back into the room a short while later, clothes dangling from his hand and a stunned grin on his face. He bounces down onto the bed and hisses, "Tu hooked up with Stephanie."

Aaron drops his tablet on the bed and stares at him. "What are you *talking* about?"

"She was there—when I went to get my clothes, they were in bed together."

"Hmm. Maybe she just slept there, for some reason."

Nik's face is mischievous, absolutely tickled. "Nope. That room came with two twin beds, and one of them was still perfectly made. And I'm pretty sure she wasn't wearing a shirt."

"Oh, holy shit." Aaron laughs, rolling the other way to lie flat on his back and stare at the ceiling.

"I *know*," Nik breathes.

"I wonder if Jasmine knows," Aaron says, turning to look at Nik.

Nik pokes him in the side, overflowing with mirth. "Hurry, shower, go find out!"

Aaron laughs and rolls out of bed, pushing past Nik. "We have been such a bad influence on you."

Nik grabs his hand and pulls him back, so that Aaron is standing naked between his spread knees. "I know. Isn't it great?" Aaron kisses him on the forehead and snickers into his hair.

AARON SNEAKS DOWN TO THE kitchen to get the coffee started while Nik is in the shower. He pauses when he walks through the doorway; not a single surface is uncluttered, dirty dishes are *everywhere,* and the room itself seems hungover and filled with anxiety. He shifts piles of dishes, manages to unearth the coffeemaker, makes his way to the cupboard where the coffee and mugs are stored and gets out of there as soon as he can interrupt the brewing to pour two cups. He knew it would be waiting for him, but he needs a few more minutes before he can face it.

He's almost back to his room, just a few doors away, when Stephanie slips out of Nik and Tu's room in last night's dress. That alone is a first for a girl who always prides herself on being put together, but the second glance is revelatory. Her makeup and hair are in disarray, she's carrying her shoes, and the moment she sees him she balks and grabs his arm, sloshing coffee over her dress. She looks down at the stain and then up at him, and she appears seconds away from bursting into tears when she steels her face and drags him down the hall, pushes open the door to the room Alex and David had shared and drags him inside.

The door isn't even completely closed before she says, "You can't tell *anybody*," as she looks around the room as if it's filled with people waiting to attack her.

He leans against the door and smirks at her. It's too delicious, seeing Stephanie like this; their competition has always been intense, and it hasn't been limited to their work. Stephanie has rich parents and a pretty face and great connections, but she has never really had the kind of firm belief in herself that Aaron does and he has always thought that she scares far too easily. He doesn't know why—he's never completely understood it—but it keeps her vulnerable, and it's why they need each other: She brings the resources, and he brings the audacity to exploit them.

"Nik already walked in on you this morning and told me all about it, and I don't know who else I'd tell. Well. Jasmine, probably. But I suspect she's busy with Joe this morning, so." He shrugs.

She perches on the edge of the bed and wrings her hands, and her face is *so* earnest, so serious. "I don't do this, Aaron!"

"Oh, I'm pretty sure you do." He slaps himself a little; Stephanie always has brought out the sarcasm like nobody else could.

Her look in return is vicious. "Shut up. He's cute. And *super* smart. And you and Nik were clearly headed somewhere to screw each other's brains out and Alex and David are so in love and Joe and Jasmine were giving each other stupid crazy eyes and I just…."

Stephanie stares off into space. Aaron watches her for a moment and then says, a little more quietly, "I'm surprised you didn't come on to Josh. It must have felt like a flashback to high school, seeing him there, with you and Jasmine and Joe all together."

She's quiet for longer than he's used to. "He's with somebody. I couldn't do that to him." A long moment passes, and then she says, "Or myself." His heart breaks for her.

"Did you two ever...?"

Her nod is slow, her smile sweet. "Once. Well, once, all the way. There was—it got pretty intense senior year and there was a lot of... but *that*, just that one time. He was my first, obviously."

Aaron nods—he always wondered, and it's not the kind of thing Aaron can ask his cousin. He wonders if he'll ever know exactly what happened to keep them apart, if it was as dumb as what had come between him and Nik. Not everybody gets the second chance.

Suddenly, she groans. "God, he's still *here*, and everybody's going to know at breakfast." She face-plants into the comforter and keeps mumbling. "I don't know how you did this. I wish I could just *die*."

Somehow the theatrics are a comfort, so familiar even in this very strange situation.

He puts the coffee on the nightstand, sits next to her and pats her on the shoulder.

"Okay, princess, that's enough of that. You'll do it because you have to, and you're the one who's always on about appearances. You didn't do anything wrong; you are *allowed* to have a one-night stand. Who knows? It might even be good for you." She turns her head to glare at him, and he delivers the punchline. "Maybe there's a human interest story in it."

The worst thing about using Stephanie for a punchline is that, more often than not, he's the one who ends up getting punched. Still, it was totally worth it.

"Just for that I'm stealing your coffee," she says with another vicious narrowing of her eyes, and she leans over to snag the cup from the nightstand and cradles it on top of her chest, breathing deeply.

He rolls his eyes and says, "Fine. I can always get more. Now get showered—you look like a girl who took a tumble last night, and that is not Stephanie Baxter-appropriate. Clean it up and hold your head high. You're our host for today, still—you have to see everybody off, and then you can wallow in your disgrace on your own time."

She gives him a weak wave, and he shows her some mercy and brushes her hair back from her face. "You're fine, honey. Did you at least have a good time?" Her smile firms up, tiny and wicked, and he raises his brows back at her. "*Interesting.* So forget about regretting it, hold your head high and carry on. But my goodness, girl—get a shower first!"

She's still grinning when he slips out the door and heads back to the kitchen to grab another cup of coffee for Nik. Tu is there with his own cup sitting in front of him, his chin propped on one hand while he lazily scrolls through photos on his tablet with his other. Aaron looks at him for a minute, and can't help the smirk that he knows is stealing across his face; Tu looks fresh from the shower, but otherwise calm and unruffled.

"Well good morning! Good time last night?" Aaron says as he crosses back to the coffee machine. Tu has cleared some more space and set out a stack of mugs.

"Yeah, the wedding was great, I thought. Everybody seemed happy, and I got some great shots."

Aaron finishes pouring Nik's cup and leans back against the counter, watching Tu. He's still flipping, and he pauses and turns the tablet so Aaron can see a photo of him and Nik dancing together. It's a tight shot in profile, only their shoulders and heads very close together, with Nik's hand curled into Aaron's hair. They're not talking, just staring at each other, and Nik is angled a little farther toward the camera than Aaron. The look on his face is soft and tender and *breathtaking*.

"Oh," Aaron says, walking closer. "You... can you send that to me? I think I need that."

Tu grins. "Yeah, tonight or tomorrow I'm going to go through these and put them all up somewhere, but I'll email you this one right now."

He bends over his tablet, punching at buttons and sending the picture out immediately. Aaron watches him, staring at his fingers and his wet hair, and thinks about everything teasing he had wanted to say. "Did you sleep well?" "How happy *did* everybody seem?" Even, "Be kind to Stephanie," maybe, when he's his better self. Suddenly none of it seems necessary, and he's sure that none of it is appropriate, not *now*, so he just says, "Thank you."

Aaron holds up the fresh cup of coffee and says, "Nik slipped back to your room and grabbed some clothes this morning and is already in the shower, so I better get this up to him." Tu's head pops up and he looks at Aaron, his eyes wide. Aaron smiles at him. "We'll be back in a little bit."

Tu's voice is quiet, a little absent, when he says, "Right, of course." Aaron grins to himself on his way up the stairs.

When he reaches the top of the stairs, Joe is stepping out of Jasmine and Stephanie's room, clad in a pair of sweat shorts, and Aaron reflexively checks him out and then grins at him, shaking his head at the gobsmacked, guilty look on Joe's face and resolutely walking on. When he finally makes it back to his room he closes the door with a sigh, carefully places the coffee on his nightstand and reaches for his phone to send a text to Alex.

"Just wanted to let you know that if your goal for your wedding was to generate our own personal bedroom farce, it was a rousing success. More gossip when you're not doing whatever it is you're doing."

WHEN THEY FINALLY MAKE IT downstairs, the whole house—Mia, Nicole, Josh, Stephanie, Tu, Joe and Jasmine—are sitting around the kitchen table, bleary-eyed and agape, because a team of six strangers are standing in the kitchen and doing dishes, cleaning the floor and gathering their supplies to move out through the house.

"What..." Aaron's voice drifts off as the whole table turns to stare at them.

"Your family sent a cleaning crew, that's what," Stephanie says, tears in her eyes.

Aaron looks at Josh, who is leaning back in his chair with a big smile on his face. He raises a brow at his cousin, and Josh spreads his hands wide. "That's all them, man. You know how they are together—I don't know how they think of this stuff, but they always do."

Jasmine leans forward and pillows her head on her crossed arms. Her hair is a mess and there's mascara smeared under her eyes, but her voice is heartfelt when she says, "Your moms are my favorite. Both of them. Do you think one of them would adopt me?"

Joe nudges her arm with his. "I have dibs on Josh's mom," he says, and she turns her head to grin up at him.

"And if I get my way, I'm next in line to join Aaron's family," Nik says, wrapping an arm around Aaron's waist.

Aaron gives Nik a look and rolls his eyes; they land on Josh when the roll is over. He watches his cousin as he says, "I think my mom has enough kids underfoot. Josh is getting married soon and Joe already knows how to clean up after himself—I'm pretty sure Aunt Karen will be in the market for a replacement." Aaron grins widely when Josh starts to splutter.

AFTER COFFEE AND A MAKESHIFT breakfast of the last of the frozen waffles and the bacon that wasn't used the night before, they clear out of the kitchen so that the cleaners can finish their work in peace. Tu and Nik head to the beach to check that the poles from the bower are down and folded, and when everybody else is settling down in the living room to rest before they start to pack, Aaron grabs Jasmine's arm and says with an imperial wave of his hand, "My girl and I are heading out to walk the grounds one last time. We'll be back later." He drags her out the front door, snagging an empty cardboard box on the way out.

The rental people are still packing up the chairs and unwinding the lights from the arbor, moving slowly and lazily and laughing and talking amongst themselves. Aaron nods at them and starts to gather the jam jars from the tables and drop them in a pile on the soft, sandy grass. Jasmine follows his lead and eventually they settle there in the grass, Jasmine cross-legged and Aaron in a crouch because he's dressed for driving home, not lounging on a lawn.

"We haven't had much time to talk, just the two of us," Aaron says as he dumps out a jar, plucks the candle from the pile of sand to toss it to the side and then places the jar in the box.

"There's always been something." She picks up a jam jar in each hand and waves them around.

He hums agreement at her and dumps two more jars. "So. Joe."

"Yep."

He shifts on his feet and then glances up at her when she stays quiet. "That's all I'm getting?"

"Tell me about Nik," she says pointedly.

Aaron doesn't even care. "Oh, Jasmine. He's... still Nik."

"He's in love with you." Her voice is a friendly tease.

"Yes. I think he is." He keeps working, and then he says, "How did I get so lucky?"

"I'll be honest: I do not know." He slaps at her until she laughs, and then she tosses her hair and says, "Well, you're right—he's pretty special. But you know you're fabulous, baby. I've been telling you that since forever."

He grins at her. "And I've been telling you that whoever you're with needs to think you're as important as you obviously are. So tell me—are you important to Joe?"

She glances up at him and gives him an impish grin. "Oh hell, Aaron. I don't know how important either one of us is to the other. But it's easy, and the thing about Joe..." she drifts off, the grin still on her face.

"Yes?" he drawls.

She shrugs. "Well, he feels safe. We have a lot of history, and it feels easy with him—he doesn't make my number go up, for one thing, and you know how I feel about my number." He rolls his eyes, mostly because he can't believe that Jasmine still takes that seriously after all this time. "I know, I know, you and Alex both think it's dumb and the only other person still keeping track at this point is Stephanie, probably, and *that's* embarrassing. But I'm not over it yet and I don't think I'm going to be anytime soon. I can still count my sex number on one hand and I like that about myself. Sue me." She keeps grinning, but dumps the next jar a little more viciously. "Also, the thing about Joe is, he's not an asshole; he could never even *be* an asshole. You know him. Basically, that's it, and right now it will sure as hell do. I'm not sure ours is a love for the ages—I still don't think that everybody gets a love story—but he's never been anything but as nice to me as he can be, and I like him."

"And that's enough?" Aaron isn't sure anymore, really, what's enough for her. Once upon a time he knew exactly what would make her happy, but as long as he's known her and as much as he still loves her, he's not sure he really knows who she is right now.

"For right now? Yeah." She leans back on the grass, props herself up with her hands behind her and sighs. "Oh, hell, Aaron. I need a *job*. I have no idea what I'm doing next, and I need something to look forward to. Joe might not be able to help me find work, but he's sure as shit worth looking forward to. We have fun, and right now? That's worth a lot, because nothing else is looking all that attractive."

Aaron pokes at her knee. "I saw him this morning without his shirt on."

"Right?" Her grin is savage, delighted. "So then you see what I'm talking about. *Very* attractive."

"I have some idea, yes. And what about Mitchell?"

She raises her brow and tilts her head to the side. "Who?"

He dusts off his hands and rests his elbows on his knees, propping his chin on his hand and grinning at her. "Right answer."

They're still sitting there, finishing cleaning out the jars and talking about when Jasmine should visit him in New York, when Joe and Josh make their way out of the house, bags thrown over their shoulders. They're both rumpled and wearing sunglasses, but they're also grinning. Joe roars at Jasmine and comes at her, tackling her into the grass while she giggles and slaps at him. Aaron shakes his head and leaves them there so he can make his way over to Josh.

Josh throws his arm around Aaron's shoulders as they walk together to Josh's truck, not cowed by having to reach up a few inches. When Aaron first outgrew Josh, it was the source of so many fights—so many times they had to be separated by their moms—and now, like so many things, it's just what's normal for them. "So, man—you and Nik. That's a real thing again, huh?"

He smiles. "Yeah. I called my mom about it—did she tell you?"

Josh shrugs. "She told Mom, and you know how that goes. She was on the phone to me before she even left the house that day. I'm pretty sure they're throwing a party, just the two of 'em—Mom was talking about a double wedding."

Aaron shakes his head; his Aunt Karen had never had much of a sense of occasion, but it's very sweet of her to think about it that way. "I'm sorry Megan couldn't come yesterday."

"Naw, man, it's fine. It's just as well." He pauses for a second, and Aaron feels a little dread swell up within him, because he knows what's coming next. "Stephanie looks good, doesn't she?"

He levels his cousin with a look, and Josh starts laughing before Aaron even has to say anything. "No way, man, don't worry about it—I'm just giving you a hard time. Shit, I wouldn't even if there wasn't Megan. That ship has *sailed*—and let's be real, it was never gonna hold water anyway, was it? There was just... we were two different people, you know?" Aaron watches Josh as he makes his way through this mixed-up metaphor, but he gets what he means. Josh looks back at the house, at how its façade looms over the street. "I mean, me and Stephanie—I never had a thing like that, before or since. It was—I don't know, man, maybe some kind of opposites attracting thing? And she's still one of the most interesting girls I ever met, probably mostly because I never could figure out what that was all *about*. But that was never—I mean, I might have wanted it to? And she's always gonna be something to look at, I think. But it was always gonna be too hard, and she was never gonna like me for just the guy I am. Her mother couldn't stand me, anyway, and she was never sure if her mom was right. I don't need that."

Aaron's arm is still wrapped around Josh, and he squeezes him around the waist. "No. You don't. I'm *really* glad you know that." He laughs, a little, and blows out a breath. "God, I'm so glad that's finally really over."

"She hooked up with that Vietnamese guy last night, didn't she?" Josh's smile is crooked and dirty, and Aaron just holds up his hands.

"Not my business."

"Uh-huh. Well, I guess you were pretty busy last night, too."

"*Only* my business," Aaron quips back with a grin.

"Aw, man. You're no fun." Aaron gives him a raised eyebrow. "Still, I'm just saying—that thing with me and Stephanie, that's not the kind of thing that would happen with the two of you. Y'all have always wanted the same thing, I'm pretty sure." Josh elbows him in the side and leers at him.

Aaron laughs and scrubs his hands across his face in disbelief while Josh calls out, "Joe, c'mon, man, put her down! We've gotta get back on the road!"

AARON SLIDES HIS TABLET INTO his bag, tosses the flap closed and glances around the room one more time. Then he looks at Nik, who is sitting on the edge of the bed watching him.

"You're already packed?"

Nik nods. "I never really pulled much out—and I was in here most of the time, anyway."

Aaron quirks a brow and then grins. "True. What time are you heading out?"

"I promised David I'd stay until it's done. He's still sort of freaked out that Stephanie's parents were so relaxed about letting them use the space, and he asked me to stay and make sure it's spotless."

"Living up to that best man title, aren't you?"

"Well, I do try."

"You succeed," Aaron shoots back with a glance. He's trying for flirty, but Nik is not taking the bait at all; he smiles, but it's not quite meeting his eyes.

"Hey."

"What?" Nik tilts his head, the look on his face quizzical and fake and guarded, and Aaron *hates* it.

"You tell me."

Nik looks at him, searches his face for something, and then he sighs and reaches for Aaron. Aaron slides over until he stands between Nik's knees, and he slips his hands up to cup Nik's cheeks so he can stare down into his face.

His eyes are gone gray and so sincere, searching Aaron's. He says, quietly, "Tomorrow I'm coming to your house. I'm going to stand on your front porch again and knock on your door and wait for you to answer. Promise me that when you do, you'll kiss me."

Aaron smooths his hair, strokes his cheeks and says, "If you call before you come, I'll meet you on the sidewalk and do it there." Under Aaron's hands, Nik's smile creases his cheeks. "You don't have to be afraid of my front porch. We aren't eighteen anymore."

Nik chuckles and leans forward to rest his forehead against Aaron's chest. "It's not the porch that's the problem."

"I think the porch is at least a *little* the problem." When Nik is quiet, Aaron tugs at his hair until he looks up and says, "At least I hope it is. Is something else going on?"

Nik looks up at him then, his eyes bright. "You're not afraid to leave here? It feels… I don't know. Magical. Like everything that happens here is the exception to every rule."

Aaron watches him for another long moment, then traces the slope of Nik's nose and bottom lip with his forefinger. And then he says, "Sweetheart, that not the house. I'm pretty sure that's us."

Epilogue

A selection of text messages:

From Nik:

Hey. I'm parked in front of your house. Still willing to meet me on the sidewalk?

From Alex:

Okay, we're back in town and the parents have been appeased. Come over and look at pictures and tell me everything I missed!

From Alex:

And bring Nik if he's there.

From Alex:

Also, I'm really liking the idea that I can get both of you in one text message. Very efficient.

From Jasmine:

Baby, when exactly are you leaving? NO movement on the job front and my dad is out of work again so my parents are being real dicks about me paying rent, so guess what! I'm going down to Corpus to stay with Joe for a little bit. Just don't want to go until you're gone, too.

A post from the "Year One" blog on the "About Our Students" page from the website of an MFA program based in New York City, Tuesday, July 7, 2015:

Part of my funding from the program is to work in the office this summer. It's nothing earth-shattering; a little filing, answering some phones, that kind of thing. It's a little gift, because I have the chance to get comfortable here before classes start and get my face in front of a few people, and I will confess that sometimes I have a little time to work on some writing of my own if things aren't too busy.

I've only been on the job for about a week; I did take a little time to go home and see old friends at a wedding. I got to see my family, got to eat a bunch of food that tasted like home. It was hot, oppressively so, and there's something about the sticky heat there that is so different from what we put up with in Manhattan in the summer; it's not even the difference in the relative humidity levels, but something about what's in the water in the air—a different kind of salt, or something. It just feels different. Or at least it always has. This last trip I didn't notice it as much.

This school year that's coming up is really exciting for me. I've been buying books, been poking around on the Internet to find old copies of syllabi to try to get a jump on what things might be like in September. And I'm starting to get my personal life ready for it, too. There are a lot of blogs about life as a graduate student, and they scare me; there's a lot of talk about pleasing your advisor, and about the hours you have to work, and about how hard it can be on relationships.

And I'm sure it will be hard, but one thing I've been thinking about is how many hard things I've already done. I watched my dad walk out of my life (that essay was already published, just follow the link). I came out to everybody I knew in an unpredictably hostile climate (ditto the above). I moved across the country all alone at the age of seventeen, and I watched my first love walk out of—and then back into—my life (those essays are still baking, in part because I'm still living them). I'm really, really good at hard. I'm so good at hard that I feel like I have to do hard things and then write about it so everybody else can know how to be good at hard too. It's arrogant, and probably pathological and egotistical as all hell.

All of these are reasons why I will do well here; I will fit right in. So I'm sure it will be hard, having a life and being a student and continuing to work. But hard is where I live, it's what I do. I can't wait.

More text messages:

From Nik:
On the ground. Missing you already!

From Aaron:
Already at the office. Go home, sleep for both of us, and then start packing.

From Aaron:
And call me tonight, please.

From Nik:
Packing sucks. I really have to bring *all* of my clothes, don't I?

From Aaron:
Unless you want me shopping for you.

From Aaron:
Scratch that. As long as we're on your budget, don't pack a thing.

From Nik:
Walked right into that one. Nice try, though.

From Nik:
New York really is very far from Houston, and I am tired of the inside of this van. Turnpike after turnpike after turnpike. Just made it into

Pennsylvania and I can't believe how much more there is to go. Give me something good to look forward to.

To Nik:

Tara and Jamie left an hour ago to head to a friend's house-share. For a week. I am all alone here. Whatever shall I do?

From Nik:

Hold that thought for a few more hours. Your layabout, grad student boyfriend is on his way.

A post from the blog "A Lone Star in Manhattan," Saturday, August 1, 2015:

For the Texas friends: He's here, so please stop texting him.

For the New York friends: He's here, so please stop texting me.

For the New York friends: We'll be ready to see people by Monday, I think. Thank you for your patience. He is much more charming than I am and definitely worth the wait.

For the Texas friends: Just… thank you for your patience. So much. That's it.

From The Galveston County Daily News, Sunday, March 25, 2017:

Mrs. Laura Campbell is delighted to announce the engagement of her daughter, Megan Rose, to Mr. Joshua Broussard of Dickinson, Texas. Megan is a graduate of Texas City High School and The University of Houston at Clear Lake and is a teacher at Stephen F. Austin Elementary School. Mr. Broussard, the son of Karen Broussard of Texas City, is a graduate of Dickinson High School and an employee of Marathon Oil.

Josh and Megan will marry in late July and, following a honeymoon to New York City, will reside in Texas City.

A voicemail message left on Aaron's phone, May 11, 2017:

Aaron! Oh my God, why aren't you answering your phone? I got it! My first byline above the fold, Aaron! I did it!

You have to come out tonight to help me celebrate. You and Nik. *Promise* me you'll come out! Put down your thesis stuff, forget about the recitals and the grading and the portfolio and all of it, forget everything, just… just give me one night, Aaron. Because I earned this, and you owe me. And I'll pay for everything, I *swear*.

Aaron! Oh my God, call me back. Immediately.

A post from the "Writers Gotta Write" blog section of www.aaronwilkinson. com, Thursday, November 1, 2018:

It's cold here this morning, icy and gray and still, and the world feels a little bit hungover from the revelry of the night before. Last night our front door was barely closed, the energy of the frigid air in-out-in of the house with every little sticky-fingered Buzz Lightyear. (This comeback of Mr. Lightyear's, by the way, this early resurgence of something I remember from my own storied trick-or-treating days, is the kind of thing that will make a young man feel old.) The price of being partnered to an arts academy's very favorite music teacher, the cost of popularity among the prepubescent set, is that Halloween will always be a big deal.

(I say that as though I'm sorry. My mother made beautiful little stuffed cloth pumpkins and sent them to us along with two batches of pumpkin bread. The house looks and smells fantastic. We both come from a warmer, stickier climate and will always be grateful for fall. I *love* Halloween.)

The frost is on the punkin, just as the poet said; the frost has *been* on the pumpkin, and the jack-o'-lanterns have been in danger of freezing for weeks. Thank God for the candles, because in this weather every little bit of warmth helps. But the poet was right—it's good energy. It must be, because last night I heard from my agent that the book has sold. I double-checked this morning, now that the witching hour has passed, and the email is still in my box, so it must be true. Somebody wants to publish that collection of essays.

The book. Has sold.

It's cold here every morning now. I have to remind myself that it's cold in New York now, too—maybe not quite like this, not with this bitterness so early in the year, but soon even there it will be cold enough to leave my eyes watering. But this is the time for fallowness, for the days to grow short, and it was always hard to see that in the city. It's easier to see here, grounded as we are in the rhythm of the school year and surrounded by more trees, more things that grow than just people. It's time for me to lock myself in my house with the person I love and let the music he loves to make fill our home. It's time for my own stories to grow just big enough to fill one book, and then they can start to fill another. We're aiming for publication in the spring, right when everything else will be shooting up anew.

Fall is the season to celebrate the harvest and prepare to live off of its bounty. We've worked hard through what feels like a long, sweaty slog of summers; we've toughed out some hard times in a blazing, merciless sun to make it here. We've earned the right to close our doors and sit quietly by the fire that we built and enjoy ourselves, just for a season.

And we will, as soon as I call everybody I know.

With love and gratitude, Aaron Wilkinson

THE END

Acknowledgments

I need to begin by thanking the Interlude Press team for their support, hard work, and understanding. This book has taken a terribly long time to see the light of day, and it would not have made it here without their help. Annie, in particular, was a relentless champion of this book and for that I am grateful. Thanks are also due to C.B., the artist whose work you see on the cover and throughout the book, and to the IP team for making that happen. I couldn't be more honored and pleased.

To Donna, Lucie, Christine, Leta, Tessa, Kerry, and anybody else who read drafts: From its very beginning to the latest version, this story has been made better by your advice and your feedback. Special thanks to those dear friends who were in that London apartment for its inception; I'm hosting the next eternal brunch, and even once the dishes are cleared I will continue to be grateful for your patience, your eternal good humor, and your love.

To the fans this story took root within and among: It has been a ride, hasn't it? I've been so grateful and happy to take that ride with you. Thank you for your support and your friendship, and as always I wish you courage.

To my kids, who barely knew this particular project was happening, but who learned to roll with a bump in the "mommy is working" time with better grace than I did.

And finally, thanks for everything are due to my partner of twenty-two years, who makes me feel like the luckiest every day. Thanks, baby. This project is finally done. Now: What's next?

About the Author

Mila McWarren grew up in Texas, but has happily made her home on the East Coast for the last decade. In her day job she works as a social scientist and she has spent the last ten years developing her fiction writing online. She lives with her husband and their two kids. When she isn't working, writing or hanging out with her family, she likes knitting and watching television, because they go together like peanut butter and chocolate, two of her other great loves.

interlude**press**™

 interludepress.com
 @InterludePress
 interludepress
 store.interludepress.com

interlude press

you may also like...

The Bones of You by Laura Stone

Oliver Andrews is wholly focused on the final stages of his education at Cambridge University when a well meaning friend upends his world with a simple email attachment: a video from a U.S. morning show. The moment he watches the video of his one-time love Seth Larsen, now a Broadway star, Oliver must begin making a series of choices that could lead him back to love—or break his heart.

ISBN (print) 978-1-941530-16-0 | (eBook) 978-1-941530-24-5

What It Takes by Jude Sierra
Publishers Weekly Starred Review Recipient

Milo met Andrew moments after moving to Cape Cod—launching a lifelong friendship of deep bonds, secret forts and plans for the future. When Milo goes home for his father's funeral, he and Andrew finally act on their attraction—but doubtful of his worth, Milo severs ties. They meet again years later, and their long-held feelings will not be denied. Will they have what it takes to find lasting love?

ISBN (print) 978-1-941530-59-7 | (eBook) 978-1-941530-60-3

Jilted by Lilah Suzanne
Foreword INDIES Book of the Year Finalist

In Lilah Suzanne's new romantic comedy, Carter, a weary architect, and Link, a genderqueer artist, bond over mutual heartbreak when their respective exes run off together. Against the eclectic and electric backdrop of New Orleans, Carter and Link have to decide if a second chance at love is in the cards.

ISBN (print) 978-1-945053-64-1 | (eBook) 978-1-945053-65-8